In deepest Hell, dawn comes up like rolling thunder in New Houston.

At the edge of the Harry Chapin Memorial Forest, this futuristic city, carved into the foothills of the jagged mountain range, is a stunning vision in pumice and steel, soaring glass and resins. New Houston is the capital of the 2nd Federation of Hell and is where The Masters now live.

On a ridge five miles away, a young man with smoke-white hair puts down his combat binoculars. Dressed in animal skins and sleek, rubberized Kevlar combat gear, his name is Bill and he is next to The Fence, which stretches away to the horizon. It is a double cordon of cyclone link mesh fifty feet high, topped by concertina wire. On the fence, right behind the young man's head, is the sign: ANYONE ATTEMPTING TO BREACH WILL BE SHOT ON SIGHT.

This is the border.

MASTERS IN HELL
JANET MORRIS WITH
C. J. CHERRYH, DAVID DRAKE,
BILL KERBY, MORE!

BAEN

MASTERS IN HELL

Copyright © 1988 by Janet Morris

A Baen Books Original

Baen Publishing Enterprises
260 Fifth Avenue
New York, N.Y. 10001

First printing, December 1987

ISBN: 0-671-65379-2

Cover art by David Mattingly

Printed in the United States of America

Distributed by
SIMON & SCHUSTER
1230 Avenue of the Americas
New York, N.Y. 10020

CONTENTS

THE RANSOM OF HELLCAT

Chris Morris

It may be that Hell is just a state of mind, but to the damned who populate its blasted reaches, it is a state as varied as sin and as unremitting as the human condition. And it's big—bigger than Texas, bigger than Australia. It would have to be, to incarcerate every mortal sinner ever born of woman.

Never mind computing that number. Hell is as big as it has to be; that will have to do. And since each of its inhabitants, to paraphrase the words of Pericles, has exactly the Hell he deserves, it contains as many stories as it does fools, and none of them happy.

We will concern ourselves with just a single story here. It is the story of a small pack of fools called the Dissidents, who thought to make Hell a better place or find a way out of it. You can recognize a Dissident by the hopeful faraway look in his eye, or by the *HELL—Love It or Leave It* bumper sticker on his BMW.

In the sorrowing city of New Hell, where the

1

Dissidents were losing badly against the Legions of Roman Hell and the Fallen Angels and the dark forces of the Pentagram, three Dissidents came together over the last ditch that they still controlled, hoping to hatch a plot to save the Movement.

This ditch was out behind the Toxic Waste Recreation Area and Daycare Facility, and most of New Hell's raw sewage ran through it, so the meeting was bound to be short, if not sweet.

There were three BMWs parked by the ditch and all of them had *Hell—Love It or Leave It* bumper stickers. None of them had windshields, since everyone in Hell knows that BMW stands for Break My Windows, and there wasn't a soul in New Hell who could refuse a proposition like that. One still had its radio. The car with the radio was a very dirty white, and in the grime on its trunk, someone had scrawled with a greasy finger *Let's Get the Movement Moving*.

The white car's owner, Jeb Stuart, an American Confederate general from the Civil War, found the graffiti to be the final indignity. "Wall, lookit dat!" he drawled. "Ah cain't stand it nuhmore! We gotta do sompin'." He pounded a gauntleted fist on the car's trunk, and the radio began playing an ear-splitting rendition of *Sympathy for the Devil*.

"The hell you say!" yelled the second Dissident, a bearded, long-haired Pole named Copernicus who was in Hell for heresy—more specifically, for enunciating the principle of heliocentric planetary motion in defiance of the Church. "Turn that infernal radio *off!*"

And before Jeb Stuart could reply, the third Dissident, a brother-murderer named Cain from somewhere in the Lebanon, strode over to the white car and, with three practiced flourishes of a crowbar he'd had under his striped robes, ripped the radio from the

BMW's console. "Verily I say unto thee," Cain proclaimed in the sudden silence, holding up the radio with its dangling colored wires, "this is the way thou dealest with the opposition."

Then he strode to the edge of the sewage ditch and, holding his breath, cast the radio into the sluggish stream of chemical and human waste.

By the time Cain had exhaled the breath he'd been holding, Jeb Stuart was stroking his goatee and muttering, "B'Gawd, he's right; the fellah's right as rain!"

"About what?" demanded Copernicus, scowling. "That was the last car the Dissidents had with a working radio! I don't understand!"

"What," Cain asked Copernicus, a wicked light in his brother-murdering eyes, "doth thou getteth when thou crosseth a Mafioso with a Serbo-Croatian?"

"I don't know," Copernicus admitted.

"A proposition thou cannot understandeth!" Cain explained, and began to laugh uproariously—until he ran out of breath and had to gulp some of the foul air.

Neither of the other two Dissidents were laughing.

Jeb Stuart hated to be one-upped.

Copernicus didn't know what a Serbo-Croatian was. And he had more important things on his mind. He said: "Che Guevara is disgraced, deposed as Leader of Our Cause—in the—how do you say?—hoosegow once again."

No one responded to that; both of the other men looked away from Copernicus, at the river of offal flowing by in the ditch, carrying a decapitated Briar Patch Doll toward the treatment plant.

Copernicus continued implacably: "Alexander of Macedon, our latest and brightest hope, has disappeared—probably into the Devil's dungeons. And he's not the only one of our Dissident leaders to have been lost—or captured. We must face it, gentlemen, we are losing the War against Evil. We are no longer Masters in Hell, but slaves. We are on the run, falling back, living in fear that, if we don't surrender, the Devil will nuke us back to the Stone Age!"

Jeb Stuart raised his head and his eyes flashed. "Nevah! We'll nevah surrendah!" He pounded his fist again on his BMW's trunk. This time, the engine started up, coughed, nearly died, then caught, roaring. The car lurched, shook as if it were waking from sleep, and then started to roll inexorably forward toward the ditch.

"Lawd, Lawd," exclaimed Jeb Stuart, running around to the front of the moving car and jerking on the driver's door. "Aw plee-uz, plee-uz, not da de-itch. Not da de-itch!"

And, while Cain laughed and Copernicus puzzled over the phenomenon before his eyes, Jeb Stuart, unable to open the car's door, dived in through the broken window and ground his gears into reverse just before the white BMW plunged into the ditch.

Panting but triumphant, Stuart glared at the other two Dissidents and said: "Ah've got a ple-an. An' by Gawd, it'll woik! It'll woik if y'all do whaddah sez! Ye game?"

"Game?" said Copernicus, who was still puzzling over Serbo-Croatians and cars that started when you pounded their trunks.

"Game, fool," said Cain. "Willing . . . able." He grinned nastily. "And . . . ready. *I'm* ready, Jeb, as long as it's . . . action." Cain's brother-murdering eyes gleamed brighter.

"Axe-shun, ah guarantees. An' ex-citin'! Y'all lissun heah: We gots ta git ow-uh boys ouddah the Devil's clutches—all of 'em. We gots ta git Alexanduh ouddah de Devil's clutches, iffen he's-a in 'em. An' Che Guveruh, too. An' Hitluh!" Jeb Stuart's eyes were glowing like Hellfire. "Iffun we had Hitluh on ow-uh team, things'd be a fah sight diff'rent. So how's ta do it? Ransom, I says! Ransom!"

"Excuse me," said Copernicus. "I don't understand."

"Thee? Thou never understandeth anything," said Cain, because he did understand—sort of. "So who's the target? Who's our hostage?"

"Not a 'who,' but a 'what,' de-ah boy, a 'what.'" And grinning from his car, Jeb Stuart again pulled on his billy-goat beard. "Da Devil's got hissef a pet—a lovin' familiar, a thing half like a cat and half like a bat, name o' Michael. It's this pet I propose that the noble warriuhs of ow-uh Cause kidnap—or petnap. We c'n trade it back fuh all 'o ow-uh officers."

"Yea, and verily! Halleluja! Yea-uh!" Cain agreed, and ran for his own car, whooping with glee. "Verily, I shall getteth Lee Harvey and some of the boys. Thy will be done in no time!"

Copernicus, too, wanted to get away from the stinking ditch. But he walked to his own car slowly, squinting up suspiciously at Paradise, that tantalizing orb in the ruddy sky of Hell that defied reason, muttering, "I don't understand. How can you think to take something away from the Devil, when all of Hell—we three included—belongs to Him?"

But the other two Dissidents didn't listen to Copernicus, even though what he said was obviously true. Like the relative positions of the Earth and the Sun, truth was beside the point in these deliberations; and Copernicus's plight in Hell was the same as it had been in life: to suffer fools, of which Hell had just as many as Earth had ever held.

Lee Harvey Oswald was an inch taller than you've

heard he was; he also died a little later, under different circumstances, than common wisdom ascribes to his history. But what the hell difference does that make now?

In Hell, he served many masters. Today that meant getting the cat/bat, fanged and clawed, black-furred where it wasn't leathery-winged, creature named Michael out of the Tower of Injustice—Satan's own digs.

You wanted a certain kind of man for this sort of undertaking, and Oswald was just that kind: he had acquaintances everywhere among the arms merchants and the mercenaries and the double-dealers.

In this case, he'd gone to J. Edgar Hoover, who agreed that, in exchange for a favor owed to him by a man of Oswald's . . . talents, he'd help out.

"What I want, see," said Oswald, "is some hardware and manpower: helicopter and pilot, glass cutters, black outfit, flash-bang grenades to stun anybody inside. And I want all this equipment requisitioned in the name of the Pentagram, for crowd control, or some such. We'll take care of starting the diversionary riot—of the crowd that needs controlling. Deal?"

Oswald was just J. Edgar's type, so J. Edgar said yes without a second thought. J. Edgar was still smarting from being Punitively Reassigned because of a little matter of running drugs into New Hell . . . He needed to teach the Administration that not even They could treat him so shoddily and get away with it. A man with his background, with his responsibilities, deserved a little bit on the side, no matter how he chose to come by it.

And if none of that were true, Oswald was just so . . . cute.

Six hours later, with the riot in full swing before the Admin complex, no one noticed one more black/

gray/red camouflaged helicopter among so many others—one that didn't skim the crowd's heads, but lofted high.

The Devil's penthouse had floor-to-ceiling windows on the west side. Oswald had been prepared to cut them with glass cutters so that he could lob in his flash-bangs, but there was no need.

The panes had either cracked and fallen out, or been removed for replacement. Whichever, it was a piece of cake for Oswald, as his pilot held the chopper steady, to hop across into the Devil's penthouse.

Of course, the wash from the rotor blades was blowing everything, including the Target, to the far end of the suite. Paper was swirling like snow and small objects were hurtling around like hail.

One such small object was the Target, Michael the bat/cat familiar. As Oswald, wearing rappelling gear and a safety harness, vaulted over the Devil's couch, net in hand, the creature let out a yowl to wake the dead.

In Hell, this was no laughing matter. There were demons around, and fiends, and Oswald had no way of knowing whether somebody might hear the beast.

So he slapped his helmet on his head, goggles down, and pulled the pin on his flash-bang. It was like popping the top on a can of Bud.

But the results were much different. A thunderous clap resonated throughout the Devil's penthouse. Simultaneously, the bat/cat yowled and jumped straight into the air, its tail thrice normal size.

The flash that came with the bang temporarily blinded even the pet—would blind anyone but Oswald, who had the proper goggles. Your basic terrorist equipment, in the hands of a professional, Oswald reminded himself, never failed.

But the bat/cat Thing had hooked itself onto the

very walls as if its paws were velcro, and was howling
blindly at the top of its lungs.

Oswald tripped over an ottoman, banged into an
overturned end table, and threw his net over the
Thing.

It stopped howling. It turned its blind eyes his
way. And then it launched itself at him, carrying the
net with it.

It grabbed him with its claws around the neck and
it began biting him through the netting. Oswald
staggered back and fell over the back of the sofa,
wrestling with the Thing.

He wrestled with it until he was covered with
blood and the familiar was bound up in the net. It
wasn't just a bat/cat, it was a Hellcat. He'd forgotten
that.

Chewed and bleeding, half blinded from a well-
placed scratch, Oswald stumbled toward the open
window with Michael, flailing wildly in the net, under his arm.

At just the wrong moment, the Hellcat lurched
sideways. Oswald lost his footing and dropped off
into space, the length of his rappelling line. And
when it broke his fall, he took the jolt between his
legs, and under his ribs where the harness grabbed him.

Painful indeed is the fate of a fool terrorist in Hell
with a Hellcat under one arm. As the helicopter flew
off, engaging emergency procedures, dangling Oswald
and his prize a hundred feet below its belly, Oswald
was weeping in agony, his legs drawn up, his hands
cupped to his groin. Both hands.

He wasn't holding onto Michael anymore. He hurt
too badly; his private parts were pureed and he
could barely breathe. Things were going black and
the tunnel in his vision was getting smaller by the
second.

No, he wasn't holding onto the Hellcat, but it was still savaging him, ripping at his flesh and his black outfit with a manic thoroughness that seemed like glee. Oswald didn't need to hold onto Michael the Hellcat; the Hellcat was holding onto him, yowling in a muffled fashion as it bit off chunks of Oswald and spit them onto the riot under way on the street below.

"And what of Oswald?" Cain asked the messenger who'd brought the Hellcat to his tent.

"It ate him," said the messenger, eyeing the leather satchel with holes poked in its side and a brass frame locked with a great padlock.

"Surely not *all* of him?" Cain disputed disbelievingly. The satchel was no bigger than a pet carrier for a dog; the thing inside could be no larger than a lamb, at best.

"It ate enough," said the messenger. "Now, if you'll just sign this . . ."

The paper on the clipboard said: *Received, one hostage. Type: Infernal. Species: Hellcat; predator; carnivorous. Identifying characteristics: Teeth, wings, claws. Color: Black. Name: Michael. Original owner: Satan.*

And, below that: *The undersigned agrees to keep this hostage in good condition and surrender him to Proper Dissident Authorities, on pain of penalties to be decided in case of failure.*

Below that was the line on which Cain was supposed to sign. He signed (made his mark) and got rid of the messenger.

That left him alone with the leather satchel. Inside it, something was moving. The satchel sides would occasionally bulge, as if a head were butting it or a paw pushing at it. Once in a while, a piteous moan, a meow or a growl, would come from it. Then the yowling began.

Cain sat for a long time on his stool in his tent, chin upon fist, staring at the satchel and listening to the soul-wrenching yowling, until the Queen of Sheba came in to see what was making the racket.

She was black and she was beautiful and the very sight of her always drove Cain to distraction with desire. Of course, he could never have her. This was Hell and she was part of his punishment. She loved every beast of the field, and every stray dog and cat; she went on dates with the shepherds and to the movies with the Chaldeans. She danced the night away with men of Nod and debauched with boys from Pompeii.

But whenever Cain would approach her tent, next to his, she would send him away with a sneer, saying, "Who could love a man who killed his own brother? Who would listen when such a man speaks to her of devotion? Get thee hence, creature, for you do not know the meaning of love. I have been loved by David, and I can tell you, you're not man enough to hold his lambskin!" And so forth.

But this time, Sheba didn't immediately begin taunting Cain. She seemed unaware of his presence at first, which allowed him long moments to study her fine black rump in its sarong of African cloth, strained tight as she knelt down and put her ear to the leather satchel.

Cain was contenting himself with a time-honored fantasy when Sheba turned, still on her knees, and said, "Thou most cold-hearted of men, how can you keep this poor creature in a leather satchel?"

"Poor creature?" Cain exclaimed. "Let me say unto you, lady, this poor creature didst eat Lee Harvey Oswald alive!"

"Then he must have deserved it," said Sheba, straightening magnificent shoulders so that even more magnificent mountains jutted forth beneath them. "Any man with a bit of compassion in his heart can hear that the poor thing is frightened and lonely. If you are any kind of man fit to pitch his tent next to mine, you will free this poor creature instantly and let me comfort it, feed it, give it love!"

"I am exactly the kind of man fit to pitch his tent next to yours," Cain blurted. "I am a man with compassion in his heart," he added hastily, "who can hear that the poor thing is frightened and lonely. I was only waiting for you, Sheba, to come along and tell me to let you comfort it, feed it, and give it love!" The very mouthing of that last word gave Cain hope that his eon-long wooing of Sheba would finally be consummated, thanks to the Hellcat in the satchel.

"Good," said Sheba, crossing black arms over her magnificent mountains. "Then bring it forth and give it unto me."

So he brought it forth, to give it unto her. But as he opened the satchel's brass lock and parted the brass frame, a thing of wings and claws and huge teeth came exploding out of the satchel. It fastened itself upon his face and began biting his nose. Its belly muffled his screams and its claws dug into his eyelids and pulled them down over his eyes. Blinded and unable to issue forth a coherent scream for help, he stumbled backwards and fell to the tent's floor.

The last thing he heard was Sheba saying, "Oh, is that not the cutest, finest thing I have ever seen? I have misjudged you, Cain, as a man who would never cuddle a poor animal to his cheek."

And all the while the Hellcat was sucking out his soul, he kept trying to tell Sheba that, though he might be a man who would cuddle a poor animal to

his cheek, he was not a man who would let a Hellcat
scratch out his eyes and bite off his tongue and suck
out his soul through the stump, let alone eat his flesh
from his bones while he was still alive.

But you couldn't reason with the woman, even if
you had a tongue—not where poor, dumb animals
were concerned.

The Queen of Sheba brought a leather satchel to
Jeb Stuart's field headquarters in the dead of night.

Stuart was busy composing his ransom note and
made her wait until he'd got a final draft.

"Read it to me aloud, Demosthenes," he said.

The man with the pebbles in his mouth mumbled:

*"Dear Lucifer, Your Most Satanic Majesty, friend
and colleague:*

*"By now you may have noticed, sir, that your famil-
iar (known variously as Michael, Hellcat, That
Damned Thing) is missing. Have no fear for the
safety of your beloved pet, kind sir, since we are all
officers and gentlemen. But do be advised that, unless you find it in your heart to release certain prisoners of war, to wit: Alexander of Macedon, Che
Guevara, Adolf Hitler, and fifty lesser Soldiers of
the Revolution whose names are on the appended docu-
ment, we will be forced to Deal Harshly with your
pet. According to the Rules of Engagement and the
Laws of War, we will expect your reply immediately,
and upon the release, unharmed, to us of the
Abovementioned, will return Your Creature.*

*This message delivered by hand from the Dissi-
dents to the Great Satan this day, unsigned for obvious reasons.*

*P.S. Any attempt to find The Thing will result in
its further suffering: it has already eaten two men
alive and we are Not Happy."*

* * *

When Demosthenes had finished, Stuart said, "An' you're shu-ah you added the names o' Oswald and Cain ta the appended list?" It wouldn't do to have Oswald and Cain interrogated at length, after they woke up in the Mortuary, where all Hell's dead were reborn for further torture—and debriefing.

"Sure," Demosthenes mumbled, and held out the draft, and the rubber stamp that the Dissidents used to mark their communiqués as official.

When Demosthenes turned to go, Jeb Stuart said, "Y'all can send the gentlewoman on in, na-ow."

When she entered, carrying the satchel with The Thing in it, Stuart would rise up, welcome her with all flourish and ceremony to the Cause, wine her and dine her and . . . who knew? After all, she was one of the Bible's most famous seductresses. It had been too long since Jeb Stuart had experienced the Ultimate Pleasure.

When the woman entered the field headquarters, Stuart was so shocked he sat down, inelegantly hard, on his campaign stool. She was . . . black! A person of color! It had never occurred to him that she really was . . . one of those kind. The Bible hadn't said it for sure, not the version he'd read as a man. He was speechless.

Sheba walked over to him with that sway of hips that made a man want to forget he was a white man, that sway that only the darkies back home dared display, and Stuart closed his eyes. The Confederacy was inspired by hips like that, because men couldn't get enough of women like that, because women like that made men want to make them slaves, because . . .

Sheba cleared her throat and her voice made Stuart's balls ache: "I have brought this po' sweet animal, massah, fer y'all to do with as ya please."

There was something wrong about the voice—not the words, which were perfectly in keeping with their relative stations, but the tone. There was a taunt in the tone. And there was something odd about Sheba speaking good Southern darkie patois . . .

But she was so beautiful, and so black . . .

"Open up the satchel, li'l filly, and lessee whadidis y'ev brought me. Besides yousse'f, uv course." And he grinned the lecherous grin that no slave of his had ever misunderstood.

The long black fingers of Sheba unfastened the brass lock and then the brass frame of the satchel, and something black and huge like a vampire bat launched itself at Jeb Stuart. He pulled out his pistol, but there was no time . . .

He heard the voice of Sheba, over his own muffled screams, telling him how kind it was of him to aid this poor animal, who was "fairly starvin', massah, until you offered to help it."

The Thing's lashing tail was in Stuart's mouth, like a gag. And no matter how he tried, he couldn't pull its jaws away from his crotch. Its teeth were sharp as razors, and when he raised his eyes, begging the black woman for mercy, all he could see was her nappy head as she disappeared out the door, telling someone beyond the threshold, "Your master doesn't wish to be disturbed for at least an hour, soldier, while he interrogates the hostage."

When Sheba brought the satchel to Copernicus's observatory on its windy peak, Paradise was just rising in the east. Hell had no regularity in its days and nights, no celestial motion that Copernicus could determine. Paradise, the single orb that lit Hell's ruddy sky, rose and set—sometimes. It was both Sun and Moon to Hell, and yet it was neither. This irregularity, this illogical taunt of Heaven, made Copernicus miserable.

So he was already out of sorts when the Queen of Sheba knocked upon his tower door. He let her in himself, demanding, "And what do you want, Madam? I have not yet succeeded in building a model to predict day and night in Hell, if that's what you're after." He waved around the observatory, where crude telescopes pointed skyward and unfinished orbits of Paradise gleamed like bicycle wheels on his workbench.

"That's not it, Copernicus. *It* is in this satchel, and you know very well what it is." She put down the satchel with a thump and from inside it came a muffled growl.

The woman was as black as the Devil's heart. She was part of the Bible, therefore part of the Church so far as Copernicus was concerned. Copernicus had had enough trouble with the Church. More than enough. So he said, "I certainly don't know what it is. I don't understand."

"Well, open it and then you will," said the black woman with a toothy smile.

Copernicus had seen such smiles before. She was teasing him, tempting him to open it. "If I open that satchel," he said cautiously, "then I'll understand? What will I understand? Will I understand the nature of day and night in Hell, the nature of Paradise, of Hell itself?"

"You will understand the nature of Hell itself, I promise," said the black woman, and bent to open the brass padlock holding closed the brass frame of the satchel.

Copernicus didn't trust Biblical women sent bearing gifts. "I haven't time to open it now," he said. "I'm expecting a guest. If you wish to be here when I open it, you'll have to wait."

"I can't wait. Are you the kind of man who will let a poor creature suffer in a cramped and musty satchel while you carouse with a guest?"

"I'm exactly the kind of man who doesn't open satchels from strange women when he's expecting a guest with an appointment. As for poor creatures, perhaps you'd better tell me what's in there."

"Don't you remember," said the Queen of Sheba, throwing back her shoulders so that her breasts jutted in vulgar display, "that you agreed to help Jeb Stuart and Cain ransom the Dissident prisoners? To hold the hostage?"

News traveled fast in Hell. "Now I understand. This is The Thing that ate Lee Harvey Oswald, Cain, and Jeb Stuart alive? And you expect me to let it out of that satchel?"

"It is That Very Thing. And, yes, you must let it out of the satchel, or else it will starve and die and there will be nothing to trade for the Dissident prisoners." She crossed her arms.

"If I let it out of there, it will eat me alive as it ate Lee Harvey Oswald, Jeb Stuart, and Cain," said Copernicus. He was a scientist, and scientists were very careful about matters like letting murderous Hellcats out of satchels. "Begone, foul emissary of the Church," Copernicus declared. He'd thumbed his nose at the Church before. He thumbed his nose now, at the Queen of Sheba.

"Hrrmph!" she said. "You are a foul and cruel man, and ill-mannered to boot, not to let the poor creature out of his satchel and then to thumb your nose at the Queen of Sheba. I will leave you with your prisoner, who will surely chew through the satchel and eat you alive well before Satan responds to the Dissidents' demands!"

And she flounced away, out the door, before Copernicus could protest.

He sat on his bench and studied the satchel, which quivered where it sat, as if a head were butting its sides or a paw pushing at its top. He listened to its meows, to its growls and its piteous moans. And then began the yowling, but still Copernicus did not open the satchel.

If you're a scientist, you don't let a man-eating Hellcat out of a satchel brought to you by a Biblical vixen; no, you don't. Not without a good deal of preparation.

It was hard to think, what with all the yowling coming from the satchel. So when his visitor arrived, Copernicus still hadn't contrived a way to feed the Hellcat without feeding it from his own flesh.

Copernicus's visitor was Hell's only Angel commissioned from On High, a volunteer called Altos, who aided the Dissidents and who had come to consult with Copernicus on the nature of the orbits of Paradise and Hell.

"Well," said Altos, crossing his white-robed arms and lowering his golden head to peer at the satchel. "You called me here to consult with you on the orbits of Paradise and Hell, but I see you have another problem."

"Yes," admitted Copernicus. Then: "Yes and no. I want to consult with you on the nature of the orbits of Paradise and Hell, a conundrum which makes all my days and nights here miserable. But first I must do something about the hostage Hellcat in that satchel."

A squalling, yowling tremor rocked the satchel.

"Do something? Do what?" asked the angel with a rustle of wings. "If you let the Hellcat Michael out of that satchel, he will eat you alive. Then you won't have to worry about the orbits of Paradise and Hell."

"But I don't *want* to let the Hellcat out of the

satchel and have it eat me alive! I *want* to solve the problem of the orbits of Paradise and Hell. I wish this hostage weren't here. I wish we had never taken the Hellcat hostage at all."

"If you do not want the hostage, then I shall return him for you," offered the angel with three beats of his white-pinioned wings. "I shall take him back to Satan and explain that this was all a mistake, that the Dissidents do not want the hostage, and that there's no need to nuke every Dissident in Hell back to the Stone Age."

"I don't understand," said Copernicus, eyeing the satchel, which was beginning to rock and quake as if The Thing inside was about to tear its way through the leather.

"The Devil," said Altos the Angel kindly, "does not negotiate with terrorists. If you do not let the Hellcat out of its satchel and return it to Satan immediately, your observatory and every Dissident stronghold will be nuked back to the Stone Age."

"But if I let out the Hellcat, it'll eat me alive!" cried Copernicus.

"Not," said the angel patiently, "if you give the hostage to me to return to the Devil. Not if you were to say to me, 'Altos, servant of the helpless damned in Hell, I give you this Hellcat to return to the Devil, no strings attached.'" The angel looked at his Rolex Submariner. "And you'd better do it quickly. The Devil is going to nuke this place in three minutes and forty-two seconds if you don't."

"I don't understand," said Copernicus. "How can you know that the Devil is going to nuke this place in three minutes and forty-two seconds unless you are in the Devil's confidence, and not an angel at all?"

"I," said Altos, drawing himself up to his full angelic height and spreading his wings wide, "cannot lie, and I know what I know when God wants me to know it. I am the only angel in Hell, here to save you from being nuked back to the Stone Age by offering to return the hostage for you. But of course, this is not a threat, merely an offer. Man has free will, even in Hell," the angel said regretfully, a single tear welling in one of his blue eyes.

"I am beginning to understand," said Copernicus thoughtfully to the angel, who was staring at the second hand on his watch. "If you cannot lie and man has free will, and the Devil is going to nuke me back to the Stone Age because he won't negotiate with terrorists, then I will freely give the satchel to you. You can return the hostage to the Devil, and—"

"Two minutes, eleven seconds," the angel interrupted. His wings spread over the satchel and suddenly the quaking and the growling, the moaning and the yowling, and the ripping sound of claws tearing at the leather stopped.

"—then I can get back to the problem of the orbits of Paradise and Hell," Copernicus finished.

"Deal," said the angel hurriedly and extended his hand.

"Deal," said Copernicus hesitantly, and shook the hand.

Then the angel knelt down to the satchel, unlocked the brass lock, parted the brass frame, and reached inside.

"Look out!" Copernicus shouted. "That Hellcat has eaten Lee Harvey Oswald, Jeb Stuart, and Cain of Cain-and-Abel alive!"

"It is true that the Hellcat ate Lee Harvey Oswald, Jeb Stuart, and Cain of Cain-and-Abel alive," said the angel as he lifted the Hellcat Michael out of the satchel. The fearsome Hellcat was purring and drooling in pleasure. Its paws were outstretched to grab the angel, who cradled it in his arms and petted it. Then the angel looked at his watch and said, "Got to fly. Only one minute and three seconds left to return the hostage, or else you'll be nuked back to the Stone Age by mistake." The angel headed toward the observatory window, Hellcat in his arms.

"But I don't understand," cried Copernicus. "That Thing ate three men alive, and yet it's gentle as a kitten in your arms."

Up on the window ledge, the angel turned and said, "It's true that the Hellcat ate Lee Harvey Oswald, Jeb Stuart, and Cain alive, but those men were sinners, willing to be eaten alive, willing to take hostages. Before Judgment Day, not only all you sinners, but the Devil himself, must learn forgiveness. Now do you understand?"

"Yes, now I understand," said Copernicus to the angel flying from the tower window with the Hellcat in his arms.

TAKE TWO

Bill Kerby

In deepest Hell, dawn comes up like rolling thunder in New Houston.

At the edge of the Harry Chapin Memorial Forest, this futuristic city, carved into the foothills of the jagged mountain range, is a stunning vision in pumice and steel, soaring glass and resins. New Houston is the capital of the 2nd Federation of Hell and is where the Masters now live. The 1st Federation was left in smoking ruin and unchecked sewage a generation ago.

1st Federation, 2nd Federation, Grand Unification, The Confederated States—the numbers or order aren't important, as this has been going on forever. Each new generation makes its adjustments, hopelessly figuring they're It as they pupate, wriggling out of a dried, paper-thin shell, graduating themselves to a new "order" from their old chaos. Same old shit.

The Government Complex houses two thousand

workers and twice that number of computers; its
levels are stacked on intricate layers of silicone and a
cedar-type substance. The building, with a million
square feet of usable work space, sits on a hundred-
foot-thick stem of optical plastic that stretches from a
granite bed, up fifty stories into the red daybreak.

New Houston is state-of-the-art, with moving sidewalks, endlessly changing displays, hospitals grouped
around the power plant. Some buildings seem to be
constructed virtually out of high-definition digital TV
and motion pictures. Here, for a tiny epoch, there is
no smog, no dirt, no inner-city decay. And, right
now, because a driving rain has just started, no
inhabitants.

It's a shared vision, of course. It is nothing more
or less than part of a movie; they all agree to believe
it, so it's real. In truth (if that's anything to care
about), this particular aspect is a carefully crafted
miniature done by the same team who did *Blade
Runner* and *Hell's Gate*, accidentally left outside on a
picnic table in a rainstorm and now quite forgotten
except by insects who will use it, just like people,
after the rain stops.

They will swarm over it, playing out their destinies just as surely as anyone could. They have bug
names and bug dreams and cut little bug farts when
they eat too much popcorn at the little bug movies.

One of which, this is.

Far away, yet only straight up—at the base of the
mountains—is Shaker Heights II, where million-dollar
houses are built into the tops of redwood-type trees.
Steam rises off damned sheep in rolling meadow
yards below. In this stunning dawn, a vee of doomed
mallards heads south.

Les Hopewell, porcine and baby-faced, is one of

the Masters' legendary film producers. Right now he is dressed in a light-blue jump suit and standing on the huge deck of his house in the swaying trees. With him is his military advisor, General "Prack" Tischner of the 2nd Federation Army, who looks through a massive Celestron telescope mounted on a tripod. Les drinks down his glass of water and baking soda. He belches.

"It is hard to believe," General Tischner mumbles, as he puts his eye to the telescope again, "that those ignorant cocksuckers will just walk in here today and be destroyed. For art, I mean."

Then, there is a tiny wink of bright amber light on his cornea, right through the telescope.

"What was that?" Les Hopewell asks, pointing out at the landscape beyond New Malibu.

On a ridge five miles away, a young man with smoke-white hair puts down his combat binoculars. Dressed in animal skins and sleek, rubberized Kevlar combat gear, his name is Bill and he is next to the fence, which stretches away to the horizon. It is a double cordon of cyclone link mesh fifty feet high, topped by concertina wire. On the fence, right behind the young man's head, is the sign:

ANYONE ATTEMPTING TO
BREACH WILL BE SHOT ON SIGHT

This is the border. Between the twin fences, two Doberman pinschers trot down its length, side by side, on patrol. They never stop, they never bark, they are always in step, and there are more where these two came from.

"Tell me a story!" a child's voice demands.

The early amber light of dawn flashes off the mirror of a burned out '55 Chevy Nomad wagon, riddled with bullet holes. The motor, melted last year by a thermite grenade, is sculpture.

"Well," responds a young man's voice, "how about John Wayne and the Rolling Stones?"

"Aww, that was yesterday. Besides, I know what happens in the end," says the child. "Tell the one about the Wolves!"

"All right," says the young man from the fence as he hefts his sawed-off Purdey shotgun over his shoulder on its have-a-nice-day sling. A child walks next to him, his nephew Jeremy, along today just because he loves his uncle so fiercely.

"Wolves . . ." Jeremy reminds his Uncle Bill, who sometimes tends to get off the subject and just wander around in mid-thought, careening from crippled sentence to half-finished phrase, hoping the intricate dance of fuzzy thoughts might lead to some new and more fertile ground beyond, only it never does, and . . .

"Story!" Jeremy grins.

"Right, right." They are walking along bombed-out Rodeo Drive. Except for them, it is deserted. None of the stop-lights work and most of the phone and electric lines are down. Burned out cars are parked at odd angles where they were left a generation ago. No birds sing—damned, doomed, or otherwise.

"A long, long time ago," Bill begins, "there were gangs of gunslingers and magic weirdos."

"Yeah . . ."

"Most of them were kids; all of them were under 30, and they had to join together just to survive their nightmare that didn't seem to be ending. As the dark months of their slavery rolled into years, they couldn't get jobs, they couldn't get into school unless they were athletes, nobody listened to them, and finally, nobody wanted them for anything except as game. To be hunted. They didn't like that."

"No way."

"So they took over a town. Just moved in. Not New York . . ."

"Nope!"

"Not Dodge City . . ."

"Unh-unh."

"Where was it?"

"Beverly Hells!" the boy Jeremy yells with delight. They walk by a deserted Texaco station. Twisting from the familiar sign is a chrome mannequin, hung by the neck. It is wearing a torn lace bra and a pair of crotchless Fredericks of Hollywood steel panties. An arrow is sticking grotesquely out of its reflective chest and one of its arms is missing.

"After the revolution, all the rich old people began to move," Uncle Bill goes on. "They played tennis and made deals and packed their bags. One by one."

They never even glance over as a pack of wild dogs, half crazed with hunger, drag a swollen human body in a red poncho into the darkness of an alley.

"Those ol' assholes went to New Houston!" says the little boy in glee.

"They were the Masters of Hell; here, they were nothing. So they went somewhere they could matter, somewhere they could control."

"But some families wouldn't go, huh?"

"Some families wanted to stay and fight for what was 'theirs.' Brave but stupid. The Masters pulled them all out, family by family, to New Houston until only one was left—just one."

"Grampy!"

"Your grandfather was a doctor, Jeremy. And he stayed to help the others. Your grandfather was a great man."

"Then what happened, Uncle Billy?"

"The Masters put up the big fence and said this will be a new kind of hip prison. Let the animals kill each other off, they said. Then, we will blacktop the whole thing and go back and play tennis—"

"And make deals," the child added.

"And screw people. But there was one gang they didn't count on . . ."

"The Wolves!"

"The Wolves."

"All right, that was great!" the Director yells. "Cut! Notch that, I think we can use it if the sound's okay."

The sound man comes loping over with his Nagra recorder over one shoulder and a Stoner assault rifle over the other. He runs back a little of the tape—
". . . and screw people. But . . ."—

"Good for sound."

"Print that sucker!" Bill and Jeremy sag against a burned out VW. The makeup girl trots over, and as they lift their faces to her, she begins powdering them down.

"I'm sorry, but you guys got no time," the Director says. "You know the drill. It's Low Budget City: we don't stop until we drop. I got a production memo from Hopewell yesterday. It wasn't good. We're behind schedule, almost out of money, pre-sold, pre-booked, and this is my last chance outta these stupid apocalypse biker movies into Something Big!"

So they go right into the next scene. As they had this one. With each passing day, there is less and less time between the setups until now, it seems nearly one continuous event. It seems nearly life.

Because it is.

On the corner of Canon and Dayton, there is a jewelry store, now bombed out and gutted with history. A machine gun rips a string of rounds across one of the old display cases with a deafening roar.

"That's enough," a young voice says.

They are two Wolves—Identifier and his young buddy, Walkalong. Identifier has the smoking grease gun in his hands. They are both clad in a pastiche of Roman armor, animal skins, and ribbons, and the older of the two is wearing Rawlings football shoulder pads.

Walkalong reaches into the ravaged display case and picks out a beautiful diamond-and-emerald wedding ring. He grins. "She'll like this!"

"How do you know, squirt?" Identifier asks. "You never even met her."

"Yes I did, you big underpants!" the boy howls indignantly.

"Let me peruse that object," the older boy says, taking the ring carefully from Walkalong's outstretched hand. He looks at it with what he hopes will seem like expert interest. "It appears to be a wedding ring . . . a good one." Then, gingerly, he pockets the ring.

"I'm thirsty," Walkalong says.

"Move back. I want to get a few identifying shots of this place." Identifier brings up his battered old Pentax 35mm camera and takes a picture. *Kershack*. There is no film, of course, but this boy has an eidetic memory, triggered by the sound of the shutter. "Now, we can go."

Later, after walking south for nearly a half hour, the two boys have come upon an abandoned boat yard. Identifier is taking pictures of a half-completed Mathews cabin cruiser, up on pole braces.

"Where're the wheels?" Walkalong wants to know.

"They don't have wheels! It's a bow-at. They go in the water."

"No way."

"They do! They float . . . like this . . ." Identifier shows him with his hand. "I seen one. In the water."

"Y'drink water," the boy tries to explain to his older friend, "you wouldn't put these in it."

"It's the ocean, you little dipshit!" exclaims Identifier. "You can't drink ocean; it's got doodoo in it."

"ASSHOLES!" a loud voice yells. The boys freeze. All the color drains from Walkalong's face. Slowly, they turn to the sound.

Upstairs in an adjacent building, a Crusader stands in an open doorway. He is a dirty old man of perhaps 25, wearing a huge red poncho emblazoned with a cross, and below it, a patch proclaiming—"Crusader—Jerry Falwell Brigade." This Crusader is wearing mirrored sunglasses, his face ticking to an amphetamine metronome. He is holding a deer rifle on the two Wolves below him.

"What're you doing here," he yells down at them. "This is a Holy Place!"

"It's not marked!" Walkalong yells, quaking.

"We're Wolves—we have a treaty!" Identifier calls out.

But the Crusader only laughs. "What do I care about Wolves? The body and blood of our savior Jesus Christ was MAN, not some goddamn animal!"

"We repent!" yells Identifier.

"All our sins," adds Walkalong, "even though I don't have too many yet." The boy's eyes have shifted upward, to the roof of the building. "Oh-oh . . ."

Another Crusader; this one a likely STP casualty, but heavily armed. "Well, well," he yells out, "what do we have here?"

"We have Wolves, Caleb!" yells his buddy down in the doorway. "At least that's what they claim. They look more like pussies to me . . ."

Walkalong's face is reddening as he glares up at them. "Wait a minute. No Crusader jerk calls me a pussy, especially when I didn't do nothing!"

The Crusader in the doorway elaborates, ticking off the charges: "Felonious curiosity, rank defiling of Most Holy Place, and nonspecific weirdness. Case closed."

"Awww, BULLSHIT!" the boy screams from below. Identifier is trembling at his young friend's nerve, reaching out to pull him back, calm him down. "I know what I'm doin'," the boy whispers, winking.

The Crusader in the doorway now has an exploding white phosphorus grenade in his filthy hand as he howls down to them, livid with rage, "The Lord God is a jealous God—dig that, you little faggots! —lest His anger be kindled against thee. Say, how'd you like a little willie-peter?" Just then, as he starts to pull the pin, an arrow slams into the side of his head. The grenade bounces harmlessly on the floor.

"They're here!" Walkalong sings out in glee. Identifier almost faints with relief. "Wolves forever!" they both yell at the same time.

On top of the roof, the Crusader tries to see down in the doorway below. He can hear nothing. He calls out his friend's name. Silence.

"Oh, Jesus Freak . . ." a voice calls out.

The Crusader turns to the sound of the voice and his face falls flat. Don Eagle, a tightly muscled young Wolf warrior with a Mohawk, faces him. The Wolf opens up with his grease gun, walking a string of bullets up the tar paper, into the Crusader.

Out in the street, all hell has broken loose. The Wolves' combat Volkswagen Driver at the wheel, roars away toward the boat shop. Sleepy, a sloe-eyed young Wolf, braces himself against the roll bar and begins blazing away with the AK-47 in his jumping hands. In the building, windows shatter, the plaster is chewed up, water and gas lines explode in pure havoc. Behind them, even the parking meters seem to be on fire.

A cameraman runs past a window with his Arri BL and almost gets shot. His soundman ducks down, pulled along behind him by the sync cable. In the courtyard, suddenly, a bank of arc lights come on, searing the daylight. "Blow 'em, blow 'em!" howls the Director to the SFX man, who fires pack after pack of his gelignite into the already hellish explosions that rain wood, dust, and junk.

In the building, now it's quiet. The Wolves survey the damage proudly. "I think the Forces of Good just ate the big one," says Sleepy.

Don Eagle agrees, lighting a smoke, adjusting a Vega wireless mike on his shirt. "Does this thing still work?"

"We got the wedding ring, guys!" says Walkalong.

"We almost got killed, but we got it," adds Identifier.

"Lemme see it," says Sleepy. They show the ring to him and his face positively glows. "Which one of you picked it out?"

"He did," both boys say at once, sharing credit in their feast of friendship.

"She'll love it; it's really beautiful. Thank you," says Sleepy.

This conversation, this story is about love in the ruins; on this side, females are rare. Even down here, nature (such as it is) is puzzling. This is about a wedding. And the forces that do not want it to happen.

"Saddle up, let's go," says Don Eagle, in command here. "We got a war council with the Black Angels."

"Are we in the flashback yet?" asks Identifier, who

always likes to know these things. But nobody seems to know.

In what used to be the residential district of Beverly Hells, above Santa Monica Boulevard, there is an old German car in front of an old Spanish house next to an old Canadian pine. All have been scorched, battered. Down the street is the antique wreckage of a C-47 Chinook helicopter, half on an overgrown lawn, half in the street. The pilot, now a skeleton, sits in the left seat, slightly canted, waiting to take off. He's been waiting like this for eleven years.

At the entrance to the house is a mailbox—unused, of course—with a rusting wrought-iron name above: DR. DAVID GRIFFIN.

In their kitchen, the Griffin family eats breakfast. Griff, the doctor, is Dad. He has an Uzi and a signal flare pistol in the front of his bowl of Wheaties. Janet, his wife, has vodka in her coffee and hopes no one will mind. They love her; they don't. Next to Mom sits Bill, the young man who is telling this story, his hair just as white although a year younger, now dressed in civvies. "This *is* the flashback," he says to no one in particular.

From a discreet shadow in the dining room, a camera crew, half hidden, zooms in on the girl sitting to Bill's right. His sister.

Robin is absolutely stunning. She is sixteen, just, with auburn hair and wild green eyes—a Griffin family anomaly, prized.

"Someone forgot to close an armored shutter last night," says Griff quietly.

"It was probably dorkface," says Bill, smiling at his sister, who gets suitably outraged.

"Kids . . ." says Mom. "Just eat your cereal, okay?"

They do. Finally, Bill breaks the silence, looking

at his father. "Dad, why're there so few Wolf babies? Why do they all die?"

His father stops chewing, almost as if he were in a trance, and looks up at his son. "What?"

Bill repeats his question. It seems to have an enlivening effect on Dr. Griffin. "They don't really know, son."

"But what do they think?" asks Robin.

"They think it's some kind of chelated lead compound." He takes a sip of his cold coffee. "Carried in the water supply that comes in from the 2nd Federation."

"The Masters," breathes Bill.

"The lead is well under the adult tolerance. And yours. But terminal to infants." He clears his throat. "That's the theory, at any rate."

"Poison," says Robin. "God . . ."

"It'd be a humane end to the Wolves, honey."

"Humane?" asks Bill. "All their babies die. What's humane about that? Could doctors fix it? The lead compound, I mean."

"Doctors could!" exclaims Robin. "I bet they could."

"I wish one would fix my washer," says mother, smiling sadly at her husband.

"Cut," says the Director softly. "Print."

But Bill's eyes are still dead on the frozen expression on his father's face. Griff feels it, too, but he won't turn and engage this boy's eyes. He reminds him too much of his real son, gone so long.

In the shadow of the other room, the camera has now disappeared along with the dolly tracks, the remote lights, the mike booms, everything. And the Griffin family keeps on eating breakfast, pretending not to notice Mom, who is pretending not to cry as she pretends not to notice Bill's anguish as he pretends not to be affected by his sister Robin, who is blinking back tears and is pretty much unable to pretend about anything here.

Riding hell-for-leather, up what used to be Wilshire Boulevard, are fifteen black Cossacks on horseback. Behind them, Hancock Park is in flaming ruin. Big Ned Cooley, their leader, is on a steel-black stallion named Zero, galloping out in front. He has a Thompson submachine gun in one hand and a chrome mannequin's arm in the other. He's the biggest, baddest black man to ever swing his dick up on horseback. He used to ride with the Errol Flynns in the old days when they had motorcycles. But now he's the head of the Black Angels. His two mulatto lieutenants pull up even with him in the dying day as the sound of raking small arms fire fades away.

At the corner of a bombed-out Beverly Hells street corner was a church. Shortly thereafter, it was a field hospital. After that, a pillbox. And after that, it was nothing, having been completely destroyed for a 2nd Federation air-strike sequence. Right now, it is where the Wolves are waiting to meet the Black Angels in a war council.

Over there is an open faucet, continually spewing an oily, slightly orange water. Wolves never drink it (except in dire emergencies) until it's been boiled and filtered. The water comes from illegal taps in the 2nd Federation's mains, and it is rumored to have everything from saltpeter to Master urine in it. But it doesn't stop them from playing in its spray.

Identifier holds his thumb over the opening so Walkalong can dance around in the rain.

Over by the combat VW is SuperJeep, a hot rod battle wagon which is the pride of the Wolf Cav, because it is the only other vehicle in Wolf Cav. It's a modified CJ-9 with twin camera mounts, drag slick tires on the back axle, wheelie-bars, and in its open engine well, a full race Corvette motor. The armor-plate body sports a fabulous airbrushed paint job, twin .50-caliber machine guns are mounted on a swivel to the roll cage, and a set of Voice of Theatre speakers are bolted on top, connected to the 500-watt Alpine cassette player in the dash. This month, the Wolves seem to favor a tape they mysteriously found, possibly from another lifetime, by one David Byrne. Whoever he was.

"What was the body count?" Don Eagle asks.

"Four definites, two maybes," Sleepy replies. "This is getting bad, even for here. I think they're mounting some kind of kamikaze attack or something."

"The Angels'll help, man," says Don Eagle.

"Right when I'm getting married, the fucking Crusaders have to go apeshit. What a drag!"

Just then, Big Ned Cooley rides up with his Black Angels. There is much yelling and handshaking as the ponies prance and wheel around, lathered and quivering and covered with the blood of others. These two factions go back farther than even they know.

"How's the bridegroom, man?" Big Ned asks Sleepy. "Nervous?"

"Me?" Then, Sleepy does a Woody Woodpecker laugh, dunce-sprung from some distant cellular shore. And antiphonally, all these friends' synapses jump at once with the same odd recall. It makes them laugh, too, and feel unaccountably good for the moment.

Identifier brings his camera up to his face. *Kershack.* On the building across the street someone, years ago, spray-painted the words: ARMED LOVE.

"Let's find a church," says Don Eagle.

"One that be hot shit!" agrees Big Ned.

"Nothing's too good for my baby . . ." smiles Sleepy.

*   *   *

Upstairs, in the studio of the old Spanish Beverly Hells house, the steel plate shutters are thrown open and brown sunlight streams in.

Bill and Robin are across a table from each other, both studying on their computer-learning machine. Each has a separate keyboard and video display. Bill's screen shows a music score, bar by bar, as the symphony plays softly over the external speakers. Robin has her earphones on and clicks her teeth absently as she contemplates a solid geometry problem on her screen. She hits a button on her keyboard and the figure twirls, increases in size. Bill gets up and comes around behind his sister. She looks up at him with a smile, and he takes the earphones off her head.

"Come on, I'm trying to study."

"I want to talk," he says.

"About what?"

"About you. You were sick yesterday morning."

"So?" She looks away.

"You were sick this morning, too."

"Sometimes I just don't feel so good, that's all!"

"How long has it been since your last period, little girl?" he yells at her.

"You big shit," she yells back and begins to cry. But he won't let up. He turns her chair to him.

"Whose is it? Identifier, Sleepy, Don Eagle?"

"Don Eagle?" she howls, horrified. "No, no! No. It's Sleepy and we're in love! Billy, you have to help me. Please? We're so afraid." Then, after a moment, something occurs to her. "How do you know about the Wolves? I mean, their names?"

"I dreamed them."

"What?"

"Before we came here, to this godforsaken hellhole,

we were other people," he says as he puts his hands on her shoulders. She looks up at him uncomprehendingly. "Nobody seems to remember except me. But we were. And Robin, even then, I had dreams full of death and misery and screaming. People in these dreams would kill each other just to pass time."

"Billy, help us . . ."

"I saw a man on fire cut in half with a sword. I saw a boy who wore a human hand around his neck from a gold chain."

"Please . . ."

"Even in that other life, I dreamed night after night. About being here, about the babies dying, all the little bodies swollen with lead poisoning. I dreamed that I was in a nightmare where there was only one doctor left! And then, I woke up and went down to breakfast."

Robin is crying now.

"That was the first day I was here, playing this part, with all of you, and I knew the dream hadn't been a dream. It had been my destiny. All our destinies." Bill touches her face gently. Tears run down her face as she looks up at him. "This child will live," he says simply.

At the far end of what was once an upscale supermarket named Gelsons, a bunch of Crusaders are gathered around the bashed-in meat counter, smoking cheap (but holy) cigars, drinking lite (but sanctified) beer. These Crusaders look bigger and much meaner than the drug-addled hunter-gatherers from the boat yard. This is, in fact, the legendary "Hit Squad." Their poncho patch proclaims them to be in the Jimmy Swaggart Brigade—the most fearsome of all.

Two Crusaders are taping sticks of dynamite to the

legs of a rail-thin, 6'7" Crusader, a former Great White Hope basketball power forward from the Cavaliers who came down from too much crack and too small a brain. He has been rechristened (for this one day only) as "Banzai."

"I ain't droolin'—baby, you need foolin.' I'm gonna give you every bit o' my love . . ." he sings absently as another Crusader wires him up.

"How're we doing?" All heads turn in fear and reverence as their leader walks up. The Preacher—mountainous mastodon of God, 287 lbs. of wild evangelical hell—lifts his hammock arms out of his brilliantly hued raiments.

"God's thunder is gonna be on his enemies like white on rice!" Preacher bellows. He reaches out and clasps Banzai's head between his massive hands. "Ain't that so, boy?"

"Yes sir!" Banzai agrees.

"You know your speech?"

"Yes sir."

"Then, you'll be great."

"Yes sir?"

"You may have to blow yourself to smithereens to get their attention, but what the fuck?" The tall boy is galvanized by Preach's voice; most are. "We ask it all in Thy name, Judas Christ, in whose power we bask and get our spirits tan . . ."

"Ahhhh-men!" they all intone together.

"Okay, kid," rumbles The Preach. "We'll get the maiden. You go get one for The Gipper."

The edge of Beverly Hells is a corner of two strips of craters that used to be repros of Santa Monica Boulevard and Doheny. Now, all that's left is the old Troubador Club, a Crusader outpost.

Banks of brute arc lights come on, bathing the area

in an eerie white shimmer. "Cue the rain!" someone off-camera yells. From pipes high across the intersection, it begins to rain.

"Scene 135337554, take 1." The clapstick clacks and the scene begins.

Preacher is standing next to a '59 Buick convertible, looking in at four Chinese Bandits.

"You are going to help us kill Wolves. You are going to kidnap the bride Robin. The Lord has decreed it."

"Hey, why not?" says gawky Bandit leader Ling Ting Tong (formerly Boonie Lipshitz from Hellywood High) who is behind the wheel. Most gangs down here have a loyalty to each other or to a dream. The Chinese Bandits are famous because they have no loyalty to anything. "We already got a couple of chinks down at the wedding site." Not one of the Chinese Bandits is oriental.

"What's in it for us, Preacher?" asks another. "I mean, let's cut to the chase."

"When we kill all the Wolves, you can have her." The exact same oily grin spreads across all their horny, pimply faces.

The best little kidnappers in the business, three of them in black Reeboks, drop silently over the back fence of the Griffin house. They could look up in the windows and see Bill, see Griff and Janet, but they have to wait hours with no smokes and no pee breaks until Robin comes back to dump a sack of garbage. In the dark, Ling Ting Tong quickly glances from a grubby picture to her and back. Satisfied, he swings down behind her and knocks her cuckoo with a sweat sock filled with pennies. She drops into unconsciousness without a sound and one of the others catches her.

"She's not all that pretty, I mean, for a bride," one grouses.

"She's better-looking than anything you ever saw, mung-breath!" Ling whispers as he hefts her over his shoulder.

The night shadows swallow them up. Gulp. And in the window above, Bill is gone.

In Griff's room, it is dark and quiet. The good doctor is on the bed in the silence, staring at the dim outline of his son's form in the doorway. The flare pistol is in his hand.

"Yes?" Griff asks softly.

"It will take both of us," the boy says with little emotion in his voice. "You know it; so do I. We'll have to pull together or we just won't make it."

After a moment of silence, the man replies. "Sometimes I don't even remember who I'm supposed to be. Or why we're here. Does that ever happen to you, Bill?"

"No. My problem is that I can't forget," says the boy, running his hand through his white hair. "You know Les Hopewell, Dad, you were his doctor! You know where he lives, how he thinks. Are you going to help us?"

"Sometimes I wake up and look across at your mother and it's not even real to me. Like it's a movie of my life. A horror film."

"It's real," says Bill.

The wedding cathedral is warm and joyously smoky with incense and Wolves. A choral director conducts a Wolf Chorus as they croon their way a capella through "Crying in the Chapel." Other workers set up portable grandstands on either side of the altar. Applique banners are being raised to the huge hewn (and miraculously unscathed) beams. One young Wolf stands in total awe, looking up at a streamer he has just lifted into place. On it are extraordinary representations done by Rockwell Kent of Sleepy and Robin. Bride and Groom.

In the sacristy, the driver of the combat VW from this morning's skirmish, who will officiate at the wedding, is going over his speech with a young prompter. "Tonight, in love and sacrifice, we're brought together to ask for just one more day of life with each other . . ."

"Wow," the young Wolf whispers, as the moment's nougat center hits him.

In the church kitchen, Wolves on galley detail are setting up cake and ice cream service for the reception. They scoop out balls of peppermint sensemillia onto slabs of chocolate layer cake on fine (if somewhat chipped) china. Bridegroom Sleepy comes in, all nerves, with Walkalong and Identifier.

"Where's Robin? She was supposed to be here an hour ago. Did she stand me up? I bet she did, who could blame her, I'm a piece of shit anyway—"

"She always runs late," says Bill, walking through the door. They all turn to their leader. Here, with his contemporaries, he looks better, in the way kids always do among their own. Identifier takes a picture of Bill with his old Pentax. *Kershack*. Bill is carrying a bizarre four-barrel shotgun—two over, two under. War Feathers are tied to the end.

"I want her to be here. Something's wrong . . ."

"Let's go, then." He turns and walks back out of the room. They follow him; they know he means business.

They walk into the cathedral, when suddenly everyone freezes at the sound of a loud, booming voice, singing sourly.

"The son of god goes forth to war, a kingfish crumb to gain!"

Wolves everywhere in that huge cathedral look up to the sound of the voice. And Bill, in one fluid motion, twirls his four-barrel, cocking it.

High up in the darkness above the organ pipes is Banzai, wrapped in his dynamite and red Crusader poncho. He steps out, grinning, into a lost beam of light.

"It's Armageddon," he yells. "We got Robin the Chaste, and if you . . ." He thinks hard, trying to remember the order. "If you don't kill up, we'll give her—wait, wait!"

Below, one of the younger Wolves' nervous giggling is silenced with a glance from Don Eagle.

"If you don't upchuck, we'll give—no, wait! Aww, goddamn it, I didn't wanna do this shit anyhow!" In a purple fury over his tied tongue, Banzai begins to jump up and down.

Just as the organist hits an ear-shattering G-major chord—

Banzai grabs his ears in howling pain, staggering back off the beam, and falls down through the smoke and mighty organ noise, FLOP-CHUNK, to his sainted end at the feet of Bill and Sleepy. The robber bridegroom screams in mortal agony, tearing away from Bill's grasp. Suddenly, in Sleepy's hand, is a Samurai sword; he flings aside its scabbard in an effortless and beautiful movement.

Just then, Big Ned Cooley, who was out on guard with the Black Angels, comes bursting through the massive oak doors behind them. "Crusaders! They're everywhere!" he yells. From outside, already they hear the sound of gunfire and screaming.

In the kitchen, hearing the warning, the galley detail puts down its ladles and aprons. "Aww, shit,"

one of them complains. "Just when we get the fuckin'
ice cream out . . ." The boy turns around and puts a
quick burst from his grease gun into a Chinese Bandit, who is blown back through the open door. His
mace and marlin-spike clatter harmlessly to the floor.

Outside the cathedral in the gathering dark, a
pitched battle is seen in muzzle flashes; the tableaus
are etched so distinctly that even darkness cannot
take it. The combat VW blows sky high, tossed into
the air like a Corgi toy. At its zenith, the gas tank
explodes into a steroid orange mushroom that envel-
ops a body in its white center. Bandits and Wolves
and Crusaders run and howl in the pitched battle's
madness as bullets whiz and spang overhead. A
second-unit camera crew is killed in a mortar barrage.

Down a side street, adjacent to the stone cathedral, two Crusader Salvation Vans are tucked together under the arcs of tracers. A few Crusaders
buckle Preacher into his steel-plate armor suit as he
takes a battle report from a wounded soldier.

"They went crazy! Alls we said was we had her—"

"Well, I guess we'll have to send them all to the
Lord," says the Preacher. "It'll be completely your
fault, you luscious little piece of ass."

Robin is trembling, handcuffed to the open door in
two places.

"Unlock her."

In the empty church kitchen, the sounds of the
firefight outside are deafening. Walkalong runs in,
out of breath, white-faced. "God almighty," he sighs
just before he is caught full in the chest with a
hurled Crucifix, sharpened to a spear point. It pins
him to the wall. The Crusader runs out. Walkalong's
grubby little fingers feel the head of Jesus.

"I better jus' sit here," he says in shock as he leans
back. "Until I feel better." Then, "Please . . ." look-

ing over forlornly at the bullets trotting across the wall to meet him.

The light in the little chapel off the main floor of the cathedral is from a stained glass window. Flashes bathe the room from the explosions outside. In here, two Crusaders are fighting with an overmatched Wolf and his long pole. Still, he beats their machetes and sabers back. Suddenly, a Crusader with a burp gun comes running in. Just as he is about to level the Wolf, Big Ned Cooley jumps down off a balustrade with his straight razor, slashing and hacking. It happens so fast, the Crusader looks down in disbelief, and drops his weapon into a pool of his own blood.

In the reception hall, away from the fight for a blessed moment, several Crusaders are hungrily slurping up the melted ice cream and cake.

Bill and Don Eagle step into the doorway. Don Eagle is carrying two more four-barrel shotguns like the one in Bill's hands.

"Where is she?" Bill yells out to them. The Crusaders turn nervously to the sound of his voice.

"God'll strike me dead if I tell," says the Crusader as he wipes cake off his quivering mouth, "so fuck you!"

Bill fires his shotgun, and the blast tears the back out of the Crusader, who is dead before he flops grotesquely to the floor. Then the two Wolves walk, firing, toward the Crusaders. Blood and ice cream are splattered everywhere as they come through the smoke. The carnage is beyond belief. Finally, they are standing next to the last Crusader left alive.

"Where is she?" Bill asks.

"Preacher'll kill me!"

"I'll kill you worse. Where is she?"

The boy starts to cry.

Near the cathedral, back on the other side of the

rutted parking lot, the night sky is stitched with rockets. The gunfire and screaming roll in like waves. Ling Ting Tong, his pants loaded with death's own fear, panicked and shaking, lifts his face out of the dirt to look at his watch.

"Only five minutes?" he howls in disbelief. "Nooo!" He goes stiff when he sees a pair of boots straddle his head. He looks up, very carefully. It is Sleepy, the bridegroom, and his samurai sword is about an inch from Tong's neck.

"Get up!" yells Sleepy. Tong does. "What's your name?" asks the Wolf.

"I hate this shit!" yells Ling Ting Tong. "I didn't know it was gonna be a WAR! I'm a lover, not a—"

Sleepy grabs a handful of Tong's beard, spinning him around. "What's your fuckin' name?"

"Ling Ting Tong! Gonna sing that song, I sumokem boo—"

"I am just about," says Sleepy, "to take this five-foot nip razor and split you so clean you will be known as TWICE TONG! Now, where's my wife?" Sleepy is almost crying with rage and frustration.

"I'll show you!"

In front of the cathedral, two lines of skirmishers stand in the flowering cordite smoke and blast away at each other. There are heavy casualties on both sides, but it gets the job done.

Driver is on top of SuperJeep at the twin .50s, blazing away into the darkness. The ammo belt is around his shoulder and a cigar butt is clenched in his teeth as he sings, "Some demented evening, you will see a strangler . . . " Then, he finds a band of attacking Crusaders headed toward the Wolves in skirmish. He turns the hose of molten death on them.

Inside, Identifier has found Walkalong, now cradled in his arms. His Pentax forgotten, the older boy weeps, rocking back and forth, remembering.

Out on a Beverly Hells side street, two blimped Panaflex cameras are wheeled into place, already rolling as Bill and Sleepy drag Ling Ting Tong to meet Don Eagle, who has another quaking Crusader in tow. Behind them, a house blows up.

"I didn't want to be a Crusader," whines the boy. "I always wanted to be a Woof! Woof woof!"

"Shut up, shit-hook," Sleepy says in disgust.

"He knows where Robin is," says Bill, indicating Tong.

"Fuckin' A! We're gonna be pals and allies!" nods Ling Ting Tong. "Yeah!"

"I'm about to use your butthole for a hatband, Junior!" Sleepy is only inches from his face, his steel eyes drilling deep into Tong's basest terrors.

"Even if these vermin take us to her, they won't just hand her over," Bill reasons. "We fight, she could get it, too—"

"No . . ." Sleepy is nearing some kind of personal meltdown. "No!"

"So we're gonna trade them something. Something they need worse than they need my sister."

"What?" they all seem to say at once.

"Indian," Bill says to Don Eagle, "go get my old Schick razor."

Later, in the cathedral, Don Eagle and Sleepy are tying Ling Ting Tong to a huge wooden beamed cross. All the boy is wearing is a sexy little loincloth. Bill puts the final touches on Ling's new beard style as Identifier holds his head still. Ling Ting Tong looks, right now, more like Jesus Christ than Christ probably did. Right down to the sad, blue eyes and the mournful expression.

"Well, fuck me dead," says Ling softly as he sees

himself in the shard of mirror that Bill holds up for him. They finish lashing him to the cross as Identifier takes a few pictures for posterity.

In the great stone hall, now joined by other Wolves, they all hoist the huge cruciform on high.

"Waaaaaa—" yells Ling from ten feet up.

"Shut up, assbucket!" yells Sleepy.

"One more word from you, and it's the hot lead enema," says Don Eagle as he taps Christ's buttocks with the muzzle of his burp gun.

"Okay," says Bill, "let's get him out front to the auction block."

Carefully, so as not to drop their prize, the Wolves carry the Corpus Lingus back down the aisle between the shot-up pews toward the great oak doors.

Outside the cathedral, a Salvation van pulls up front. On top, hiding behind armor-plated garbage can lids, two Crusaders hold outdoor speakers, wired to the cab within.

"We have your sister!" The Preach's amplified voice booms from the speakers as the holders grit their teeth in pain. "Surrender, Heathens, or else!"

Up on the great stone steps, the cathedral doors are still closed.

"I will kill her myself!" bellows Preach, and with that, the side doors to the van burst open and Preach steps out, dressed in his flak suit. Choking under one of his bulging arms is Robin. The Preach still has the microphone in his hand. "You'll be washed in more than lamb blood, by god!"

Then, from the cathedral, the charred oak doors slowly creak open. From within comes the sound of the organ. Someone is playing "The Old Rugged Cross." Here they come.

Bill and Sleepy carry the cross with its swaying, mythic savioroid on high. Ling, thinking of the murderous look on Don Eagle's face, is acting his ass off, giving a brilliant version of Jeffrey Hunter's Christ. In case anybody doesn't get it, the director insisted that Identifier scribble a last-minute sign above Ling's head that says, simply:

—JEZUS—

In the middle of his Crusaders, the Preacher is absolutely stunned. His jaw hangs. Finally, he slowly sinks to his knees and others follow suit. In Preach's rheumy brown eyes, tears are welling as he gazes up in profound shock at the icon center to his life. Robin, next to him, now unhanded, is also stunned.

"We found him inside," Bill calls out to the Crusaders by way of explanation. "All the bodies were gone. And when the smoke cleared—there he was, in a sunbeam, kinda!"

For many, during this fat, wondrous moment, a mystic legend is aborning. People on either side (even stuntmen) drink in every millisecond; the smells, the ambient sounds, and for a few, feelings.

"Wanna do a swappie?" Bill asks the Preacher. Above them, Ling looks up into the night sky in holy pain (getting into it, now) as if his salvation might actually be up there, nestled where the stars used to be.

"Anything you want . . ." Preach is devastated, unable to take his eyes off his very own christ.

"Send her over!" Sleepy yells.

"Come on, Robin! Just walk toward us, real slow," Bill calls out. He looks back at the Wolves. "Okay, guys, take him down, cross and all. Carefully."

Only now, next to Preach, a soldier slowly stands up. He is one of the Chinese Bandits from the '59 Buick. His eyes are on the top of the cross. "Wait a minute . . ."

"Down, Centurion!" Preach bellows. "Down on your knees to the Living God!"

"That ain't no god, that's my boss!" yells the Bandit.

"Get me the fuck down from here!" Ling Ting Tong howls. Robin, edging toward the cathedral, makes a break for it, sprinting across the street for the Wolves. The Crusaders jump to their feet as they all realize who their "savior" really is. Preach rises slowly, an atomic apoplexy bursting across his face in dancing red fistules.

"FREE FIRE ZONE!" he screams, actually peeling some paint off the van next to him. He lifts his assault rifle, firing into the air.

Enter the Black Angels on horseback! Taking this exact moment to arrive, like the cavalry they are, they ride like the wind, flashing midnight steel and spitting automatics, swooping down on the Crusaders and Bandits in a terrible charge. Big Ned Cooley, astride Zero, flails with a sword in one hand, the splintered mannequin's arm in the other. He almost decapitates a Chinese Bandit.

Ling Ting Tong has somehow gotten the cross member loose from the crucifix and, screaming and spinning like a mad dervish, is knocking down Crusaders and Wolves alike.

The mulatto Black Angel lieutenants are standing back-to-back, combat style, laying down a murderous field of fire with their bucking BARs. Behind them, their battle ponies rear up, pawing the hot air.

Taking slug after slug into his flak suit, the Preacher walks inexorably forward, as the rounds thud into the armored chemical weave. " 'He will repay him tenfold, for the end of the law is obedience!' " he roars. "That's Deuteronomy Seven, Ten!" The mighty Colossus keeps coming.

Up on the stone steps, in nightmarish pitched

battle, Bill and Sleepy try to hide Robin from harm and are almost overrun by howling Chinese Bandits. One spins Robin around, his bayonet high, only to be blown away by Sleepy's magnum. Bill picks up yet another Bandit and heaves him down the steps, but not before he is cut across the chest. Robin kicks one of them square in the face as the Wolves back in tightly together to form a redoubt around her.

They are all fighting for their lives—shooting, punching, kicking, biting, stabbing the hordes of Crusaders and Chinese Bandits. A grip is shot dead, toppling over his applebox. There is fear and finally terror on all their young faces; they look like wild animals who are trapped in a forest fire. They are drenched in blood (panchromatic and otherwise) and they are losing.

Driver is dropped with a shot in his upper back. Bill is cut again, this time flayed to the bone. Don Eagle is brought to his knees, clubbed half to death with a baseball bat. And yet, they fight on, one foot in glory, the other in darkness.

At the bottom of the stone steps, now running in gore, the Preacher looks up at his victorious fighting troops with pride. Here is the moment he has been waiting for. With his ungodly strength, he holds out his huge battle broadsword, steady as a rock.

"Cease fire!" he yells into the night. Instantaneously, there is silence, except for heaving breath and the moaning of the dying.

Up on the steps, Don Eagle has the last bullet chambered and his Winchester pointed dead on the Preacher. Showing his scorn, the behemoth tears his flak mask away from his face, revealing the eyes, now glowing slag.

"You only have *one* chance left," he says, heard by all. "Send me your leader!"

Bill lowers his samurai sword. Robin grabs his arm. "No," she whispers.

"Man to man—one on one!" he roars with a deep rolling laugh from down in his guts. He has been waiting for this moment forever. This is why he loves war, why he became a Christian soldier, and in the end, why he came to lead them.

"Let me do it," Don Eagle hisses. "I know how!"

"But it's me he wants," says Bill simply, in tight closeup. For a second, their eyes all connect in that terrifying way where nothing is hidden. Robin buries her face in her brother's side. "You want to help, put a tourniquet on my arm," he says. Sleepy does. Bill's word is law for Wolves. It's how they have survived this long, and there is no thought of leaving it now.

"I heard he can't go to his left," says Sleepy.

"Neither can I," says Bill.

"Now!" bellows Preach.

With that, Bill hoists his bloody samurai sword, kisses his sister, and begins to descend the stairs.

Below, Crusaders and Bandits cheer as their leader divests himself of the armor, throwing it off, piece by piece. His muscles ripple in the ambient firelight. Then, he hefts his huge broadsword and steps into the middle of his cheering throng. Bill is now across the circle from him, looking like some tiny, white-haired David facing a Visigoth Goliath in the middle of a sweaty, howling mob of warriors.

"If you win," says Preach with a smirk, "we go home. If I win—and I'd say at this point it looks like your basic mortal lock—I am going to cut your dick off—"

"My what?" Bill asks incredulously.

"And then, I'll lop off your head, just like John the B., and I'll jam it down all goggle-eyed on my Crusader battle flag!"

Cheers, here from Crusaders and Chinese Bandits. Up on the steps, Wolves are stilled to a cold glare.

"After we vaporize the rest of the heathen Wolves," the big man continues, "that little girl up there—YEAH, I MEAN YOU, BABY—is gonna pull the train. She is gonna take on every man left alive in my army—crazy, crippled, or blind!" With no warning, he takes a quick swing with the huge broadsword!

Bill falls to one knee, dropping his own sword as the foot-wide bloody blade whizzes through the night air inches above him. The fight is on.

The Preacher's movements are spare and fluid for such a big man, and his recovery time with the gargantuan weapon is nearly instantaneous. Bill can only jump and duck, spinning away from the edge of death. The Preacher roars with laughter as his broadsword clangs a shower of sparks against the pavement.

On the steps, the Wolves all pull back at once from the blow, an almost telepathic move of group body english for their warrior. Robin is trembling as she clings to Sleepy. Behind them, Don Eagle quietly inserts a banana clip into his burp gun. "I ain't goin' gentle into any good night . . ."

Now, to the edge of the mob, Griff comes unnoticed. All their young faces are turned toward the fight. The doctor makes his way through them.

In the circle, Bill jumps back—but not far enough—as Preach cuts his arm, laying it open to the sinew. The pain is awful. The Bandits and Crusaders cheer. Preacher moves in methodically for the kill. Bill is helpless now, exhausted and nearly unconscious from lack of blood. Still, he won't give ground as the huge man comes toward him, swinging his weapon in beautiful arcs, an awesome display of swordsmanship.

Now, the moment is at hand. Bill sinks to one

knee. Above him, the howling evangelist lifts his sword in both hands, bringing it higher and higher.

"Billy—," says Dr. Griffin.

Bill looks back to see his father, at the edge of the frenzied crowd, simply reach inside his shirt, draw the signal pistol, and blow a white phosphorus flare the size of a baseball into the forehead of the Preacher. Stunned, Bill leans sideways as the sword clatters to the pavement.

Preacher's screams are drowned out by the spectacular nova in his brain that explodes his eyeballs, sends his fried tongue curling in and out like a window shade, and tears the top of his head off, lifting it into the night like a little hairy rocket ship.

"CUT! CUT! Print that!" screams the nearly orgasmic Director. "Jesus fucking Christ, that was better than David fucking Lean. That was great! Somebody better call 911 for Arnold, though," he says as he hops over the writhing form of the Herculean actor. "Okay, men, I know you thought the wedding scene was next. I'm sorry. But the pull-down claw jammed in the Mitchel; we have to do another take of the battle scene—"

He is hit full in the chest with a quick burst from a burp gun.

Staggering back, the Director looks down at this new hamburger in utter disbelief, just under the tiny coke spoon and St. Chris medal, miraculously untouched on his gold chain. Looking up at his cast and crew quizzically, he topples over on the Preacher, dead before he can feel that huge hand jerk in Death's final spasm, grabbing the Director's balls in a vice grip.

No one has moved.

"All right. Set up for the wedding scene," says

Bill, next to his father, handing the burp gun back to a wide-eyed Crusader.

"The cover-set for second unit will be the funeral pyre. We're coming out of this flashback with a happy ending. Or my dad and I are gonna know the reason why!"

They all cheer.

In a deserted schoolyard, down from Sunset, two ancient horses pull a flatbed truck with no motor, which is piled high with bodies. Graves Detail supervises the careful placement of the fallen onto a rusted jungle gym. Wolves in gas masks with clipboards take names off dog tags. A Crusader douses the jungle gym with alcohol from a battered red can. The body of Walkalong. And a Black Angel lieutenant. And the Preacher. And Ling Ting Tong. And Driver.

Big Ned Cooley rides up with some of his Black Angels. "Bill says to come on. Finish this up."

Don Eagle lights a Molotov cocktail. For a second, he looks at it, and then, up into the heavens. "Some we loved," the warrior starts his prayer. "And some we hated. But, fuck it, take 'em all in anyway, Lord. We're doin' our best down here."

With that, he heaves the bottle in an orange arc onto the jungle gym, which bursts into a flaming pyre. The mulatto lieutenant screams into the night. His buddy is gone and a lot of others feel the same way. Now, they all leave and the fire burns blue in its purity.

Over there, against the darkness, a few hungry, skulking dogs come out, sniffing the redolent air.

Inside the cathedral, music and warmth and singing and joy are carried by the dancing light of a thousand candles. The war has been cleaned out completely, and marriage has been rolled out magnificently in its place. In the pews, which seem to stretch out beyond the confines of any imaginable church, hundreds . . . thousands sit in tears and smiles, Crusader next to Wolf next to Bandit next to Black Angel. Now, they are together.

At the altar Sleepy waits, his heart a stuttering drum, and in his hand already the diamond and emerald ring. Don Eagle, his best wolf, is at his side.

In the first row, Bill is next to his mother, holding tight to her hand. Up at the ten rank pipe organ, Wolf-gang Mozart is wheeling and dealing a fantastic trill from his Coronation Mass, Part XXII, and the shower of music comes down over them all like fireflies.

Then, the famous bum-bumpa-bum intro of the Wedding March. Every eye turns back to the door and . . . there she is! Holding tight to Dr. David Griffin (whose face is glowing with pride and a sad, thrilling envy that every father is one day forced to find) is Robin in her wedding dress, as bright as the midday sun of a past life. Its glorious train seems to stretch away forever. Her eyes are young and alive, and in her womb sleeps something else young and alive. She is holding tight to her father's hand, hers almost lost in his. She brings their trembling hands up to her face and kisses his fingers.

"Let this be a new beginning," she says, looking into his eyes. He blinks fast, tears forming too quickly to be hidden. "You're all we have, Daddy. You and Billy. Find us peace."

"I will," he says, and she knows he will somehow do just that. Here the bride begins the longest journey of her life. Her father takes her to her husband, who will take her to her destiny. Daddy to Sleepy to glory. Tinkers to Evers to Chance—triple plays, even here.

Now, the great smoky cathedral fades away; the dark is replaced by a new brightness. And instead of just Robin drifting down the long night stream of radiant, smiling faces . . . they are all walking.

The day is arrived and it has become their road out of hell.

It's brighter, hotter, and windier than it has been in some time. Identifier is taking pictures that he will remember and teach for always and ever. *Kershack. Kershack.* There are hundreds now, thousands. Ahead of them is the Main Gate at the Border.

Wolves, Crusaders, all of them have here put down their arms, leaving everything behind them. Out in front of them walks their leader, talking to his nephew at his side, who is looking up at him with childlike adoration.

"We're out of the flashback, aren't we, Uncle Billy?" says Jeremy.

"Yes, we are." Bill reaches down, touches the boy's head.

"Where's my daddy?"

"He's here. With my daddy and the Indian. Don't worry." Behind them, the crowd has become a river of young people. Some are walking, some carrying the lame, some riding in carts, coming any way they can. Even those clusters of sculking wimps in dark glasses—the Moles, a gang of nerds who, out of sheer terror, moved into the sewers, where most of them saw no light their whole lives. So many. . . .

And above them, on the great motorized Chapman Titan cranes, the Panaflexes are rolling, ultra-wide-angle lenses sopping it all up, every angle covered.

Down the road, at the Border, the barbed-wire gates swing open. Behind those gates, where the

Masters live, there is a huge crowd of extras, waiting. They are clean, sleek, protected, yet this day these thousands who have petitioned their government for peace (and longer lunch breaks) will try to heal a generation of loss. And to that end, someone in that huge crowd starts to cheer. It is taken up by others, and still others. The cheering sweeps through them like a summer brushfire, building, echoing. Its greeting washes over the Wolves and Crusaders and Bandits and Black Angels like clean, cool water.

"This is better than Christmas, Uncle Billy!"

"It's just the beginning, Jeremy."

"If this is the happy ending, what was the other one?" the boy asks.

High in the redwood-type trees in Shaker Heights II, the producer Les Hopewell is on his balcony with his military advisor for this scene, General Tischner, and a colonel from the Army of the 2nd Federation. Les is looking in his telescope.

"Are they all inside, yet?"

"Almost, General. Another few minutes."

"We'll have the best seats!" exclaims the colonel, rubbing his hands together. "I should've brought my video camera! All those lefty peace-scummies . . . it'll be like shooting fish in a barrel!"

"Plus the added attraction of being able to get rid of our labor malcontents and social duds at the same time. Not too shabby!" exclaims the general.

Mrs. Hopewell is bringing ice-clear vodka martinis out to them on the deck on a platinum tray. She stops cold. In her hands, the tray begins to shake. The men look at her, the tinkling glasses, and then, their eyes slide over to see what she is looking at.

Dr. Griffin, Sleepy, and Don Eagle have stepped out quietly from behind the drapes, through the sliding glass doors. In their hands, a small armory: a sawed-off over-and-under Baby Bretton shotgun, a Bushmaster auto pistol, a Weaver Nighthawk, and the ever-popular Mac 10.

"Griff?" Les asks incredulously.

"It's me," says Griff.

"It's great to see you, boy! You look fantastic— thin. How do you stay that thin, Griff? I was hoping to see you. In the final scene. Down there. We were going to have a dinner party for your whole family! Didn't you call, hon?" He turns and glares at his wife. "You cunt! She didn't call. It's like her, though, trying to sabotage my career. She asked Selznick—it was some Jew holiday or other—why he wasn't at temple, can you believe this moron! You are out of here, bitch! Griff, Griff, it's great to see you. How do you stay that thin?"

"Hello, Les. How're the ol' herps?"

"The what?"

"Your herpes simplex sores, Les. That you got from the funeral parlor in Tijuana. How are they?" The colonel visibly shrinks away from the producer.

"You bastard."

"What are you people doing here?" General Tischner demands. He gets up.

"Motherfucker, sit back down," suggests Sleepy.

A brace of armed sentries walk in and freeze, scoping the situation. The colonel takes this moment to reach for his pearl-handled pistol, as General Tischner sprawls across the table, jumping for the nuke-remote switch.

"Wolves forever," says Dr. David Griffin, as he opens fire.

Below them, straight down through the warm breeze that carries away the sound of gunfire from above, is a picnic table at the base of the redwood structural tower. The amazingly detailed movie miniature for the government complex has dried from the rain and is now crawling with thousands of insects, on the way to their work in the intricate layers of silicone and cedar-type substance. They are on the moving sidewalks, being carried along past little walls that seem to be made entirely out of moving pictures.

Two ants have stepped off the sidewalk to watch one of the larger screens, which is showing something amusing. Their antennae wave in laughing little hiccoughs. They turn from each other, fascinated, back to the screen.

Where, in deepest Hell—for take two—dawn comes up like rolling thunder in New Houston.

HELLBIKE

George Foy

He wondered for the tenth time where they found wood like this in Hell.

The supports they were crouched beneath were massive—three hand's-breadths square, black and shiny, and very closely grained. The trees they came from had to have been at least 20 meters tall, yet he had never seen a tree like that, much less a forest, in all his eternity here.

Not that he'd seen all of Hell, by a long shot. There were some areas where even a compulsive traveler had no wish to go, ever: not once he'd known what they were like.

Such as the area they had just visited.

The supports trembled again, harder. They were nailed together with inch-thick iron spikes, laced together with huge iron bands, strutted with thousands of iron stays.

The trembling grew. It was not wind, though winds blew constantly in Hell, or at least this part of it, playing the scale from a low moan to a hurricane's howl, but never ceasing entirely. The man swallowed the rage that always puked up in his throat at the mere thought of the Royal Geographical Society, put a hand out flat to warn his companions, then cautiously crept out of the shadow of the wooden supports till he enjoyed an unimpeded view of the top of the bridge, maybe 100 meters above them, and the cliffside approach to its span. From this perspective, almost vertically uphill, he could see only a shallow angle of the roadway, but what he saw was enough to make him draw in his breath quickly.

Too quickly. The freezing, stinking, choking smog that passed for atmosphere around here made him cough worse than a desert sandstorm. He ducked, stifling his convulsing chest as best he could, wrapped the burnous tighter around his mouth, and peered upward again.

Angels. More Angels. He had no idea there would be so many. He could see the left handlebars of at least a hundred motorbikes poking over the steaming roadway like chrome gargoyles, their ebony streamers and pennants all ashimmer in the fog. The animal roar of the BSAs rose and fell at frequencies so low your bones picked them up before your ears did. The bikes' electronics were Lucas—another sadistic twist perpetrated by Those Who Must Be Obeyed— and their perpetual malfunctions caused an almost uninterrupted flow of backfires, under and behind the thundering exhaust. The red flash of their strobes glinted distantly off the uppermost timbers of the bridge, sometimes reflected off a drawn cutlass blade, a black helmet, or the steel-spiked toe of a jackboot.

The bikes moved fitfully back and forth as the riders gunned their engines, and the roaring grew louder still as more and more Angels screamed down

the approach road and braked to a halt in the molybdenum tailings uphill from the bridge. If another 20,
30 motorcycles joined the crowd, their line would
stretch as far as the abandoned flume, and they
would not fail to notice the escape route.

Sir Richard Francis Burton shuddered despite himself, and drew back under cover.

Once they saw the chute they would guess. Three
men on two stolen bikes could not have jumped a
60-foot gap in an uncompleted bridge a mile and a
half high. That feat might just be possible for an
unencumbered Angel, though, and Burton had hoped,
a little fancifully, that they would commit mass suicide like lemmings, trying to leap the gap, victims of
their own hellish macho ethic. But as soon as they
spotted the flume, they would come roaring down its
wooden chute after them, and the jig would be up.

The ledge on which the bridge supports were set—
the ledge on which they hid—was an ancient strip-
mining level, a narrow shelf cluttered with rockfalls,
shattered mining equipment, and acid seeps. It was
also a dead end, for it broke off in a sheer drop,
2,000 meters in either direction. If they were spotted they must indeed, abandon all hope; the only
choice he and his companions would have at that
point would be whether they preferred burning to
death in the river of fire in the ravine below, or
being lovingly and slowly minced to pieces by the
blunt, rusty cutlasses of the Angels. Which was the
easy part.

Because after that came the Undertaker.

Burton had escaped a lot of expert tortures in his
time on Earth—there was that time sneaking into
Asmara, for example, where they used cauldrons of
hot oil for infidels—but nothing compared with the
Undertaker's slab. The true horror of death in Hell
was that it was only temporary.

One of his companions stirred uncomfortably, scratching and cursing at a moly-bug. He pulled down a red bandanna from his face, licked grit from his lips.

"Now what, Rich?" he whispered.

Burton shrugged, and loosened his own burnous so he could stroke his moustache, which was long and full and handlebar-shaped, and had been unmatched in the Indian regiments.

"For the 100th time, I wish you wouldn't call me Rich," he replied.

"Sorry."

"*Ya Sheikh?*"

The other man was just a silhouette in Tuareg dress against the darkness of the timbers.

"What?"

"If they find us, *effendi*—" behind the burnous, the man's voice was drenched in fear. It seemed to sweat off his words and permeate the atmosphere. "They will kill us?"

Burton sighed. He wondered once again how and why this man, who went by the appropriate name "End-of-Time," and was the most venal, cowardly, dishonest, lickspittle manservant he had ever traveled with on Earth, could track him down among all the screaming millions of all the eight Circles of Hell. Unless it were part of Burton's own MSQ— Maximum Suffering Quotient—planned by the same people who had put John Speke in charge of the Royal Geographical Society, Hades Chapter.

Speke, the effeminate fraud who had "discovered" the source of the Nile instead of Burton. Speke, who had picked the fruit—after Burton carried him up the tree.

Burton unclenched his fists.

"They will do the thousand cuts, End," he explained, not without vicarious relish. "Each Angel gets a chance to make a tiny cut with his saber; they make the Ndebele look like choirboys. There must be a hundred of them up—"

"Cut it out, Captain," the man in the red bandanna said.

"I would have thought that after the desert—"

"Leave him be. He's scared enough."

The third man of their trio, the man with the bandanna, was an American, a musician. He was a small man with a rather insignificant moustache, dressed in blue desert robes, with a battered molybdenum trumpet strapped around his chest. He was a member of Burton's club by virtue of his reputation as a practitioner of jazz, and a member of this expedition because of his reputation as an arms smuggler in a previous life.

For some reason Burton could not quite fathom— perhaps because of its syncopated similarities to Arab melodic lines—Burton had become obsessed with this "jazz" music. Obsession, in Hell, was as close as Burton got to enjoying anything, and Jack Purvis was a virtuoso, the only man he had ever met who could play "Flight of the Bumblebee" forwards and backwards from start to finish on both trumpet and trombone. The effect, in one of the abandoned mine shafts, was truly astonishing. Purvis claimed there had been better than he—in particular, 20th Century American Negroes named "Satchmo" and "The Bird," but they had all passed North, as the saying went.

Heaven, Burton thought then, must be good jazz music, endless jamming through eternity. The Duke, and Gershwin, Purvis had agreed, lifting his eyes to the North.

A cracking sound above and to his right jolted him sharply from his reverie.

It came from the flume.

Following the line of the structure with his eyes,
Burton could make out a biker, foreshortened by
distance, teetering on the flume's top section, the
back wheel of the machine locked in the channel of
the chute, the front edging over the void. The figure
struggled against the eternal reddish sunsets of Hell's
sky—or rather, the reflection of sky on the three
vertical miles of molybdenum strip mines that lay
above the fire ravines.

They were trapped.

A quick glance up and down the roadway con-
firmed Burton's suspicions. The line of bikes now
stretched past the top of the flume. From that angle,
the rotten wooden chute that once funneled molybed-
enum would be clearly visible to Satan's bikers.

The Angel was trying his best to investigate this
discovery. He leaned delicately to the right, trying
to correct his balance. He turned the handlebar and
gunned his engine. The locked rear wheel broke free
with a screech of breaking wood. The front wheel
skidded off the rim, back into the chute, hit a nail,
and bounced up and over the rim of the flume. The
motorcycle reared up on its own power, hung vertically: there was a sharp, fibrous crack and it suddenly toppled into thin air, dragging its rider with it.
His scream of rage, muffled by the smog mask, cut
off sharply when he hit the ledge below. Man and
bike bounced once, then rolled down the slope of
the ledge, followed by a solid billow of rocks and
dust, rolling, sliding, picking up speed till, with a
whine of uncontrolled backfires, they shot over the
vertical cliff that immediately overhung the fire ravine and were swallowed by smoke from the river.

From the top of the chute came bellows of hoarse
laughter, that soon dwindled into grunts of predatory
interest.

Black Schutz-Staffeln helmets bobbed over the lip of the roadway, examining the chute. One of the Angels, more enterprising than his fellows, took the launcher off his bike and lobbed a rocket-propelled grenade into the pilings beneath the bridge.

It landed ten feet from where Burton and Purvis and End-of-Time crouched, but failed to explode. Nevertheless, End-of-Time began wailing, and tried to jam his body into a three-inch gap between two timbers. Burton smacked him on the ear.

High above them, someone kicked the Angel with the rocket-launcher, sent him screaming over the edge: apparently a policy decision, such as these were among the Angels.

Or perhaps, Burton thought, their commanding officer was one of the ancient Romans, who routinely punished initiative with "translation."

The Angel bounced off the flume and landed in a confusion of boulders 200 feet lower, twisted in three different bad angles.

A couple of the Angles' bikes wound up lustily.

A minute passed, and another. The wind blew sulphur grit into their eyes as they crouched and watched and waited.

A week of the worst kind of desert travel, Burton thought bitterly. A week of privation and thirst, not to mention the strange horror they had found at the desert's edge and the doubts it raised, but they had made it back. Then, just when they were getting close, *this* had to happen.

Suddenly a shape hurtled off the roadway. It flew over the cracked section of flume, landing square in the trough. Picking up speed down the slope to control his direction, the biker shot off the end of the ramp and slewed sideways in a wide, braking skid that covered them all in a sharp rain of pyroclast pebbles where they lay hidden, a mere 20 paces away.

A second motorcycle followed, and a third. The fourth over-balanced halfway down and tumbled straight and without fuss into the ravine. The fifth skidded to a halt less than ten feet from their hiding place. Burton, hopeless, had to jam the cloth of his headdress into his mouth to muffle his coughs.

But it was too much for End-of-Time. Before Burton could anticipate him, the Arab had leaped out from under his sheltering timber. Sobbing in terror, stumbling over struts and supports, he clambered through the black maze of beams and joists to where their stolen motorcycles lay hidden under the giant-gerbil pelt.

"*La!*" Burton hissed, desperately—"No!"—and Purvis threw himself after the Arab. But End-of-Time, powered by fear, had levered one of the huge BSAs upright and was kicking the starting pedal. Burton went after Purvis, tearing his robes on nails, whacking his head on invisible beams in his haste.

And then it was too late.

End-of-Time's motorcycle thundered into life. The last Angel turned his head in time to see the Arab, screaming madly, gun his wildly slewing motorcycle down the ledge on the other side of the bridge, away from his pursuers. The Angel shouted a warning and powered his own bike slowly into the darkness beneath the bridge's pilings, looking for a way through.

Purvis and Burton had both frozen in shock and fear when End-of-Time's bike started into life. Now Burton found Purvis's shoulder in the gloom, dragged him into the shelter of a wishbone-shaped timber, and brought his mouth close to the musician's ear.

"Wait," he whispered.

There was only one gap, in the thousands of pilings that made up the bridge's underpinnings, to offer itself readily to vehicular passage. For this very reason Burton had not used it, preferring to find another, more tortuous way into the structure.

This Angel's only concern was speed, however, and the bloodlust of hunting. He focused his strobes, switched on his headlight, found the obvious path, and entered it. The arches trembled with the roar of his exhaust. Burton caught one glimpse of the Angel through two black timbers, his cutlass drawn, the black chains readied, the smog mask and black visor giving him a buggy look that was the Angels' hallmark.

Then he was gone, in a roar of doppler, an occasional backfire, a burst of afterburner. The bikers who had already negotiated the flume, never original, followed the same winding path through the timbers.

Then, in a seemingly endless procession down the flume and under the bridge, came 100 or more Angels from the advance guard. Burton wondered how long it would take to catch his old servant, and felt a wincing pity, a sympathetic horror. Even in Hell, End-of-Time had been too pathetic to be evil, or deserving of what the Angels would dish out.

Silence returned, to the extent it was ever silent in the inferno, where 100,000 mines and steel foundries worked day and night; where water caught fire in spontaneous combustion, and the roadworks never ended or began. This was background noise, however—something your brain screened out, like the wind. Less common, and therefore louder to their ears, was the sound of groans coming from Angels who had not quite managed the flume, many of whom lay in a broken heap, 20 or 30 yards away.

"Rich."

He let it pass.

"Let's get out of here."

"Hang on another minute." Burton checked under his robes to see if the map he had drawn was still there. The map to the desert, its mysteries, and its agonies. It would be too ridiculous if they escaped, against all odds, only to leave the whole point of the expedition behind.

Once he had satisfied himself that the scrolled parchment was still there, Burton moved. He felt his way slowly to the edge of the bridge supports, then peeked around and up.

The ledge they stood on was now deserted. So was the flume leading up to the roadway. No bikers were visible along the edge of the road either but he could hear, like the evil snoring of some enormous cat, the faltering idle of dozens of motorcycles coming from behind the cliff edge. The reserves, the Angels' rear guard, Burton thought. Satan grant there were no liches among them. He had a real horror of zombies.

"Right," he said. "Purvis?"

"Yeah."

"We're going to break our way out with the motorbike."

"No shit."

"What?"

"I mean—what choice have we got?"

"I'll thank you to avoid profanity when addressing a man who holds the Queen-Empress's commission."

"Jesus." Purvis leaned forward, trying to tell if Burton was serious. "We're in Hell, buddy. Can't you get that through your fat head? The British Army and all the Queen's horses and all the Queen's men don't mean jack-shit in—"

"Purvis!"

The American's hand drifted toward his curved Tuareg dagger. Then he drew a deep breath. It was so easy to get mad in this place.

"Forget it," he muttered, through clenched teeth.

Burton waited to see if the American would come at him, but nothing happened. Finally, Purvis muttered, "You think?"

The Englishman put his own anger away, for later. It would keep.

"No." He answered the unspoken question. "Not a ghost of a chance, really. But it's all we've got."

A moly-bug had found its way into the fold around his neck and sunk pincers a quarter-inch long into his throat—pincers the insects used to grind molybdenum ore into paste to feed their larva colonies, that scientist had said (What was his name? Darwin?). At any rate, those pincers made short work of flesh. Burton grunted, picked the bug out. It squirmed in his fingers, thorax flashing red in that idiotic insect code they had, huge mandibles clacking crazily, excreting metal. He smashed it into the wood, where it made its characteristic scratching noise, then lay still.

"Purvis." Burton tried again.

"Yeah."

"Will you do something for me?"

"Shoot."

"If I don't make it, I'd like you to get the map we made to a chap called Kropötkin. Prince Pyotr Kropötkin. And tell him what we saw, most importantly."

"About the desert."

"The desert, yes, but especially Djougaschvili and the Irish bloke—"

"Kennedy, Jack—President Kennedy."

"Yes."

"I still can't believe it." Purvis's voice held disbelief, over and above his nervousness. "I mean, I knew the Kennedys had influence, but that much?" He continued, "Do you think the Tuaregs will have gotten the message through?"

"There's a possibility. They have good contacts with the dissidents, especially the Viet Cong in the Park. Look," Burton said, "come on, what are we doing, wasting time like this?"

More to comfort himself than anything else, Burton pumped his closed fist up and down in the "cavalry forward" signal. Purvis hitched his trumpet to a more comfortable position.

Silently, staying well inside the shadow of the huge bridge, Burton slid through the black timber to where the second motorbike lay on its side, still covered by the pelt of giant desert gerbil.

After they had peeled the pelt off it, Burton lifted the black-chrome monster upright with a grunt, felt for the clutch. With Purvis behind him he wheeled the big bike in and out of the bridge supports till it stood, just in the shadow, facing back toward the flume.

"Right."

Without a word Purvis straddled the bike, checked the grit filters, the fuel cock, the clutch, the throttle. He flipped down the kickstart, readjusted the bandanna around his mouth. The distinctive sweet smell of fire-fuel touched his nostrils, overcoming for a moment the permanent back-ground odor of sulphur and naphta.

Burton climbed on behind the musician, feeling irritation over his own fear. He was not used to riding pillion, but he was even less used to motorcycles. There was something about Hell that made it difficult for a gentleman to adapt. End-of-time, an expert camel driver, had somehow found the motorcycle an easy transition, and Purvis was eminently at home with the infernal combustion engine, having operated flying machines as well as motorcars and motorcycles.

"There's a break in the chute, from the first one," Burton said. "He caught his wheel."

"I saw. We'll have to jump it, I guess. Ready?"

"Well, come on, then."

"Hold on tight."

"Go!" Burton ordered. The habits of command died hard.

The bike jerked once, twice, three times, as Purvis's heel mashed down on the starter. Burton laced his fingers around the musician's stomach, and remembered at the very last moment to keep his feet clear of the afterburner.

Then the engine caught in a stuttering roar, and without so much as a by-your-leave, Purvis had opened the throttle wide and headed straight up at the flume.

Jack Purvis must have been in tighter situations in his previous life, but offhand, he could not think of just when.

Of course, in those days, he'd been scared of dying; now he was just scared of the Undertaker. It did not seem to make much difference, as if the human brain, incapable of grasping the big picture, the reality of no-time, focused instead on the pains and losses that defeat would bring.

Such as the Undertaker. And Cutlass Death. The fact that End-of-Time, unknowingly, had given them even this infinitesimal chance only made the fear worse. The pains of translation, as they called the provisory deaths of Hell, were anything but small. He put the thoughts from his mind, checking instead to make sure his trumpet was secure. As he twisted the throttle as far as it would go, Purvis heard the same riff from "Legends of Haiti" that he always heard when things got tight: the slowly accelerating beat of the congas and the follow-throughs of the cornet. He leaned forward to kill the surging bike's tendency to do a wheelie, and felt Burton lean with him.

A good fellow, Rich Burton, for all his touchiness and Regimental pride. Weird, of course, even for a Limey, but you could count on him, unlike his Arabian friend; and a good sense of balance. Came from being in the cavalry, he said. But he couldn't steer a bike for shit. Purvis leaned to his left to line up with the flume, reminded of the time he had taken off from an airstrip made of ironwood logs in Bolivia during the Chaco wars, flying a full cargo of mortar shells while government troops potshot at them the whole run . . .

The powerful engine pushed at the small of his back. A jolt, a cracking of timbers, a change in the angle of attack, and they were climbing the wooden chute. He risked switching on the headlight now, looking for the break in the flume.

There was a "whoosh" in front, and a deep bang behind them: a grenade launcher that worked, for a change. They had been spotted. At 60 IUMs, or Infernal Units of Measurement, up this rickety stack of kindling, the acrid smog made his eyes stream with tears. Two men leaning back and forth doubled the chances of overbalancing, but he had the break in his headlight and it would be no problem as long as he could see, as long as the smog did not thicken. His thumb stroked the afterburner switch and he let the front wheel lift a little, over the gap, sensing the empty space with his muscles. He hit the afterburner, felt the push, saw far below and to his right the orange poppings and the ribbons of smoke from the burning torrent, almost two miles down. Then they were over. There was a sickening jolt as the rear wheel hit ground. He gave her more after-

burner and leaned face-down over the handlebars.
The bike settled on up the last stretch of flume. They
leaped the lip with three feet to spare, and landed
easy on the roadway at 70 IUM, in the middle of a
crowd of Angels skidding and diving to a halt on
every side to avoid being hit.

Purvis jammed down three gears, used both front
and back brakes, dodged a cutlass, slewed the bike
around using his left foot to keep them level. By
some miracle they managed to stay upright. Behind
him Burton yelled something, but there was no time
for discussion or thought. Uphill he had seen only an
impenetrable mass of Angels swarming like moly-
bugs, all black and red in the blacklights, completely
blocking the broad access road on which they had
driven down to the bridge.

There was a mighty roar of triumph from the Angels as he pointed the bike downhill, toward the
bridge, and opened the throttle and afterburners as
far as they would go.

"What the hell are you *doing*?" Burton yelled.

"Shut up!"

"—suicide!"

"It can't be worse than the desert!" Purvis yelled,
but his words were lost in the slipstream and he had
not convinced himself anyway. Still, they had no
choice—no choice at all. The trumpets from "Haiti"
blared close to their crescendo. They would go in
style and rhythm, and they would be translated,
because there was no way two men on one bike
could jump that gap, however fast they went. But at
least they should die quick and clean. For the moment.

There were Angels behind them—he could feel it
under the roar of his own burners—but none of them
could catch up to them in time.

He wondered what the Undertaker's slab would

be like the second time around—if the Undertaker's breath was as bad, his stories as excruciatingly boring.

Purvis felt a grenade hiss by within a foot of his head. They were going 130 IUM, near enough, coming off the pyroclast gravel onto the bridge roadway now, the timbers grumbling under their weight. He could see the gap widening as they approached, the timbers their bodies would smash into on the other side flickering with the reflection of the flaming water they spanned.

At the very last minute he saw the grenade blow away that exact section of bridge he had been aiming for as a take-off point. The explosion bent down planks and lifted up a row of timbers like a series of piano keys, or shallow steps. Automatically, he adjusted his course to hit the steps, his pilot training taking over. Altitude and speed on takeoff, the training said. Altitude and speed. He had the speed, the steps would give him altitude. He jammed both throttles harder against the stops.

When they hit the raised timbers they were going 145, and it was all Jack Purvis could do to keep their bike upright as they took off in a series of gut-wrenching jolts from the unfinished bridge and disappeared into the smoke of the burning river. Flying, he thought irrelevantly—he was flying again. The engine raced, the afterburner roared. The stench of sulphur seared his nostrils through the bandanna. Far below, a blur of orange lights from distant mines winked out of the smog. It was almost pretty, but it gave him no comfort. He waited for the bridge to break them.

Then—too early, much too early, he saw the other side coming at them, too fast, much too fast—and, in an arc of intuition like the parabola of flight itself, he realized they were going to make it after all. They were *over* the roadway.

The jolt of their landing almost broke his coccyx. It loosed his grip on the handlebars and smacked his face on the headlamp, breaking his nose. Behind him Burton shouted something. He lost control of the bike for a second, twisted the handlebars with his elbows. The bike skidded the other way, slewed, jackknifed in the gravel. Then they were falling, still going uphill, the wheels sliding from under them, up a slope of moly tailings that tore at their skin but cushioned the truly harmful shocks.

Grenades landed around them, some impotent, the others going off and throwing up huge clouds of dust that further obscured the aim of the launchers. In the glow of the river of fire Purvis saw an Angel gun his motorcycle off the undamaged section of the bridge, glide gracefully, and plunge gracefully into the void.

Their BSA still worked. His nose would hurt for eternity. They picked themselves up and motored slowly up the mine-road, looking for a way back to the Great Edge. When they got to the top they could see far away across the Mesa of Misery to the million lights of New Hell, towering for hundreds of stories through the smoke of ironworks and strip mines.

Then they ran down again, into the roadblocks.

HOUSEGUESTS

Nancy Asire

Once again, seated in the same cab he had taken hours before, Napoleon rode through the night down the streets of New Hell, deserted at this hour, not long before dawn. Most of Hell's more decent folk were long abed, leaving the streets and alleys to the vagrants; shabbily clad men in large overcoats pawed through trash bins set behind bars—aluminum miners were the more serious of that ilk. Whores accompanied their latest tricks down the sweaty sidewalks, backlit by oppressive sodium streetlights. A few drunks sat on deserted corners, feet in the gutters, their empty bottles of Ripple forgotten in the paper bags that drooped from numbed hands, staring vacantly as the ordinary—oh, so ordinary—cab rattled its way out of the industrial warehousing area.

Napoleon looked away from the cab window: no matter how much one chose to ignore such sights, one could not banish their existence. Such things were as much a part of New Hell as the towering skyscraper of the Hall of Injustice, and *that* building could be seen from any point in the city and beyond.

But the plight of the vagrants, the presence of the Hall of Injustice, took second place behind the situation he faced.

Having ascertained that Napoleon's clandestine contacts, made earlier by discreetly coded phone calls, had produced the results they waited for, the Romans (all Horatius' lads, men who would have looked at home at a Mafioso wedding) had let him go, sent him back to his quiet neighborhood on the south side of Decentral Park, to his house which, God willing, the Romans had guarded through the night. He had played his part in this affair, for the most part not knowing—an elementary precaution—what was going on.

Memory took him back to the warehouse, stood him again facing the redoubtable Mouse, brought back Mouse's words: *Caesar asks a further favor,* Mouse had said. *Hadrianus—Hadrian—will be delivered to your friend Wellington's house.* Mouse's ever-expressionless face had gone grim. *This is to be kept quiet, mind you. Very quiet.*

Napoleon frowned, leaned back in the seat, and stared forward through the cab, his eyes focused on the bobbing rabbit's foot hanging from the cabbie's rearview mirror. Hadrian. Once Supreme Commander of all the armies of Hell . . . once *his* superior officer . . . and now—now in Caesar's hands, a pawn in a game Napoleon was certain he wished to avoid.

Avoidance, however, seemed out of the question.

There will be no neutrals, Mouse had said in Mouse's matter-of-fact way, and Napoleon had known at that moment the Roman was right. No neutrals. He and Caesar were friends, had been friends for years upon years, and Napoleon knew himself and

Wellington in Caesar's debt, and Augustus', for the peaceful life they continued to live on the far side of the Park from Caesar's villa.

But Hadrian? Napoleon winced: what must Wellington have thought, rousted out of his sleep, presented with the drugged ex-Supreme Commander, and instructed—assuredly in Roman understatement— that he was to sit on the Emperor Hadrianus until further notice?

Damn. Another fine mess we're in, eh, Wellington?

The cab left New Hell behind, turned out into the suburbs, skirting Decentral Park on the east end, then swung down the street that ran on the south side of the Park. Even before the cab had reached his street, Napoleon kept a wary eye on the passing tangle of trees and undergrowth, alert for the smallest sign of Viet Cong, but even the Cong seemed to be elsewhere, perhaps on the opposite side of the park, spying on Caesar's villa. Caesar professed that the Cong were shadowy puppets of Mithradates, but Napoleon believed otherwise: like the weather, the Cong simply *were*. No matter how many times routed, killed, or bombed out of existence, they always turned up the following day, denizens of the Park, confused as ever, as if nothing had ever happened.

The cab slowed as it neared Napoleon's house. He glanced at the house next door, but it sat reassuringly dark, Goebbels more than likely asleep. One point for our side. Another glance ahead: his own house sat dark, the porch light on, a cheery welcome. But a few lights shone at Wellington's, not all that unusual, for the Duke sometimes suffered bouts of insomnia, and prowled about at the oddest hours.

The cab pulled up into Napoleon's driveway, and

the cabbie—an unremarkable man; the sort one would expect to see in any large city—reached over the seat and opened Napoleon's door. Napoleon scanned his yard, Goebbels' and Wellington's, climbed out of the cab, nodded to the cabbie, and hurried up the walk.

Marie stuck her nose out from beneath the sheets, heard a car ease up the driveway, and flipped on the bedside light. Napoleon! It had to be Napoleon! She slipped out of bed, pulled on her robe, and walked down the hall. Still not sure who had driven up in front of the house, she hesitated at the end of the hall, patted the large pocket of her robe, and felt the reassuring hardness of the small disruptor lent to her by the Egyptian god-queen. Napoleon would disapprove of her going armed inside the house, but Kleopatra (on one of her rare visits when Napoleon had been gone) had assured Marie that times were changing, that she *must* take precautions. The small disruptor was easily concealed, and in this case, what Napoleon did not know could not hurt him. She hoped.

Yes . . . it was he. She recognized his step as he came up the walk, but still she stayed in the hall, having learned a healthy distrust for nearly everything in Hell, no matter how innocent it seemed.

A key rattled in the lock, the door opened, and, peering around the corner, Marie saw Napoleon's figure outlined against the street lights. The knots in her stomach loosened and she breathed a quiet sigh of relief.

"Marie?"

She could tell from the tone of his voice that he was tired, on edge, and preoccupied.

"Napoleon," she said, rounding the corner of the

hall as he closed and locked the door, meeting him halfway to the center of the entry hall. He hugged her fiercely, kissed her forehead, and tightened his embrace, his arms fortunately well above the weapon in her pocket.

"Ah, Marie, *amour*, you're all right. Has anything odd happened since I've been gone?"

Where to start? Coffee first, instant at best on such short notice.

"Several things," she said, slipping from his arms, taking his hand and leading him toward the kitchen. He followed, silent, waiting for her to go on. She flipped on the kitchen light. "Goebbels had company around one or two o'clock. I heard a car drive up and got to the window just in time to see a couple of fellows carrying large boxes hurry up his driveway."

"*Merde!*" Napoleon sorted through the cups on the drainer by the sink, found his favorite, then turned to watch her as she set a tea kettle on the stove. "They were gone when I drove up."

"The car left immediately after the men went inside." She leaned back against the counter. "And someone's over at Wellington's."

He grimaced. "We've got trouble, Marie."

"More of Caesar calling in old debts?" she asked.

"You might say so." He crossed the kitchen, leaned back against the counter at her side. "It's Hadrian, our illustrious ex-Supreme Commander," he said quietly, as if he feared the kitchen was bugged. "Wellington and and I are supposed to keep him out of sight for a few days."

She lifted one eyebrow. "You're yanked out of bed in the middle of the night, dragged off God-knows-where, and *now* gifted with Hadrian? It seems to me that pretty soon Caesar will start owing *you* favors."

He grinned slightly. "Have you heard from Wellington?"

"Not a word."

"Huhn. Well, believe me, Marie, if things go as I'm afraid they will, we'll hear a lot of words from him, and none of them especially nice."

She met his eyes. "At least you're home again," she said, her hand stealing into his. "That's all that counts right now."

"Crocodiles! Ah, Gods, the crocodiles!"

Wellington glared at his bathroom door, winced as the yowling behind it began again. Glancing out his bedroom window, he saw the subtle change of light that passed for dawn in Hell. The moaning began again, and this time Wellington retreated into his living room, to come face to face with one of the four Romans who had delivered that—that wailing, *stoned*, totally out-of-it creature who was Hadrian . . . Publius Aelius Hadrianus, Emperor of Rome.

"Antinoos!" The voice coming from the bathroom raised a full decibel. "ANTINOOS! The *crocodiles!*"

"I say, fellow," Wellington began.

"Marcus," the Roman said, looking decidedly un-Roman in his disguise as an electrician, one of the sort who worked for any number of 24-hour emergency companies.

"Marcus." Wellington glanced over his shoulder and hooked a thumb toward the bathroom. "Will he *ever* shut up?"

"Oh, eventually, sir," Marcus said, the least little hint of a smile touching his face. "The injection we gave him should wear off in another ten hours."

"Oh, glorious! Simply glorious!" Wellington prowled around his living room, from the Chippendale chairs by the front window, across the lush Persian carpet, to the Regency couch, then back again. "He's been here two hours, and I'm ready to kill him."

Marcus, the Roman-turned-electrician, remained silent.

"And you had to take the phones out, didn't you?" Wellington accused, stopping at Marcus' side. "Now I can't even call for friendly reinforcements from next door in my time of need—*if* you understand what I'm saying. You *do* understand, don't you, Marcus?"

"Sorry, sir. We couldn't take the chance of him getting to a telephone. Gods only know *who* he'd try to call. I reemphasize, sir, we can't let any hint of his whereabouts leak out."

"Well, then, sir," Wellington said, looking down his long nose at the Roman who stood a head shorter than he did, "will you kindly tell me again just how long it is that I'm supposed to keep—" a venomous look aimed toward the bathroom "—him out of sight?"

"Three days, sir."

Wellington threw up his hands and began pacing again.

"And we'll have to be leaving sometime this afternoon," Marcus said, following Wellington on his circuitous route of the living room. "Hadrianus must *not* be linked to Caesar *or* Augustus. I therefore urge you, sir, to avail yourself of your contacts, to call in your own men to guard Hadrian, so we can leave."

"How the deuce do you suggest I do *that* after you've pulled all the phones?"

Marcus answered calmly. "You'll find a way, Caesar trusts your resourcefulness."

Caesar trusts my resourcefulness! Wellington snorted, pulled the tie to his silk and velvet night robe tighter, and stalked off into the kitchen to fix some tea. Marcus did not follow.

The water was boiling in the kettle now. Wellington took his cup to the stove, settled his tea bag to exactly the correct level, and lovingly drowned it. The aroma rising from the cup was as heavenly as anything could be in Hell.

Something was going on—something big—else the Romans would never have turned up on his front steps, the rubber-legged, portly figure of Hadrian supported between two of them. And since the legionaries considered live phones to be a liability, and had relieved Wellington of that particular concern, he could not call Napoleon to ask what the hell was going on.

Wellington pulled a chair out from his kitchen table, sat down, and contemplated his cup. Napoleon had to be in on this: an hour ago—though it seemed eternities—Wellington had seen a cab pull up in Napoleon's driveway. Napoleon had hastily exited, the cab had driven off, and the neighborhood had returned to its usual nighttime quiet.

Now where in God's name had Napoleon been at that time of night?

Wellington snatched his tea bag from the cup to keep the brew from getting too strong, and set the dripping bag down on the saucer. He added a liberal dosage of cream and sugar, took a long, luxurious sip, sighed, then took another sip. Well . . . whatever Marcus and his three companions thought, Wellington would take a nice, neighborly stroll to Napoleon's in the not-too-distant future.

"ANTINOOS!" Hadrian howled from the bathroom where he had locked himself.

Wellington grimaced. Not-too-distant future? Ten minutes from now would be too late.

Napoleon opened his front door to find Wellington standing on his doorstep, clad as usual in his red British general's uniform, a cup in hand.

"Sugar?" he asked of Wellington, stepping back so his neighbor could come inside. "A little early for borrowing things, isn't it?"

Wellington growled something *sotto voce*, paused in the entry hall until Napoleon had shut the door, then turned to face him.

"Will you kindly tell me what the hell's going on?" Wellington asked. "What is that blubbering toad doing at *my* house?"

Napoleon tried to hide a smile. "By 'that blubbering toad,' I assume you're talking about Hadrian?"

"Don't play dumb with me," Wellington said, stomping through the dining room toward the kitchen. "*You* know what's going on. Good morning, my Lady."

Marie had come out of the kitchen, a coffee cup in her hands. "Breakfast, Wellington?" she asked. "Or have you eaten?"

"I think he wants some oatmeal," Napoleon said, stepping around Wellington into the kitchen. "He brought his own cup."

"Napoleon!" Wellington's voice was pleading as he followed. "What's going on that the Romans have dumped Hadrian on us—or me, since he's in *my* bathroom?"

"Sit, Wellington." Napoleon pulled out a chair for his guest and took one opposite, as Marie sat down in another. "What's Hadrian doing in your bathroom?"

"Howling, mostly. It seems the Romans gave him some kind of injection to keep him pliant." He snorted. "More like roaring drunk, I'd say. Moaning and wailing about crocodiles and someone called Antinoos."

Napoleon lifted one eyebrow. "Antinoos? Don't you remember the story about Antinoos?"

"It escapes me now," Wellington replied. He set his empty cup down on the kitchen table. "I do think I'll take some breakfast, my Lady," he said to Marie, "if you have anything left over."

"God, Wellington . . . why do we have a garbage disposal when you live so close?" Napoleon leaned back in his chair. "Antinoos, my friend . . . Hadrian's dearly beloved."

Wellington sat up straighter. "Oh God! I forgot. He's *that* sort, isn't he?"

"Ah, yes," Napoleon said. "Dear Antinoos, the beautiful one who drowned in the Nile, the man in whose memory Hadrian built the city of Antinoopolis. The memory of his lover's death drove Hadrianus near the brink; and yet, whispers tell, Hadrian was the one who ended his lover's life, *not* the crocodiles."

"Crocodiles." Wellington watched as Marie scrambled two eggs at stoveside. "I wish I could throw a crocodile in the bathroom with him. It would serve the bugger right." He looked back, his dark eyes serious. "Do you know what's going on?"

"As little as possible," Napoleon said. "I can tell you things are starting to heat up on the opposite side of the Park. I assume you heard me leave last night?"

"No. But I saw you come back. Where were you?"

"Caesar threw a little party for me at a warehouse in downtown New Hell. I was supposed to find Lawrence."

"Lawrence again? Whatever for?"

"I didn't ask. I just made a few phone calls, set some things in motion, and waited."

"You found him?"

"They let me come home, so I assume my contacts did."

"I say." Wellington stared at the wall. "I don't like the sounds of this."

"Neither do I, but I think things have gone beyond what you *or* I would like."

Marie set a steaming plateful of eggs down before

Wellington, handed him a fork, and placed a cup of tea to one side.

"You're a marvel, my Lady," Wellington said, attacking his eggs with uncustomary gusto. "But what should we do about Hadrian, Napoleon? You *did* know about him, didn't you?"

"Mouse told me. If the Romans want him quiet and out of sight, we're going to have to do our damnedest to comply. How many Romans have you got with you at your house?"

"Four. And they said they'll have to leave by afternoon."

"I'm sure that's right. They obviously don't want to be connected to the ex-Supreme Commander."

"And we do?"

"We could always be called back into active service again," Napoleon reminded Wellington. "There's the matter of the price we pay for our continued retirement—"

The Iron Duke harumphed something into his eggs. "And Caesar doesn't let us forget it for a moment, does he?"

"I'll see if I can get some DGSE fellows over here before noon," Napoleon said. "Then the Romans can leave."

"O, God. I'm not sure which is worse—uncommunicative Romans or surly French."

"Have you got a better idea?"

Wellington shook his head. "Not unless it's changing our names and faces to protect the innocent."

Jean-Pierre de Vauban was no stranger to modernism, though his talents were decidedly early 19th century military. Recent tours of duty with commanders as contemporary as T. E. Lawrence had given de Vauban a tolerance for the modern, while still reinforcing his longing for the return to the old days, the old ways, the comfortable routine of *l'Armée*. Drifting from one mercenary job to another, like most of the men from Napoleon's *Grande Armée* who had awakened from death to find themselves in Hell, de Vauban had been puzzled by his Emperor's reluctance to assume command of the French in Hell. Louis had that position—Louis XIV, who lived immersed in memories of the past, who turned his back on nearly everything modern, and who sought to ignore Hell and all things in it by throwing lavish party after ball after *soirée*. It was enough to make any honest Frenchman puke in his boots.

But *l'Empereur* Napoleon seemed to be not as retired as it appeared on the surface. De Vauban had been rescued from an existence of panhandling by the Little Corporal himself, and lately, had been sent into the bars and taverns of downtown New Hell as an agent for Napoleon.

To receive, again, a gunshot wound for his trouble.

And now, dizzy and fuzzy-headed from the pain medication, he crouched in a fetal position inside a large crate. The crate itself rode in the back of a large brown delivery truck, the sides of which were labeled "Onesimus-Ortega Parcel Service." It was a genuine delivery service but, as seemed to be the case everywhere, Caesar had agents inside the company.

De Vauban's wounded shoulder was bandaged and held immobile against his side, but every time the truck hit a bump, a wave of fiery pain radiated out from the wound. Yet this method of crossing from Caesar's villa to Napoleon's house was necessary, the Romans had explained. Things were happening which de Vauban should not ask about. The less he knew, the safer he would be. De Vauban had not questioned . . . he knew when to keep his mouth shut.

Try to keep a clear head until you're inside the house, the Roman physician had told him as he had been settled down into the carton. *I know this won't be pleasant for you. Once inside your Emperor's house, take another of these pills and keep taking them whenever you're in pain.*

Medicine was not the only thing the Romans had given him. Wrapped tightly in soft cloth, securely lodged in the corners of the crate, were several Uzis, along with a number of rounds of ammunition. *For Napoleon,* the Romans had said, *in case he finds himself low on armaments.*

De Vauban grimaced as the driver turned sharply again; the grade increased slightly, and then the truck came to a stop. Taking long, deep breaths, de Vauban waited inside his crate, thanking God and all the saints someone had had the forethought to provide airholes in the wooden sides.

With a screeching rumble, the back door was opened. De Vauban tensed, heard the two burly Roman agents jump up into the truck. The crate swayed and de Vauban held out one hand to keep himself from falling against his wounded shoulder. With a lurch, the crate was lifted onto what de Vauban assumed was a dolly. He closed his eyes as the deliverymen carefully rolled the crate down the ramp leading out of the truck, expecting at any moment to go wheeling off God knows where.

He peered out one of the airholes as the agents pushed the dolly up a driveway that lead to a low-built, large-windowed, stone and wooden dwelling. He glanced out of the other airholes on either side of the crate: the house was not much different from the homes that flanked it on either side. This was where *l'Empereur* lived? In such modest quarters? De

Vauban smiled despite his pain: Napoleon was still Napoleon . . . a man who, in life, detested the ornate and opulent, though he gave the public spectacles when the citizens demanded them. Even in Hell Napoleon still clung to his simplicity.

A sharp bump: de Vauban clenched his teeth to keep from yelping in pain. He peered out of the forward airhole again: the deliverymen had pushed the crate right up to the doorway. One of them reached out and rang the bell, while the other balanced the crate on its dolly, waiting to be admitted inside.

De Vauban shut his eyes in misery: it had been embarrassing enough for his Emperor to find him panhandling on a street corner, but now he would face Napoleon again, only this time staring up from the bottom of a crate, surrounded by enough guns and ammo to arm a company.

"Napoleon, there's a delivery truck in the driveway."

Napoleon looked up from his paper. "We didn't order anything . . . did we?"

"Not that I know of. It's an Onesimus-Ortega truck."

"Damn!" Napoleon leapt up from the couch and hurried into the entry hall. His hand was on the door handle before the deliveryman had rung the bell.

There it sat: a large crate, the sides of which were labeled "Acme Home Gym." Napoleon looked up at the deliveryman. The fellow was neatly dressed in a uniform the color of which matched his truck, the OOPS Company logo embroidered above his name.

"Delivery for Napoleon Bonaparte," the fellow said, extending a clipboard and pencil. "Please sign there . . . beside number ten."

Another low rumble came from across the Park,

toward Augustus' villa. Napoleon met Marie's eyes and shrugged. She had just come from the guest bedroom, where they had installed de Vauban, sedated again to counter the pain of his wounded shoulder.

The poor man had been nearly unconscious from the pain and stress of riding from the opposite side of the park. But de Vauban's pain did not seem to bother him as much as his embarrassment at being found stuffed into a crate and surrounded by Uzis and ammunition.

When Mouse had left the warehouse, he had said that Augustus would be returning de Vauban to Napoleon as soon as conditions allowed, and that the method of delivery would be by Onesimus-Ortega. What Napoleon had not counted on was the speed of de Vauban's return. That very quickness, plus the gift of arms and ammo, told him volumes about what was going on across the park, even if he did not know the particulars.

And he, most assuredly, had *no* desire to become further enlightened.

De Vauban was a clever fellow, though a bit too anchored in the past to make his way in a Hell gone modern. But he was one of Napoleon's "children" . . . his "sons" of the *Armée*, and bore in his heart a loyalty that death had not shaken. And he had more than proved his worth, if what Mouse had said in departing was true. Surely, in the future, Napoleon could find a position for de Vauban other than the one he now held as groom to an English lady of Wellington's acquaintance.

"Is he sleeping?" Napoleon asked as Marie sat down beside him on the couch.

"Finally." Another low rumble from the park. "Viet Cong?"

"More than likely. It sounds like they're after the villa again."

"O, God," Marie said, and then, with a quiet laugh: "I hope Goebbels and his guests were totally confused by the delivery."

Napoleon grinned. In addition to keeping the Romans' hands clean, de Vauban's arrival had been staged for the benefit of Goebbels next door and whoever had joined the little Nazi propagandist during the night.

"I wonder how Wellington's doing?" Marie asked.

"He doesn't seem too pleased with his 'old friends' who've come for a visit, but I don't think the DGSE men are all *that* happy to be there either. At least the Romans got out of his house. We're still under their protection," he said, glancing out the living room window to the opposite side of the street where a Parks and Recreation crew was busy filling potholes left in the street from the last Cong mortar attack. Romans, those men, but again disguised so that they could be taken for a simple road gang.

It was getting so that one looked in one's mirror in the morning, afraid to see a disguised Roman looking back.

"You think there's going to be a lot of trouble, don't you?"

He nodded. "And *big* trouble. I can smell it from here. The Romans know it, too, and want to disengage from us—keep us uninvolved in whatever's going on. That crew out there will stay as long as they can, but they'll pull out, too, if things begin to deteriorate. The quieter we keep things, the better. God knows who's over at Goebbels', or who might come sniffing around for Hadrian."

"The next two days aren't going to be easy, are they?"

"No. But if we keep our wits about us, we'll make it through all right."

She met his eyes and he smiled in encouragement. It still bothered him that she had refused to return to Purgatory . . . had given up her chance for Heaven simply because she loved him. God knows he loved her—had loved her above all other women when he had been alive—but her choice had staggered him. He felt responsible for her now, even more so than when he had assumed she had just somehow ended up in Hell when she had died. Once again, he questioned whether he was worthy of such devotion.

A warm feeling stole into his heart and he reached out, drew her closer, and kissed her forehead. Hell was Hell and there was no changing that, but it was of some comfort to know that even here, love stood as the one variable the Devil himself could not account for.

Dinner that night was eaten in silence; even de Vauban was quiet, having roused himself only long enough to eat some soup and crackers. A pall of dread hung over the Park, over the houses that surrounded it . . . over the entire area. A feeling of utter dread and utmost danger had settled in with the fall of darkness. Marie was silent, her eyes troubled whenever she looked at Napoleon; and he was just as quiet. Something was going on—something that went beyond the description of Something Big. Napoleon glanced up from the dining room table, out through the living room window and across the Park. In cases like this, the proper response was *not* to wonder . . . or even ask.

If the previous night had been blessedly quiet,

and the morning also, those facts gave Napoleon no comfort as he stared at the phone in his hands. The third wrong number of the day, and none of the callers had given him any code words he knew of. He set the receiver down in the cradle, slipped his hands into his jeans pockets, and stood rocking from heel to toe.

"'Who was that?" Marie asked from the living room.

"Wrong number." Napoleon now hooked his hands behind his back and walked slowly from the study to the kitchen. The coffee was nearly gone: he dumped the last little bit, and rummaged around in a drawer for filters.

"Marie?" He glanced over his shoulder. "Where the hell are the coffee filters?"

He heard her get up from the couch. "In the second drawer from the refrigerator." Her voice grew louder as she came through the dining room. "Can't you find them?"

Napoleon shut the drawer and counted—one, two. He had been in the correct drawer, but there had been nothing in it but balls of string, several screwdrivers, garbage bag ties, a ruler, scissors, a note pad, multitudinous pencils and ballpoint pens (not all of which worked), and a nest of small paper bags.

"Damn." He opened the drawer closest to the refrigerator as Marie joined him. "They're over here."

"I could have sworn I put them in the second drawer," she said, cocking her head and staring askance at the neat pile of filters.

"Damned things are alive," Napoleon muttered, taking one out, slipping it into the container, and following that with the coffee. "When you turn out the lights at night, they *migrate*."

He put the pot in place, inserted the coffee, and

poured water into the top of the machine: the fresh-brewed aroma filled the kitchen.

"Who do you think is calling us?" Marie asked, getting two cups out of the cupboard—they had actually run the dishwasher after breakfast. "We hardly ever get wrong numbers."

"Except the *right* wrong numbers," Napoleon agreed. "I don't know, and it makes me nervous. They never ask me anything, and the people they're hunting are never the same."

The doorbell rang.

Napoleon exchanged a quick look with Marie. "Stay here. I'll see who it is."

He crossed the kitchen, walked through the dining room and into the entry hall. It was a sign of the times that his heart gave a little jump of relief when he saw Wellington's face looking through the front door window.

"Things getting a little too interesting next door?" he asked, ushering his neighbor inside.

"I'm going to kill him," Wellington muttered and, waiting until Napoleon had closed the door: "I'm going to carve him up into little pieces and stuff them *all* down the bloody disposal!"

Napoleon gestured toward the kitchen. "Marie and I were going to have some coffee. Will you join us?" Wellington nodded and followed. "What's Hadrian done now?"

"O, Lord!" Wellington threw his hands up in the air. "What *hasn't* the blithering idiot done?"

"Put on another cup, Marie," Napoleon called ahead. "We've got company again."

"He ensconces himself on my couch," Wellington was saying, "my *Regency* couch, mind you, and expects to be *served*! I'll bloody well serve him—serve him right back into the bathroom and throw away the key! And not only *that*—" he took his cup from Marie and sat down at the kitchen table "—he raided my liquor cabinet! Went right after the best, you know, right after the flipping best! Drank an entire bottle of Lafitte-Rothschild, and you know what *that* costs . . . *when* you can get it!" Wellington's voice lowered as he leaned forward. "And do you know what the bloody idiot did? He put *water* in it! Water, for God's sake. And then he has the flipping nerve to pronounce it a 'bland red wine'!"

"Has he made any moves toward the door?" Napoleon asked when Wellington had run out of breath.

"Not with the DGSE men sitting around with their guns in plain sight. Hadrian may be crazy, but he's not stupid."

"Are you getting along with them all right?"

"Tolerably. They're good men . . . they proved that back in the swamp when we went after Alexander, but—damme! They're bloody surly fellows. Won't speak more than one or two words of English, and my French isn't the best. One of them stays in the living room at all times, keeping an eye on both the door and our besotted ex-Commander. And they've discovered my TV. God, Napoleon! I didn't know they made 'The Gong Show' in French!"

Napoleon stared. "Neither did I."

"We've had three wrong number calls," Marie mentioned in her best here's-something-you-should-know voice.

"Oh?" Wellington sat up straighter. "Just this morning?"

"Yes." Napoleon motioned toward Goebbels' house. "And with the visitors next door, I'm beginning to get worried."

"You think they've set up listening devices?"

"Why do you think we've got the radio blaring in the bedroom facing his house? Neither Marie nor I are devotees of Heavy Metal."

"Wonderful." Wellington took a long sip of coffee. "What next?"

"I think it's time we took Goebbels' mind off who might be in whose house," Napoleon said, leaning back in his chair, balancing it on two legs.

"Oh? And how do you propose doing that?"

"It's something I've threatened to do for years when a neighbor got obnoxious. Now I've got the perfect excuse. When you came over here, Wellington, did you see any of Attila's kids?"

"Oh, yes. Now that the supposed road crew is out in the street, there's a whole litter of them in our front yards watching. Why?"

"Because I think this is a job for Attila."

Before Napoleon left his house, he looked out the living room window. Wellington was right: at least four of Attila's rug-rats sat on the edge of the street, quietly (this, in itself, an event) watching the Roman road crew. The fifth child was crouched at the end of Napoleon's driveway, chalk in hand.

Napoleon left the house and strolled down the drive. Attila's son—Napoleon was never sure whether this one was Dichtdu or Yhano—never stirred, but kept scribbling on the concrete.

This was a weekly ritual: Attila's kids would go from driveway to driveway, drawing and writing unmentionable things with chalk. Each homeowner would periodically rush out of his house, yelling threats of lawsuits, and chase the offending child away. Napoleon looked down: *Dieu!* the little monster was getting more inventive every day.

"Off!" Napoleon bellowed, pointing up the block toward Attila's house. He crouched down so his eyes were on a level with the child's, grabbed the boy by the shoulders, and said, "You tell your father I want to see him down here *immediately*. This has got to stop!"

A flicker of understanding passed behind the boy's slanted eyes. He squirmed out of Napoleon's grip, gathered up his chalk, and ran down the street toward Attila's.

This has got to stop! All of Attila's children—brats though they were—had learned certain code words: learned them or had the words beaten into their thick skulls. And Attila would understand this message: danger! I need your help.

Napoleon watched the boy's retreating back, looked down at the obscenities scrawled on his driveway, and shook his head. What would it be like, he wondered, turning back to the house, to be five years old and trapped in Hell forever?

Attila arrived about a half hour after Napoleon had chased his son off the driveway. Clad in his usual off-duty clothes of baggy trousers tucked into low leather boots, topped by a blousy-sleeved shirt covered with embroidery, cinched at the waist with a wide leather belt, the Hun stood silent in Napoleon's kitchen, his cup of coffee forgotten in his hands.

"So," Napoleon said, having explained the way things stood as of this moment, "you can see we've got a problem."

"Goebbels has listening devices, heh?"

"I'd be willing to bet on it. I'm trying to mask any conversation inside the house with rock music in the bedroom. It's set loud enough to stun an elephant."

"So, why ask for me?"

"Attila, *mon vieux*—"

"Hey! Wait a minute. I don't like it when you start calling me *mon vieux*! That usually means you've got something especially nasty for me to do."

Napoleon smiled. "Not this time. How long has it been since you and the polo teams have had a party?"

"Uhn . . ." Attila's forehead wrinkled in thought. "I don't know. A while."

"Good. Why don't you invite everyone over for a backyard barbecue?"

"In *whose* backyard?"

"Don't be so suspicious, Attila. I'm a friend, remember?"

"Sorry. Force of habit. Whose?"

"Mine."

"Oh. When?"

"Tomorrow morning. Starting about eleven."

"What Napoleon's trying to say," Wellington inserted from his place at the kitchen table, "is that we need a distraction. Something to keep Goebbels' mind off who might be in our houses."

"And that ought to do it." Attila grinned nastily. "I'll make the phone calls."

"Good man," Napoleon said. "And now, to Hadrian. If we're all outside tomorrow, he *might* be able to elude the DGSE men and slip out. I think it's time we do something about that. Let's go over to Wellington's."

"And do what?"

"Attila, you'd be suspicious of your own mother."

"Justly so, heh? She never *did* like me."

Napoleon sighed. "We can't afford for anyone to recognize him, and I think a shave of our ex-Supreme Commander's face might just do the trick."

* * *

"*Où est Adrien?*" Napoleon asked Mirabeau, one of the DGSE men whose turn it was to man the living room.

Mirabeau made a face and pointed to the bathroom. "*Dans la salle de bain.*"

Napoleon walked down the hall to the bathroom and tried to open the door. It was locked. Again.

"*Pardonez-moi.*" Mirabeau stepped up to the door, fished around in his pocket, and pulled out a number of picks. Kneeling, he inserted one into the doorhandle, jiggled a bit, and the door eased open. "*Voilà,*" he said, standing and gesturing into the bathroom.

Publius Aelius Hadrianus lay stark naked on his back in the bathtub—a half-finished bottle in his hands—snoring noisily.

Napoleon nodded to Mirabeau and Anbec—the second DGSE man. Taking the bottle away and setting it on the back of the stool, they grabbed Hadrian (one under the Roman's armpits, they other around his knees) and dragged the ex-Commander from the bathtub. All through the process, Hadrian stirred only once, mumbled something about crocodiles, and began snoring again.

Wellington's electric shaver stood in its recharging base; Mirabeau snatched it up, knelt with knees on either side of Hadrian's face, and started shaving. Napoleon watched from the doorway, his smile widening into a grin. As the beard fell away, Hadrian's entire countenance changed—from a distance, few would be able to recognize him.

Attila craned his head so he could see around Napoleon. "Gods! He *does* look different."

"That's the idea. Wellington?"

"If you've got hair all over my bathroom, I'll—"

"Oh, come on. Anything for the cause. We'll get it swept up."

Wellington looked down at Hadrian. "Fat pig," he muttered.

"Perhaps. But a *different*-looking fat pig, *n'est-ce pas?*"

"Huhn."

Napoleon grinned again and walked back into the living room. "All right, Attila. Make your phone calls. I'm going back home."

"And I," Wellington disclaimed, wearing a particularly martyred look, "am doomed to spend my time here with—"

"O, Gods," Attila said, looking over Napoleon's shoulder.

Napoleon swung around: Hadrian came staggering down the hall toward the living room, his eyes mere slits, his mouth hanging open as if he were catching flies. For a moment, the two groups of men faced each other: Napoleon, Wellington, and Attila in the living room; Hadrian, flanked by the two DGSE men in the hall.

"Antinoos!" Hadrian murmured, his eyes opening wide. "Antinoos . . ."

Napoleon glanced at Attila and Wellington, but they had backed off to one side.

"Antinoos!" Hadrian said again, and came lurching toward Napoleon.

"Shit!" Napoleon made for the front door, shoving Attila in front of him. "See you around, Wellington. Have fun."

He snatched the door open, followed Attila out onto the front step, and slammed the door behind him.

"ANTINOOS!" the faint howl came from inside. "O, Gods! The crocodiles! The crocodiles are coming!"

*   *   *

After a restless night spent in the other guest bedroom, punctuated by several more very wrong numbers and the wailing of Twisted Sister, Judas Priest, et al., Napoleon had awakened convinced he had seldom been happier to see the dawn of a new day. Until the news had come over the radio.

"Mysterious dawn meetings of Cabinet!" the announcer intoned. "Possible shakeup of the government. More, after this commercial."

Napoleon had cursed, met Marie's eyes, and shaken his head. *Dieu!* A shakeup in the government? And here he and Wellington sat on their quiet side of the Park, Hadrian in their hands. If a shakeup *was* in the works, there would be a number of people who would love to get their claws into the ex-Supreme Commander.

There was no hope for it. Hadrian was hidden inside Wellington's house and Napoleon could hardly call Caesar and ask to be relieved of this duty. Best to go on with things as if nothing had happened. Now, breakfast and three Tums behind him, he and Marie set about preparing for the barbecue.

The evening before, Napoleon had driven down to the local Unsafeway grocery store and spent a fortune on ribs, chicken, and barbecue sauce. He had bought potato salad by the barrel, stuffed the back seat with bags upon bags of potato and taco chips, and then stopped at the local liquor store on the way home, arranging for several kegs of beer to be delivered to his house the next morning around ten.

Now, standing in his backyard, which overlooked the 18th hole of Hellview Golf and Country Club, he and Marie set up the tables they had rented from the club and began the process of loading them down with the food. Wellington had contributed his Webber grill, as had Attila, and now the Iron Duke stood between both grills, turning the ribs.

The sight of Wellington, still clad in his gold-braided red general's uniform, topped off with a long chef's apron sporting the words "Born to Cook," was amusing, but Napoleon was careful not to let the slightest smile touch his lips. Wellington was in a rare foul mood, muttering arcane things to himself under his breath, and glaring at anything that moved like some cornered ferret. And if Wellington knew about the "dawn meetings of Cabinet," the Iron Duke's mood would hardly be improved.

"Napoleon."

He looked up from spreading out the bowls of chips and dip: Marie stood pointing at the back door. De Vauban had wandered from his bedroom, found his way to the kitchen, and now stood wavering on his feet in the open doorway.

"*Merde!*" Napoleon hurried toward the back door just as de Vauban took a faltering step down onto the patio.

"Moscow!" the soldier muttered, catching himself on Napoleon's shoulder. "Damn ice! Damn snow! Is this any way for a Frenchman to die?"

"Marie!" Napoleon called over his shoulder, propping de Vauban up to a straighter position. The fellow stood six inches taller, weighed a good deal (despite his convalescence), and clung to Napoleon limp as a dishrag.

Marie ran to Napoleon's side: he transferred some of de Vauban's weight to his right shoulder as she opened the door.

"Hallucinating," Napoleon said, guiding de Vauban toward the kitchen. *O bon dieu!* If Goebbels had seen any of this, they were sunk.

De Vauban was weeping now. *"Ah, mon Empereur . . . je suis mort . . . je suis . . ."*

Napoleon led de Vauban through the kitchen, the dining room, and down the hall. Marie hurried ahead and waited in the guest bedroom. The veteran was mumbling nonsense now—more about ice, snow, a river, and a wagon. Drowning. Cold.

With Marie's help, Napoleon eased de Vauban into bed, pulled the covers up around the wounded man's chin, and stood watching. De Vauban muttered a string of gibberish, sighed deeply, and closed his eyes.

"God," Napoleon said. "Whatever the Romans gave him certainly packs a punch."

"It's probably the codeine. Do you think he'll be all right?"

"Yes. He's already asleep now. But we'll have to keep checking on him. We can't afford to have him stumble out into the party."

De Vauban had started to snore lightly. Napoleon turned and left the room, Marie following.

"Napoleon . . . look there!"

He glanced out of the living room window, stopped in his tracks, and stared. The Roman repair crew was still there, busy filling the potholes some child—guess whose?—had dug up the day before. But a large orange moving van was slowing to a stop in front of the vacant house that stood between Wellington's and Attila's.

"Dieu en ciel!" Napoleon stared at the van. "New neighbors? Today?"

Marie shrugged. "We can't do anything about that now. What's the time?"

Napoleon glanced at his watch. "Quarter till eleven. Attila and his friends should be arriving at any moment now. I've never known them to be late for free food."

"Napoleon!"

Wellington's voice came from outside, sounding decidedly distressed. Napoleon and Marie hurried out into the backyard.

"Platters!" the Iron Duke said, gesturing with his tongs to the two grills. "The ribs are done."

Just in time, too. By the time Napoleon and Marie had heaped the platters with ribs and transferred the chickens to the grill, Attila came swaggering around the corner of the house, the members of the Hun and Mongol polo teams following.

"All right!" Attila roared, lifting a leather drinking skin in one burly hand. "Let's get this party started, heh?"

"Eeeehah!" one of the Mongols screeched, and started the stampede to the waiting plates.

The first thing Hadrian saw upon returning to consciousness was an overhead light. Not just any overhead light, mind you, but one that looked suspiciously like a miniature chandelier. He turned his head, winced at the pounding in his skull, and found himself nose to nose with a bathtub. A *bathtub*?

The world spun around him and Hadrian closed his eyes, but that made things worse. The last thing he remembered was sitting across from Machiavelli, that bird of ill omen, being interrogated as he had seldom been questioned before by anyone . . . anywhere. And assured, in Machiavelli's smooth voice, not to worry overmuch, for it was entirely possible that Caesar (who knew all too much how things *truly* stacked up in Hell) would give Hadrian help.

After all . . . a Roman was a Roman, whatever Age he had lived.

That thought moved him. Hadrian grasped the side of the bathtub and levered himself to his knees. The bathroom spun again and settled; he put his other arm on the sink and hauled himself to his feet. For a moment, he stood breathing heavily, his eyes focused on his hands gripping the ornate marble countertop. He rubbed his eyes, tried to stifle a moan, and looked into the mirror.

Out of which a stranger looked back.

"Gods!" Hadrian's hands flew to his chin. His beard! Gone! He blinked twice, looked in the mirror again, but it was true. His carefully nourished, lovingly cultivated beard was gone.

The second piece of personal inventory followed a shiver. He looked down: he stood naked . . . naked as the day he had been born. Where, by all the Gods, were his clothes? He shook his head, groaned softly, and tried to remember. Nothing came to mind but Machiavelli's dark, suave features and silky voice.

A deep breath, followed by another and another. Hadrian looked around the bathroom, absently approved of its luxury, and slowly walked toward the door, his equilibrium improving with each step. Where was he? In whose hands? Certainly not Caesar's, but then one never knew when it came to *that* man.

Laughter filtered through the closed door. Hadrian paused, his hand on the door handle, and tried to understand the words. Laughter again: this was all he could distinguish. He eased the doorknob, inched the door open a small way, and leaned his head out into the hall.

He had seen this hall before—dimly recollected it, but *when* he had seen the hallway remained a mystery. Quietly as possible, he stole down the hall, poised to retreat to the bathroom and its door, which could at least be locked. He froze as the laughter came again, and eased forward.

Four fully armed men sat in the living room with their backs to him, automatic rifles leaning against their chairs; all four sat clustered around a large console TV, laughing and pointing at whatever had amused them.

Hadrian drew a long breath: no escape there. He backed down the hall to the bathroom and slipped into the room that opened off the hallway.

It was a bedroom, as lavishly furnished as the bathroom and living room he had just seen. But whose bedroom? Hadrian glanced around. He needed clothes—he could salvage personal dignity if he had something to wear.

He froze again: loud laughter, shrieks, and voices lifted in song (if that yowling could be dignified by such appellation) came from outside. The faint laughter coming from the living room assuring him that his captors were still engaged, Hadrian slipped up to a window, carefully pulled back a corner of the drape, and looked outside.

Barbarians! The yard next door was full of them. Leather-clad, booted, armed with long daggers, the warriors yelled back and forth to each other, waved some sort of food over their heads, and swilled from large cups.

By all the Gods! Had the Dissidents taken over Hell? Had all form of lawfulness fled? Hadrian swallowed heavily. If the Dissidents *had* taken power, his life would not be worth spit. His Trip to the Undertaker still vivid in his mind, he had no desire to repeat the performance. He *had* to escape. It did not matter where—anywhere but here, where he was guarded by four tall Moderns equipped with automatic weapons, and surrounded by a backyard full of howling barbarians.

Clothes! He hurried to a closet, eased the door open, and flipped through the clothing he found inside. Gods! The owner of this house was tall and slender. There was no chance of *anything* fitting. But wait—a robe of sorts, made of silk and edged with velvet. Hadrian yanked the robe off its hanger, and wormed his way into it. The sleeves were far too tight and, when belted, the robe came dangerously close to not covering his front. But it was far better than going naked—even a large towel around his middle would have been an improvement. Now that he was dressed, a small sense of dignity crept back into his heart.

And now escape. The bedroom sat to the rear of the house and, with the barbarians running amok next door, there was no chance to slip out the back window. Another window opened onto the side yard. Hadrian eased the window up, froze, his heart in his throat at an imagined sound from the hall, then opened the window all the way. Fortunately, the bedroom was at ground level and the drop to the side yard not that far.

With a prayer to the distant, disinterested Gods, Hadrian slipped a leg through the window, prepared to bolt once both feet had touched the ground.

The entire backyard was filled with people, for the Huns and Mongols had come with their polo back-ups. After the initial rush on the food had died down, everyone had begun to wander around, plate and cup in hand, talking in loud voices. Attila had even brought along two men he knew who played the flute and small, hand-held drums. These fellows were discreet enough, but their playing added to the general din.

Napoleon looked over the crowd, feeling vaguely pleased. He had checked on de Vauban earlier, and the veteran of the *Grande Armée* was still deep in a drug-induced sleep. Now, the steady roar of conversation and laughter filled the backyard. Let Goebbels and company hear anything through this.

He had already eaten enough to last for hours, so he merely strolled around between the groups of laughing, rowdy men, stopping to talk with each, and praising various polo matches he had seen. Marie walked at his side, not saying much, but charming even the most fearsome of the guests with her smile.

Wellington seemed to be the only one who was not having fun: the Iron Duke sat at one of the chairs by a table, gnawing on a rib—some trick, since he held it daintily between just his thumbs and index fingers.

"Wellington," Napoleon said, stopping at his neighbor's side. "Look lively, eh? We don't want Goebbels to think you're not having a good time."

"Huhn." Wellington looked over at his house. "Makes me nervous just thinking about Hadrian left in there with the DGSE men. I'm telling you, if he so much as—" Wellington's face changed. "Napoleon. Look behind. I think we've got party crashers."

Napoleon turned: two short fellows clad in black pajamas had sidled up to the table where the ribs lay, small bowls of rice held in their hands.

"*Mon dieu!*" Napoleon looked back at Wellington. "It's the Cong!"

"What do we do?" Wellington asked, his eyes wide.

"What *can* we do? Nothing. Just leave them alone
and maybe they'll go away."

"This is Hell . . . remember?"

"All right . . . maybe they won't shell our side of
the Park for a while."

The two Viet Cong picked up a rib apiece, looked
furtively around as if expecting to be driven off, and
started eating. Attila, the Huns, and the Mongols did
not seem to mind the party crashers; in fact, no one
paid them any attention at all.

"Hey, y'all!"

A new voice rose over the rumble of conversation.
Napoleon glanced over his shoulder: a portly man
walked into the backyard between his house and
Wellington's. The man wore a plaid shirt and tight
blue jeans over which depended a beer belly; all of
the above were cinched in by a wide belt with a
large buckle (on which was inscribed "Go O.U."),
and finished off by a pair of knobby leather cowboy
boots.

"Our new neighbor?" Marie whispered.

"Guess so."

"All rot," the newcomer said, looking at the platters still stacked with ribs and chicken. "Y'all havin' a
bobby-cue here? Got grells and everthin'."

"*Qu'est-ce que c'est un* 'grell,' Wellington?" Napoleon asked, staring at his latest guest.

"A grill?" Wellington hazarded. "It's hard to tell
what he's saying."

"Now who-all's throwin' this here bash?" The fat
man took a plate from the table and heaped it with
ribs.

"I suppose I am," Napoleon said. Attila had wandered up and stood at the newcomer's shoulder.

"Oh . . . a Chinee," the man said, looking at Attila. "I'm Tommy Hendron from Tulsa, Oklahoma, U.S. of A."

"Attila," Attila said, nodding his head, and taking another bite off his chicken leg.

"At-tu-lah?"

"King of the Huns," Wellington supplied from his chair.

Hendron screwed up his face and stared. "Y'all joshin' me. At-till-ah? The Hun?" He snorted a laugh. "An' who're you?" he asked of Napoleon.

"Napoleon."

The Tulsan stared and then threw back his head and roared with laughter. "Thet's rich! Napol-yun an' At-till-ah the Hun at the same bobby-cue? C'mon, y'all."

"And *I'm* the Duke of Wellington," Wellington said, rising from his chair.

"Who's thet?"

Wellington's face turned red. "Who's that? How *dare* you! Surely you know about—"

"This *is* Hell," Napoleon said, shooting Attila a sidelong look.

"Summon tol' me thet," the Tulsan said, "but I don't know. Where's all the fire an' brimstone?"

"Around," Attila hinted.

"Hail," the Tulsan muttered, and Napoleon was unsure whether it was a curse or a statement. "This cain't be Hail. I *cain't* be in Hail. Why, I sung tenor in the choir, don'tcha know. I went t'church ev'ry Sunday. An' I *never* missed a game! I *cain't* be in Hail!"

"That's what they all say," Napoleon said.

"An' you're Napol-yun? Hey? Where's yer hat and how cum y'don't have yer hand in yer shirt?"

"I don't have fleas."

"Napoleon."

Marie's voice: he looked over his shoulder. The two Cong were still quietly eating the ribs, chasing each bite with a bit of rice. But, wait. Were those the *same* two Cong? Napoleon stared. He was certain the first two had been clean-shaven. Both of these men sported small mustaches.

"Did you see them go anywhere?" he asked Marie in a whisper.

"No. They're not the same two who were here first, are they?"

"I don't think so."

"Napoleon," Marie said, cocking her head, "we *can't* feed the entire Park."

"What're all these Chinee doin' here?" the Tulsan was asking.

"They're *not* Chinese," Wellington said, staring down his long nose. "They're Huns and Mongols."

"Mon-goals? As in Gen-gus Can?"

Napoleon rolled his eyes and led Marie off into the crowd. Just what the neighborhood needed. What had gone wrong with Reassignments? Not that one needed to have been Somebody on Earth to end up in this neighborhood. There was always the couple from California who lived in the house on the other side of Attila. He stopped for a moment. Augustus had hinted that someone in his household was handy with a computer. Did that mean they had access to the Reassignment files?

"Caesar," he muttered, "I'll get you for this one."

The pitch of conversation had grown apace with the liquor imbibed. The Huns and Mongols had all come equipped with bags of *kumiss*—fermented mare's milk—and that, in combination with the beer, had elevated the noise level so it was hard to hear.

Put *that* in your pipe and smoke it, Goebbels.

Ah, well. Tonight the Romans would take Hadrian off Wellington's hands, the DGSE men could leave, and Napoleon would only have the recuperating de Vauban to worry about.

Plus whatever had happened on the opposite side of the Park.

When Napoleon and Marie had made an entire circuit of the backyard and ended up at the tables again, a *new* set of Viet Cong had turned up at the rib platters. Two of them again, clad in black pajamas, but one of this pair wore glasses. Napoleon looked away. *Don't question it. It makes about as much sense as anything* else *in Hell.*

"I s'pose I *am* in Hail," the Tulsan was saying. "I ended up with all th' things frum my house back in Oklahoma. Got my wet bar, my sectional sofa, an' my water bed. Folks who moved me had a sign on the van sayin' 'Axis Moving Company.' An' *they* said they got the stuff frum Hail Movin' an' Starge. But I jes cain't figger it out. Why me?"

Why not? Napoleon thought.

"Napoleon!"

He turned: that was Attila's voice, and the King of the Huns did not sound pleased.

Attila gestured sharply; the look on his face sent a shiver down Napoleon's spine as he rushed from the tables to the corner of his house.

"What's—?"

He looked to where Attila ran: somehow Hadrian had managed to crawl out of Wellington's bedroom window. The ex-Supreme Commander, clad only in Wellington's robe, was sprinting off toward the front of the house. For a man his size, Hadrian moved with astounding speed.

"Get him!" Napoleon yelled, pelting after Attila, knowing neither of them would be in time to keep

Hadrian out of the front yard and—God forbid—out of Goebbels' sight. Napoleon called forth a burst of speed, gaining on Attila.

And coming around the corner, still befuddled and muttering, walked de Vauban, straight into Hadrian's path.

The two men collided, Hadrian falling on top of de Vauban, who let out a yowl of pain. Napoleon reached the human tangle only instants behind Attila. *Dieu en ciel!* Who had seen? Napoleon glanced up: the Roman street crew had stopped its work and stood staring, but Hadrian had not made it to within view of Goebbels' house. Seeming satisfied that things were again in good hands, the street crew returned to its pothole filling.

"The ice! The snow!" de Vauban howled, thrashing beneath Hadrian's considerable weight. "The wagon's going under! We're sinking in the river! DO SOMETHING!"

Attila hauled at Hadrian, Napoleon assisting. Napoleon met Attila's eyes and nodded: the Hun slipped his dagger from his belt, gazed longingly at the blade, and clouted Hadrian on the back of the head with the pommel.

"ANTINOOS!" Hadrian bellowed, stiffened, and fell sideways out of both Napoleon's arms and Attila's. For a long moment, Napoleon stared at Hadrian: satisfied the ex-Commander of Hell's armies was unconscious, he turned to de Vauban.

"I'm dead!" de Vauban muttered. "Dead in the damned river! God . . . I'm cold!"

Footsteps sounded from behind. Napoleon cradled de Vauban's head on his knees and looked up. Five or six Huns had gathered behind Attila. And there, his narrow face going redder with each passing second, stood Wellington.

"That bloody slime! He's wearing my robe! Look what he's done to it! Torn it! I'll kill him . . . I swear, I'll *kill* him!"

Attila gestured the Huns forward. "Get Hadrian back inside," he barked. "Hurry!"

The Huns gathered up the unconscious Roman Emperor (no mean feat) and carried him back to the opened window. Two of them clambered inside and, assisted by their comrades, hauled Hadrian back into the bedroom.

A loud ripping sound came from the window.

"Fools! You're ripping the robe even more! I'll—"

"Wellington . . . shut up!" Napoleon had, with Attila's help, got de Vauban to his feet. "I'll buy you a new robe, I promise. Now cool it."

"But—"

"Well-l-lington."

"Damned fat, bloody pig!" Wellington stood staring at his window, closed now that the Huns had dragged Hadrian back inside. "Ruin *my* robe, will you?"

"Wellington . . . SHUT UP!" Napoleon glanced at Attila. "Get in there and see what's happened to the DGSE men. Tell them we'll have to give Hadrian another shot. We've only got one left, but we can't afford to have him running all over the neighborhood. And keep the party going. If Goebbels notices anything, we're dead."

Attila nodded, sent the remaining Huns off to the crowded backyard, and trotted around to Wellington's back door.

"Help me get de Vauban inside," Napoleon asked Wellington. Marie had rushed around to the side yard, and now stood holding de Vauban's other shoulder.

"Another new robe?" Wellington prompted. "You promised."

"Oh, for God's sake, Wellington. I'll get you *two* . . . one for the morning, and one for the night. Now grab de Vauban's other side, will you?"

Wellington muttered something, glared at his bedroom window through which the Huns had dragged Hadrian, and took de Vauban's weight from Marie.

"Moscow!" the soldier murmured, crying again. "I always *hated* winter. . . ."

"With any kind of luck—which we haven't had lately—Goebbels will think he's just another drunken party guest," Napoleon said. Wellington's only comment was another malediction aimed at Hadrian.

Attila sauntered from Wellington's house across Napoleon's backyard, adding a certain drunken list to his walk. "Idiots were watching TV," he said to Napoleon. "Now they're so embarrassed about Hadrian's escape, I don't think anything will stir in that house without them knowing about it."

"Moscow . . ." De Vauban shook his head. "Damned river!"

"And there was someone else in the house with them," Attila added, his tone of voice bringing Napoleon to instant alert. "Don't know how he got in and didn't ask. *You* talk to him. I'll help Wellington get de Vauban inside."

Napoleon transferred de Vauban to Attila and turned around as another Hun came staggering across the backyard. Another Hun? From a distance, yes . . . but close up?

"A message for you," the Roman said, pushing his leather and fur hat back on his head. "With regrets. You'll have to keep Hadrianus another three days."

"Another three—?" Napoleon stared at the Roman.

The Roman grinned a good-natured Hunnish grin that didn't touch his eyes, lifted his cup, and disappeared into the laughing crowd.

Napoleon glanced sidelong at Marie, then looked out over the party. The Huns and Mongols had settled down to serious drinking (the Roman indistinguishable among them). A few Mongols had started dancing drunkenly around the backyard, whooping with every step. Wellington had returned to his chair by the table and perched there in obvious ill humor, while Attila and the Tulsan eyed each other like two scruffy dogs, unsure whether to fight or play.

"*Dieu en ciel!*" Napoleon's shoulders slumped as he took Marie's hand. "Three more days of *this*? The Tulsan can't believe he's in Hell. Huhn. I know *I* am."

SPITTING IN THE WIND

Lynn Abbey

He lay motionless as he came to consciousness, waiting for the whirring machines and the drain of the innumerable tubes protruding from natural and unnatural orifices to tell him he was still alive. To tell him that it was all a nightmare of dying and not dying itself. It was only a hope—a half-hearted exercise he went through from habit and because it reminded him who he was. Or had been.

There was only one unnatural tube sprouting from his belly and this was not, on its best day, the hospital.

A prodigious, inherently terrifying belch erupted from elsewhere in the room. Despite himself, he cringed, the tightening of his facial muscles revealing not only that he was awake but that he was, after a perverted fashion, very much alive.

"Yuri! Open your eyes. It's a beautiful day!"

An undoubtedly filthy hand crashed down on his chest, jarring him so that he belched as well and got an eyeful of plaster dust as he acknowledged his unchosen companion's greeting. Like a yawn in a crowded room, the belch proved contagious. The bushy-browed giant sitting beside him let loose another one that reeked of ozone and glowed magnesium-bright in the dingy flat.

"Damn you—be careful!" The man who had once been Yuri Andropov, architect of the modern KGB and ruler of the U.S.S.R., snarled as he pushed the other's hand away.

Leonid gave a shrug that was part disdain and the rest schoolboy pique. He retreated to the other cot and sat staring out the window at the roiled, polluted sky. Yuri swung his feet over the bedside, carefully maneuvering the flexible tube coiling from his navel, and waited for his other inescapable companion to make his first appearance of the day.

In a few moments a white-haired, lax-faced man took shape in the corner shadows. He came forward, blind-eyed and shambling, and hefted a dark, medium-sized, featureless box from the floor at Yuri's feet— featureless except for the shiny socket that held the other end of his umbilical cord. Yuri got up before the cord was fully extended and followed the ghost into the lavatory.

The absurdity of this all-too-real afterlife was exquisitely captured by the room's plumbing. Rust stains in brown, green, and creeping magenta corroded the washbasin. The pipes coughed, shook, and wheezed, and the water, on those rare occasions when it surged as high as their sixth-floor walkup, had the color, texture, and aroma of burnt coffee. But the toilet, here in a part of Hell where a man's plumbing was short-circuited and constipation eternal, glistened like virgin snow. It gushed clear, icy water and, without a second thought, Yuri knelt down to wash his face while Konstantin wedged the box into the washbasin.

Then he vomited, flushed twice, and sat on the ring. Not having the ability to shit didn't eliminate the need to try—the compelling need to *try* that gave every resident of this region the devil's own hemorrhoids. His truncated intestines knotted in on themselves, giving the umbilical tube a nauseating tug, even as the aroma of a grease-laden breakfast crowded in beside him. With a final belch and groan, Yuri heaved himself to his feet and carried his box into the other room.

"You should give up eating," Leonid suggested.

Andropov shot him a disdainful snort as he shoved his fork into the rubbery eggs the ghost set before him. "You're bleeding again," he added.

The bearish giant opened his overcoat. His shirt and trousers were decorated with a patchwork of brown stains, indicating that the accusation had been true many times in the past, but it was not, at this moment, accurate. He patted his abdomen affectionately, belched brilliantly, and closed his overcoat.

"It's the best way. Solves two problems at once. Everybody else's having it done."

Andropov ignored him. It was true that the appearance of the Nazi doctor had wrought changes in New Hell's exclusive PND community: the men, and occasional woman, who had had the ability to usher in the nuclear winter with their fingertips and who now sprouted fusion boxes—Personal Nuclear Devices—from their navels. And it was also true that having the PND implanted inside one's belly not only solved the problem of what to do with the damn thing, but got rid of the equally damnable digestion problems. Belching white heat and having an incision that never completely healed seemed a small price to pay—but it would be a cold day in Hell before Yuri put himself under Mengele's knife.

He applied himself to the last of his charred, crumbling bacon, contriving not to notice Konstantin as he folded the cots and threw the garbage out the window.

"You're going in again?"

"I have a job to do," Yuri explained to the bear as he removed his trousers from the crude clothespress he had constructed above the wheezing radiator pipes.

The bear laughed; *that* was magnesium-bright as well. "Here?" he sputtered like some comic book character. "Whatever they've got you doing, it will go much better if you don't do it."

"I do not choose to spend my days at the circus."

"Piccadilly's more important than the Pentagram. Everyone goes through Piccadilly."

Yuri gave him a dark look. His roommate and Kremlin predecessor had a greater tolerance of New Hell than he would ever have—he hoped. Leonid Brezhnev positively throve in Satan's homeland. He had regained the boorish vigor and stamina of his early middle age and, despite his increasing indolence, this crazy world was yielding its secrets to him.

"Suit yourself, then," Leonid shrugged with what Yuri knew was sincere disappointment. The man hungered for backslapping friendship; Yuri got one of this life's few satisfactions by denying it.

Konstantin gathered the PND in his arms and the men began their descent to the streets. They lived in a part of New Hell that could have been lifted from almost any modern Siberian city. Indeed, Yuri suspected it *was* a Siberian city: Irkutsk. The signs were Cyrillic, and from time to time, he could hear snippets of what he thought were Russian conversations as they made their way toward the railway station.

Hadn't Siberia always been compared to Hell, and wouldn't it be just like Hell to extend to Irkutsk? But yesterday Yuri had been equally certain they were in Yakutsk, and the day before that, in Usk-Kut. As sure as he had become that the babushkas sweeping the railway platform around them circumvented nothing more dreadful than the Kremlin, Andropov knew that their Trans-Siberian Railway tickets were passages to New Hell itself.

There were other discontinuities in this existence. Language, for example: Why could he think in Russian, dream in Russian, but speak only English or, worse, Archaic Greek? And what had happened to Konstantin Chernenko? Could anyone else in this world or the previous one see him? Did the PND appear to float above the worn upholstery—or was it a ghost as well? Was the tragic-faced man's twilight existence the ultimate condemnation of the Kremlin's gerontocracy?

Yuri had discussed Chernenko's condition with Leonid shortly after the ghost had first appeared, but his counterpart had simply shrugged off the questions.

"This is Hell, is it not? Do not seek philosophy or reason here. He is a ghost, and you and I, we are little bombs. Who would have thought that we, good atheists purged of religious idiocy, would come to a socialist Hell?" Leonid had laughed, then, at the absurdity. This was before Mengele and his laughter was not brilliant, merely inflammable. "But Yuri, of everyone who is here, is it not remarkable that we're the only ones who're prepared? A socialist Hell run by amateurs! Don't teach your grandmother to steal sheep, eh?"

Andropov had taken that advice, or at least he no

longer sought philosophy and reason from the man
Hell's justice had set beside him for, he suspected,
all eternity. He still sought answers in the shattered
corridors of his mind—corridors that veered dangerously close to insanity. Not, he feared, that insanity
had any meaning in New Hell.

The train rocked its way through the featureless
Siberian landscape; storm clouds gathered along the
horizon. They always did, never in the same place or
at the same time, at least once during their daily
journey. Darkness enveloped the car as the electricity failed. Yuri gripped the armrests while Leonid
settled back for a nap. Sometime in the next few
moments, when the lightning crackled and grounded
itself in the metal around them, they'd make the
transition. He wanted to see it happen—wanted
proof that his personal Hell sent him to Siberia each
and every night—but the lightning was a thousand
times more brilliant than Brezhnev's belches and his
eyes were either shut tight or blinded.

When he looked again they were in a crowded
subway car that had been stolen or copied from New
York City's IRT. It stopped, with a half-dozen bone-
jolting lurches and squealing brakes that did, indeed,
bring blood to some unfortunate passengers' ears, at
Piccadilly Circus, where Leonid, after a final invitation, took his leave. A hundred lost souls, give or
take a dozen, shoved their way into the car. They
battled for Brezhnev's vacant seat; battled to the
death—or to the Undertaker, which was worse. But
no one ever attempted to sit in Konstantin's seat, so
perhaps they *could* see him or the PND.

Leonid claimed Piccadilly was the probability gen-
erator for the afterlife—an infernal Siege Perilous
designed to speed the damned to their appropriate
fate, although it was both grossly and subtly imper-

fect, like everything else here. Andropov conceded that the bear was probably right—but that it didn't matter for him. He would always pass safely through Piccadilly—because he would have preferred any destination but Mendenham Station, which was, invariably, the end of his personal line.

He was the only one from his car to leave at the soot-stained underground station; the only one from the whole train, unless one counted Konstantin, still patiently bearing the PND, as an equally damned soul. But then, Yuri'd never seen anyone else exit or enter the station. The same drab ticket-seller with the onion-ring glasses was always on duty, still struggling with the same crossword puzzle. He had wondered what the little man had been—had even tried to strike casual conversations with him the first few times he had exchanged Hell's faded, greasy currency for brass slug tokens. But the gnome could be neither tempted nor taunted into revealing his other life.

The stairway ended in the lobby of some long-abandoned hotel, but a hotel such as never existed in the U.S.S.R. There were distinctions to be made in monumental, oppressive architectural styles that Andropov had never appreciated in mortal life. The Soviet state—indeed, almost all socialist states his own had influenced—was gray and massive; it *looked* like it would endure, even if the plaster began peeling before it was fully dry. Mendenham Station, however, was both old and unfinished—as if its creators had run out of imagination three-quarters of the way through the job. It reminded him of those backwater towns that his agents had hated so much in South and Central America.

The dust, the heat, the flies, the indolence and suspicion of the inhabitants who watched him emerge from the hotel: they all oppressed him as he crossed the plaza to the chipped stucco edifice Satan deemed appropriate for his esteemed chief of security. One of his many chiefs of security, Yuri reminded himself as he slid the warped plastic card into the encoder a half-dozen times before it registered and the door swung open.

Andropov heaved a sigh of relief as he stepped into the sumptuous, if slightly flawed, facsimile of a Palladian library. On better days, an admittedly relative judgment in this life, he often played a mental game of "what's wrong with this picture," still finding a source of pride in his accurate memories of all things English and American. Today, however, what was wrong with the room was all too obvious.

A knife-hilt was protruding from the computer's video display.

Unmindful of the wrenching in his stomach as the ghost struggled to keep up with him, Yuri made his way across the room.

"Bloody Hells," he muttered, his tongue making refined English out of the lengthy Russian phrases rattling through his mind.

Flickering green light flowed from the bottom of the shattered glass. It would take weeks to get the damned thing repaired or replaced—as if that were the greatest of his problems. Gingerly, he took hold of the very end of the hilt and eased the blade out. The knife fell to the desk top, putting a gouge in the rosewood that went through to the chipboard beneath. Yuri cursed again: Mephistopheles himself had sworn the wood was genuine.

"Look at this!" he complained. The ghost opened its eyes and looked—in the other direction.

Andropov shook his head that a member of the politburo—a man he had never liked, but whose power and influence he'd been wise enough to respect—should have come to such a fate, then turned his attention to the note that had dropped beside the knife.

NOW

S.

The marks fairly ate through the human parchment Satan used for his most personal correspondence. Yuri sank into his chair too fast for Konstantin; the tube tugged at his gut. He was wracked by spasms of nauseated agony that almost equalled the promise of the note.

When the physical and mental shocks subsided, he had the presence of mind to study the knife—not as a weapon against either himself or his boss, but because it was the devil's own knife. Andropov was no great judge of weaponry; he'd always done his fighting from behind a desk, but he judged this a deadly little blade, and all the more valuable because the steel showed no pitting or corrosion. There were others here in Hell who'd give anything to have a knife like this at their sides—if there were anything in Hell worth giving or having.

Yuri tucked the knife deep in the bottom drawer of his desk and, with a timely nod to the ghost, headed back for the street.

The Underground didn't go to the Pentagram. Satan didn't leave himself exposed to his subjects, not even here. But if you were summoned, then transportation usually manifested itself. Andropov had paced the sidewalk no more than a few minutes before the brightly painted jalopy pulled up alongside.

"Gedin," its driver commanded.

He settled into the open back seat, reminding himself that appearances in New Hell were the ultimate deception. He had been summoned by the head honcho and he'd arrive there in one piece, shaken and nauseated from the potholes and the twisting of the PND's cord—unless it was the devil himself driving.

"We're smarter than *He* is," Leonid was apt to say when he felt the urge to demonstrate how much he trusted his roommate. "We can see through him. Try it sometime: let your mind go blank and listen. He always gives himself away."

And though Yuri could not bring himself to turn Leonid in, he'd never felt the urge to test the bear's outrageous theories. Until now. It couldn't hurt to have a little foreknowledge—no matter how much worse things were going to get. He closed his mind to the jolting and shaking, to the belching and heartburn, and like some decadent Christian saint (of which there were several here in Hell), he waited for a SIGN.

"Dusenburg."

First it was a word. A meaningless word—probably some polluted city in Eastern Germany where he'd lost an agent or two—but then it was an image: an automobile utterly unlike the one in which he was a passenger. It was a huge thing with leather and camel-hair upholstery, a chauffeur, a wet bar, and an unsavory past.

Gangsters. American gangsters—so that was the lay of the land.

Well, it could have been worse; it had been worse before. At their first, explosively disastrous interview, the devil had been a 1960s American businessman who had a parody of Marilyn Monroe pretending to be a secretary-receptionist. Andropov tried to repress that afternoon—his first clear memories of the afterlife. He remembered their second meeting better.

The summons had been hand-delivered by a spectacularly wigged gentleman claiming to be Cotton Mather; the journey had been accomplished in a four-horse coach with worse suspension than this Third-World reject jalopy and, rather than meeting in a Howard Hughes construction dis-stravaganza, he'd spoken with a Louis XIV version of evil incarnate in a not particularly well-done recreation of Versailles.

"I expected better from you," Lucifer had said scornfully, the reports in his lace-edged fist bursting into flames as he spoke. "This—" He opened his hand, and the paper and flames vanished. "—is garbage."

Konstantin hadn't been visible long, then, and they frequently jostled one another when Yuri made a sudden or nervous move—as he did when the monarch's hands manifested long, black talons. The umbilical cord jerked taut, and his apologies were transmitted through a succession of belches.

"It has taken me some time to get established, your . . .?" He hadn't even been able to remember the appropriate form of address for Satan disguised as a French king. "Most of my best operatives and agents have already been co-opted: the Fallen Angels, the Insecurité, the Reich's Norm Snoopers—"

"Louie, just Louie," the boss explained in a more conciliatory tone. "Stop looking; Hell doesn't work that way. Take what you can get; you've dealt with worse—I've checked."

Lucifer adjusted a rococo mirror until a parade of computerized text marched across it. Andropov had swallowed hard as a series of KGB improvisations and indiscretions scrolled past.

"I thought you'd gotten the knack with the Tania gambit, but since then— Yuri, Yuri, your information about the rebel forces I can get from anywhere.

"And the rest? The rest: Joseph Smith and the Mormons migrating to the fifth level; Savonarola running a *samizdat* operation; Richard the Lionhearted and his mother organizing a Crusade. A *Crusade* here in Hell. Yuri, if you can find some sort of pattern to all this, then I'll be forced to conclude that the source of our problem is at a higher level."

He'd said nothing in his defense. What could he say? His operatives weren't so much incompetent as nonexistent. Everything he'd put together had come, one way or the other, from the bear's reports about Piccadilly. Even Tania had been Leonid's discovery; he'd recognized her dragging two worn shopping bags through the station and taken pity on her. As Louie had taken pity on him—the devil's own pity, and a fate worse than death itself.

"Englishmen," the French king had said at the end of their conversation. "I'll find you some Englishmen. They're always good at this sort of thing."

And for a few days Andropov had been encouraged. Englishmen *were* good at this sort of thing. The KGB hadn't been the only force recruiting in their insufferable public schools. Then the recruits showed up: the Hellfire Club, as useless a lot of ex-eighteenth century profligates as Hell supported. They were intelligent, witty, energetic and, to a man, utterly insane in a way only New Hell could appreciate.

These men had, after all, dedicated their mortal existences to the pursuit of damnation. They had not adjusted well to the petty irritations that greeted them instead of debauchery and brimstone. If Che Guevara was running some reformist exercise in futility out in the wilderness, then the Earl of Sandwich and his friends were the reactionary rear-guard, determined to put some zest and heat in everyone's eternal damnation.

He stared bleakly out the open window. They had entered the section of skewed, official-looking building, a cross between his own Moscow and Albany, New York, where such authority and organization as Hell had called home. Uniformed guards and half-naked barbarians strode blindly past each other on the wide, cracked pavements. The poison ivy creeping up the walls was, at this distance, almost attractive, and, deep in his own thoughts, Yuri Andropov was convinced that the Hellfire Club had done it to him again.

It was Monroe's day off, or Lucifer had finally gotten himself an efficient rather than attractive secretary, for the woman (a nameplate on her desk had identified her as *Ms* Anthony) who led him through the warped doorway was the ugliest broad this side of the Urals.

No amount of illusion or disguise—and today he looked like Edward G. Robinson—could hide Satan. Yuri felt his presence, felt fear twisting through the vestiges of his bowels, and was grateful for the chair those terrible hands pointed toward. So compelling were those magnetic, endless eyes that it was some moments before he realized that he wasn't alone with the boss. The Undertaker, wrathful and stinking, was the third point of an uncompleted pentagram marked in the carpeting, and the one who began the conversation.

"I only got so much time to waste with reconstructions," the cadaver whined. "My real work is in original vitalizations—and I'm falling behind, Nick. Ya gotta do something about it."

"I'll try," the man in the cantilever-shoulder suit soothed.

As far as Andropov's, or Leonid's, information went, the Undertaker had come to Hell at the beginning—right behind Satan himself. With his unspeakable breath and worse humor, he was one of the few Hellacious institutions of which the Hellfire Club approved. Yuri's bad feelings about this interview were intensifying.

"Keep 'em the Hell outta my lockers! I got better things to do than put 'em back together again. Even in No-Time I got no time to fix up no dumb-ass gentlemen, not if you want me in phase with you *at all*, Nick."

The gangster turned to Andropov. "You can see we've got a problem here."

"The rebels are moving?" he answered, twisting in the wind of Lucifer's attention. "Caesar's army has launched its assault?"

"Suicide," Satan corrected.

"Suicide?"

"Suicide—regular, repeated, and multiple."

There were a few things that simply didn't happen very often in Hell. Suicide was one, largely because of the malodorous apparition reeking in his corner. It was rumored that each false resurrection put one's soul deeper into Hell's mire, but the real reason that no one tried suicide, more than once, was the eternity one spent, in very naked pieces, lying on a slab listening to the Undertaker's transcendentally stale jokes.

Andropov had tried suicide in this very office and spent an unpleasant portion of eternity in the Undertaker's presence. He'd protect his miserable existence and his PND as he had never protected his mortal flesh, to buy freedom from another eternity in Hell's morgue.

"I find it hard to imagine, sir," he said after a moment, then added: "He's a great deterrent," because, ironically, it was impossible to lie in the devil's presence.

"I am relieved to know that some things around here do actually work, Yuri, but I'm afraid it *is* happening, and I'm afraid that the ones doing it claim to be under your orders."

Once, in the previous life, fear had had its limits, but in Hell, certain emotions were open-ended. Andropov pushed the envelope of dread and terror as he contemplated what the Earl and his friends might be up to. "It can't be," he said, as much to himself as to his interrogator. "They wouldn't do that to me. They couldn't. The instructions are clear: infiltrate the rebel cells, gather information, and return.

"I thought they were starting to get the hang of it. The reports were coming in regularly. They were even starting to turn up interesting data . . ."

"An' killin' 'emselves every chance they get. Every damn night for the last— Shit, every damn night for a long time now. Polo it was, last time. *Polo*, and with the Huns, no less. Bodies all mashed up in one heap an' the heads blasted through the goal posts."

Yuri had wrapped his umbilical in his fist, knotting it, adding to his private agony. "No," he whispered, tears starting to form in the corners of his eyes. "They come back. *They come back.* They couldn't keep coming back—not after every night."

"It happens—sometimes," Satan confided, giving a baleful glance toward his not-quite-feline familiar. He seemed almost embarrassed. "Affinities—damnations, if you prefer—occasionally require certain, ah, souls to remain linked until Doomsday." He nodded toward Konstantin; the ghost's eyes opened and he seemed aware of his surroundings for a fleeting moment. "You have considerable nexus potential yourself. It seems to have extended itself to your agents."

Andropov's bitterness got the better of his judgment. "Dammit, what've I done to deserve them?"

The Devil's eyes smoldered. His gangster persona grew fuzzy at the edges. "Don't push your luck," he hissed on wind that reached back to eternity. "It can be worse—worse than you can yet imagine."

Absolute danger burned the fear out of Andropov. He felt more alive than he'd ever been as premier, at least. His nerves steadied and the umbilicus dropped from his fingers as he got to his feet.

"So be it. *Fait accompli*—the Hellfire Club is mine and they amuse themselves by committing suicide. I remember the other world; I remember Beria and the Thirties. I've got a dozen lunatic Englishmen. If they're enough to throw him off his production quotas, then, I humbly submit, your problem is much greater than mine."

"It ain't that simple, Boss. You know that," the Undertaker whined as those still-red eyes refocused on him.

"But my man has a point." Satan's manicured fingernails clicked across a keypad. "Even with seasonal adjustments, volume is below peak."

The cadaver twitched like a deranged marionette. His arm extended and grew long fingernails that brushed against Yuri's ashen, but unquivering, flesh. "Him. Him an' his Limeys. Nothin' neat with them. No, not at all. They come through all mashed up, in pieces even, pickled so badly the harpies won't touch them. No, nothin' simple puttin' 'em back together. Takes forever with 'em lyin' there, laughing at me.

'Quaint,' they call me. Quaint! How can I work? How can I do my job? Get rid of him—"

Yuri felt his cheek split. His body flinched of its own accord as chthonian pestilence escaped into his bloodstream. It took more than a lifetime's worth of steel and backbone to spin around on his heels to Satan, the wound lengthening as he moved, and extend one silent thought: *Call off your dog.*

"Enough!" Lucifer's hands flashed with blood-red fire. The Undertaker shrieked; Yuri felt the flames dancing on his face. "Susie, get your ass in here."

"You will address me as Ms. Anthony," the harridan's disembodied voice replied through a desk speaker, "if you desire my services."

The speaker exploded, and the door burst open to hang limply from half-melted hinges. Yuri actually felt his heart stop as the devil's wrath froze time in its tracks.

"I don't desire your damned services. I desire your worthless ass in here!"

He snapped his fingers. Andropov's heart shuddered back to work and the steel-haired female marched stiffly through the door. She took her place on the fourth point of the pentagram. The devil pried Michael from his shoulder, where the familiar had climbed for a better view of the confrontation, and tossed it at the fifth point. Fluffing its spiky fur, Michael bared its fangs and spat acid.

Ms. Anthony hissed right back. "Mrs. Pankhurst will hear about this," she muttered before her embattled master sealed her lips.

He snapped his fingers again. Yuri found himself wrenched through the void of eternity, his body arriving in the Undertaker's workrooms well ahead of his nerves and his courage. Falling to his knees, he was oblivious to everything except the dry heaving of his stomach.

"Are you quite finished?" Lucifer inquired as Andropov gulped air.

Yuri tried to nod his head, but the motion kicked off another round. His spit was blood before a taloned hand closed over his neck.

"I could fix him," the Undertaker volunteered. "Fix him up good."

"Umm," Satan replied, giving Yuri's neck a final squeeze. "Remember, you're behind already. Don't bite off more than you can chew."

Andropov remained on his knees while the boss inspected bottles and jars, the contents of which Yuri had no desire to know. The nausea was gone, and with it the bloating that had plagued him since his second resurrection. He wished for a men's room. Tremors were rippling through his bowels; they felt like the real thing.

They had something out on the slab by the time Yuri resumed reluctant control over his intestines and studied the room that was, with its racks of spotted glassware, rusted scalpels, and shredded tubing, the source of his most hellish nightmares. It could have been the morgue below KGB headquarters.

Emboldened by that thought, he moved to join his superiors by the slab.

But the miniature mounds of flesh quivering beneath the Undertaker's skeletal fingers were beyond, or beneath, even the KGB's destructive talents. All the memories gushed back into Yuri's consciousness. He gripped the enameled table, its icy solidity keeping him on his feet.

As field operatives, the Clubmen were unmitigated disasters, but surely they had done nothing to deserve the Undertaker's shiny black slab. Tiny naked arms and legs folded and twitched like freshly aborted embryos, but Yuri nevertheless easily recognized the faces of Francis Dashwood, John Wilkes, and Thomas Potter, the most charming and impetuous of his charges. He could have endured that sight, even as the Undertaker poked and prodded to display some obscure feature to his master, but each homunculus sprouted an artery from the base of its spine, connecting it to a throbbing mound of unformed flesh.

Immediately Andropov understood the cause of his, and certain other hellish citizens', physical deformity. It was knowledge that demanded nausea but, in keeping with Hell's perversity, Satan's touch still numbed his gut.

"God, no," he whispered: the translation reflex that turned his properly Communist thoughts into English was as defective as his bowels.

He withered under the boss's raised-eyebrow appraisal. Expecting the worst, he kept his mouth closed and gripped the table tighter.

"And our information about the rebels?" Lucifer asked in a softly modulated voice.

Andropov opened his eyes as the Undertaker brought out another protoplasm blob and set it beside the Hellfire Club. Another trio of partly formed miniatures were spat out with an unpleasant, liquid sound.

"Incomplete. This one—" The Undertaker used his scalpel to spread its arms; even Yuri could tell it was horribly deformed. "A Slope, a big one: Uncle Ho himself—maybe?"

"Maybe?" Lucifer's incredulity froze the air.

"Look at it! How'm I supposed to print that? Damn Cong always understood body counts. Well, they aren't just carryin' 'em home anymore—they're keepin' 'em home. Creation ain't exactly our long suit, Boss."

"Face it—" Susan B. Anthony had found her tongue and was putting it to use again. "The Deceiver's been deceived; the Old Trickster's been foiled again."

The devil raised a fist that could have consigned her soul to another Hell, but the harridan didn't blink.

"Did you think you were above your own damnation?" she continued, warming to her harangue. "Did you think Hell wasn't big enough for you? The rebels are His agents sent to curb your infernal pride. They'll build a tower to Paradise before—"

An obscene gesture sealed her lips again, but not before she had formed them into a triumphant smirk. Watching the two of them glaring at each other, it occurred to Andropov that Hell was home to certain souls not because of some great evil committed during their mortal lives, but because Hell deserved them. The flashing-eyed Anthony would have been out of place in any heaven but Hell.

"Well, what about it?" Satan inquired. "These others—is this some widespread new tactic on their part?"

The Undertaker shrugged, a gesture that accentuated his resemblance to a poorly reassembled skeleton. He unrolled the second homunculus. It did not appear deformed but, unlike all the others, it was completely motionless. "This one—Caesarion—he's got some interesting notions in his head. Came through intact—or so's I thought—but he's not growin' neither, so I gotta add juice. Everything inside gets fuzzy once I do that." He turned his attention to the last twitching bit of crypto-humanity. "And this one—Lawrence, Thomas Edward. Another pickled Limey—empty as the day he was born."

"But is it systematic? Something breaking down *here* or something they're doing out *there*?"

The Undertaker shrugged again and went back to tormenting the unfortunate Lawrence. Yuri watched the pathetic creature writhe and scream in high-pitched agony. The infernal calm within his gut had faded. A ripe belch bubbled loudly—a harbinger of louder and more massive things to come. Lucifer turned to stare at him.

"You. You find out."

"But I," Andropov protested, stepping away from the table even as he gestured to the tiny lumps that were in some way his field agents.

"Will find out what is happening in the rebel camps and you'll put a stop to it."

With the Undertaker cackling in the background, Lucifer made a green-glowing gesture with his index finger. Yuri felt the air rip out of his lungs faster than he could scream.

He was clinging to his PND, squeezing right through the ghost, when his thoughts cleared again and he found himself standing in front of his office on the dusty, generic Latin American street above Mendenham Station. The local peasants were studying him as if he'd grown another head. Relinquishing the PND back to Konstantin, Yuri neatened his thread-bare jacket and approached the door with more *sang-froid* than he felt. His fingers came to an abrupt halt inches above the sonic lock; the Club was in session in his waiting room.

"They were the same jokes, I'm telling you. The old boy's run through his repertoire already."

"No, there was one about this bloody Hitler, the Italians, and some little furry creatures I hadn't heard before."

Andropov shuddered; he recognized both the Earl's

and Wilkes' voice. It would be just like the pair of
them to collect the Undertaker's humor. Hadn't it
only been moments ago, a few painful heartbeats at
the most, that he'd seen their miniature forms on the
Undertaker's slab, and whatever else the ghoul had
been doing, he hadn't been telling jokes. Expecting
the worst, he tapped a five-tone movie theme onto
the sonic pad.

But Francis Dashwood and his companion looked,
as usual, better than he did. Sprawled across the
furniture, several empty port-wine bottles on the
table between them, the rakish pair radiated a glow
of health and contentment that, in Hell, was obscene. Gaudy as silk peacocks, it seemed certain that
they'd come to Hell with their mortal possessions
intact and had never had to venture into the Black
Market for any of their daily needs or desires.

The fourth Earl of Sandwich saluted him with one
of his eponymous creations that overflowed with slices
of rare, juicy meat and horseradish.

"*Fay ce que voundras,*" the aristocrat announced,
as if Yuri were an unannounced intruder, rather than
the rightful resident of the suite. "We've been waiting for you."

"Dashing good time last night," Wilkes added, a
sidelong glance toward the Earl, who chuckled with
appreciation. They loved puns and schoolboy humor,
these determinedly debauched young men; perhaps
that was why they cultivated their suicidal relation-
ship with Hell's Undertaker.

"You were supposed to be at the Country Club
measuring the rebel presence," Andropov chided
sharply, "'not playing polo with Attilla's boys."

"But, Andy," Dashwood replied, unwinding from
the chair, then draping an elegant arm across Yuri's
shoulder. "Polo is *the* game at the Country Club

these days, and Attaboy's in the thick of it. It's all in the report, just like you wanted."

Yuri glanced at the vellum sheets on his desk. Resurrection had taken care of the worst of the Earl's anachronistic English accent and vocabulary but, in keeping with the general traditions of Hell, it had done nothing for his handwriting or his spelling. Untangling the report would take hours.

"You got creamed. You've lost Potter," he reminded them, thinking of the third homunculus he'd seen on the slab.

His agents took this for a joke. Dashwood, who could not seem to comprehend nuclear war and who did not, therefore, clearly see the PND, much less the ghost, pounded Yuri's shoulder until the cord in his belly ached.

"Stewed, not creamed," Wilkes calmly corrected from his chair. "He'll be back ere long."

The incompleteness of Hell, once planted in a man's bowels, extended to his gonads. Most such men reluctantly accepted a vow of eternal chastity, but not the one-time Mad Monks of Mendenham, whose jaded tastes apparently included eternal frustration. Each had taken the loneliness of Hell's street-walkers as a personal challenge.

"Well, you're to preserve your lives, if not your dignity, from now on. The Undertaker doesn't want to see any of you again."

"I told you he'd run out of jokes," Wilkes injected.

"I'm serious. I've met with the boss and something's gone wrong. They might not be able to bring you back—"

Both men raised an eyebrow—Wilkes the left one and the Earl his right—and stared at him with mock astonishment.

Andropov shrugged away from Dashwood and retreated to his high-backed chair behind the desk. Nothing, absolutely nothing, in his vast store of experience prepared him for the herculean task of converting the Hellfire Club into reliable operatives. Secure in their cynicism, the only motivation they understood was one that approximated their own quest for the Hell they'd seen in Hieronymous Bosch's painting.

Yuri glanced at the digital clock facing him on the desk. One P.M.—though time, like everything else, was unreliable here. It read seven P.M. by the time he'd done his best to bend his agents to the tasks Lucifer had assigned.

The street was dark by the time he sealed the office and led the ghost to the Underground station. They waited for what seemed like another hour before an empty train screeched to a halt and spread its graffiti-coated doors. Absently he counted the stops to Piccadilly: nine, ten, eleven. He remembered counting to twelve in the morning, but it was eleven now. A half-dozen or so lost souls found seats in the car. Yuri found himself hoping that Leonid had waited, but the bear wasn't in sight.

In the morning it was thunderstorms; on the return trip the car simply plunged into darkness for an instant before emerging onto the Siberian steppes. A niggle of curiosity nudged Yuri to ride the last car some evening and observe the landscape as the transformed train rose from the Underground; it was an urging he hoped he'd always be able to resist. Leaning against the window, he let the rhythms of the uneven track ease some of the tension in his neck. If he got lucky, he'd fall asleep. He needn't worry about missing his station. Wherever he was, wherever this train happened to be going, he would ride it out to the end of the line.

Snow was falling when the train powered down. Shoving his hands deep in his coat pockets, he hurried through a lobby that was as drab and unremarkable as any other, and yet was subtly not the one he had used in the morning. He turned left at the front door and started counting his steps, hoping the snow wasn't causing him to change the length of his stride by too much.

Nine hundred steps, and he was almost at an empty, wind-swept intersection. Left again—into the teeth of the wind. Clutching the coat tightly across his chest, his head tucked as deep into the thin collar as he could get it, he counted aloud. One hundred . . . Two hundred . . . Was it possible for a man to freeze solid in Hell? Six hundred and sixty-six, an auspicious number and a shadowed doorway on his right. Fingers numb and almost useless, he fumbled with the latch until it admitted him to a naked vestibule.

Not trying to count now but just to climb to the uppermost flat, Yuri stomped his way up loudly protesting stairs, Konstantin plodding noiselessly behind him. As he rounded the last landing the aroma of greasy boiled cabbage overwhelmed him. The bear—if he had counted correctly while outside—was cooking dinner.

And it was Leonid who opened the door to greet him, dripping utensils in one hand.

"Greetings, comrade! I thought maybe you'd finally gotten yourself lost. Relax. Sit by the pipes—they're steaming tonight. Dinner's almost ready."

The bear enveloped him in a hug that made both of them belch, but Yuri was grateful for the warmth, just as he was grateful for the promise of food. Leonid was a far better cook and scavenger than was the ghost.

"But you don't even eat," he commented, almost apologetically, as he leaned against the heating pipes.

"You do, and he does—I think. It's the least I can do."

Leonid didn't mean the ghost but a fourth presence in the room— a man Yuri hadn't noticed at first but whom he recognized at once.

"Lawrence," he whispered.

"Ah, you know him. I thought so. I found him in the men's room at the Circus. He doesn't seem—quite all there."

When snapping his fingers in front of Lawrence's brilliant blue eyes failed to elicit a blink, Yuri was forced to agree with the bear. What had the Undertaker said? Empty as the day he'd been born? It seemed that way until Leonid put great steaming bowls of soup on the table. Then the Englishman roused himself enough to ladle it into his mouth like there was no tomorrow.

"Did you meet with the Devil again today?" Leonid asked as they watched a second bowlful disappear. He had found Tania, the agent they'd sent after the guerrilla chief, Guevara, the same day Andropov had gotten the assignment to free Hadrian and send the Cuban to the Undertaker.

Yuri hesitated a moment, then inclined his head in confirmation.

"So, where do you send this one?"

With the girl the matter had been clear-cut. She'd had a vital connection with the rebel leader; had, in fact, been the one to send him here in the first place. She'd been a logical choice and, though disoriented when the bear had found her, she'd warmed to her assignment with professional enthusiasm. Yuri didn't remember a lot about Lawrence of Arabia, but what he remembered didn't encourage him.

"Back to Piccadilly Circus," he said slowly.

"Ach, you don't think he's the right one?"

"He's part of the problem—"

The blond man looked up as if to dispute that claim. "Seven pillars," he said, his eyes focused on something only he could see. "Seven pillars of wisdom. They're out there. I've seen them."

"What's the problem?"

Yuri took a sip of his own soup. There was no proscription against telling the bear, or anyone else, about his problems. In Hell, a breach of security had a way of becoming its own reward. But tonight he needed to talk, so he told his predecessor in the Kremlin what he had seen and what he'd been told.

"He's your man," Leonid affirmed, nodding as if it all made perfect sense to him.

"He's an idiot! Seven pillars of wisdom. In Hell?"

"I don't know how I got here, Leonid, but I'm here and I've been given a job to do. Maybe you don't care—but I do. I've done my job wherever I've been and I'll do it here in Hell—the best I can. And that doesn't include sending lunatics on fantasy quests. If there's a breakdown at the Undertaker's and the rebels are exploiting it, then I'll get to the bottom of it if I have to go into the field myself."

The bear folded his hands across his ample abdomen. "No, Yuroshka. We are Russians and Hell is very much like Russia. And you are the idiot."

"Because I try? Because I refuse to give up? I'm pushing on a rope; spitting into the wind. But I'm a man and I don't give up."

"And your enlightened parents refused to swaddle you as an infant, no doubt?"

"Yes. No. No, my family was educated—not barbaric peasants. I was certainly not swaddled like cordwood—whatever that has to do with it."

"Your Russian soul is flawed, Yuroshka," Leonid said, nodding sadly to himself. "You never learned the secrets of survival. I always suspected as much. Ach, well, I will tell you the secrets of the barbaric peasants. Mother Russia will mend your soul, even here in Hell."

Yuri took his bowl to the iron sink, his back to the bear, pointedly ignoring him. "I'm not going to waste my time listening to nonsense about souls—Russian or otherwise. Or swaddling—as if wrapping an infant in dirty rags for its first two years could improve anything!"

"Yuri!" the bears voice deepened to a growl.

"Don't bother me."

"You *will* listen to me."

It was a command—not like the boss's commands, which stripped one's will away, but a command nonetheless. Andropov turned around and met his roommate's angry glare. It was Brezhnev in the tiny room now—Brezhnev, who had dominated the Kremlin by brute presence, who had physically intimidated and humiliated more than one member of the inner circle. Andropov went meekly back to his chair.

"That is better," Brezhnev agreed, opening his hands. There was blood on his fingers; his PND wound was weeping again. The new Brezhnev, the great overfriendly bear, was dominant again, but there remained a shadow of the old Brezhnev, and Yuri made no move to escape the oncoming lecture.

"The first thing a Russian—a real Russian—learns is the futility of resistance. Bound to a board, he can scream and struggle but *it will make no difference!* He exhausts himself, but food and everything else come when they will, not when he wills. Broken, he shrinks back into himself and learns— He learns that food still comes when it will. Resistance is worthless.

"It is a lesson he never forgets. It's a lesson he's never forgotten. He remembered it when Napoleon came, when Hitler came, when *we* came. Retreat into himself and leave the rest to God."

Yuri's head came up. "I cannot, will not believe in God."

"The Russian peasant doesn't believe in God—he believes in evil. He knows that evil is real. He remembers it holding him to that board—and he remembers that resisting evil exhausted him and that not resisting it brought him enough to survive. Let God take care of evil, the peasant says, it's none of my business. Yuroshka, we took their churches away—did they change? We took their land away, their customs, their languages—did they change? The Russian peasant will outwit us all and he will outwit Hell itself if you let him."

Andropov thought of the Hellfire Club. Its members embraced Hell, gloried in it, and, after a manner of speaking, throve where men of greater substance withered away. Even the bear himself, though his gut was bleeding, did not dread eternity. And he had learned more about the inner workings of the place by seeming to do nothing but wander an Underground station than Andropov had for all his well thought-out schemes.

"So you think I should let the Club run rampant and send this Englishman off on his quest?" he asked wearily.

"Seven pillars. Seven is the magic number, the sacred number. Within the pillars lies wisdom," Lawrence intoned.

Leonid stood up, wiped his bloody hands on his trousers, and went to the window. The snow had stopped. If any of them had ever known the patterns of the stars, they might have gazed up and known if this were Siberia or some other place.

"No," the bear said slowly, "I think you should go with him. He is not an accident."

"Go off on some crackpot search for wisdom? He'll know. He'll find me and drag me back."

Leonid shrugged. "If he does, what difference does it make? Have you got better solutions for him or yourself? You've got eternity and you need wisdom. The devil thrives on your struggling, on your opposition; he *is* the Rebellion. If you do not resist him, but make your way like a single drop of rain in the river, he can do little to stop you."

"What about you?"

"I'll be at Piccadilly. I'll know how you're doing."

There was a long silence, punctuated only by their belching and Lawrence's mad monologue about his pillars. Yuri wondered anew just what the bear's infernal assignment was, then pushed the thought aside. The discussion would go on for a while—for appearance's sake—but the decision was already made.

GOD'S EYES

Michael Armstrong

"Turn away from me so I can have a moment's joy
before I go to the place of no return
to the land of gloom and deep shadow,
to the land of deepest night
of deep shadow and disorder,
where even the light is like darkness."
—Job 10:20–21

Job stood in the hatchway of the armored combat earthmover, scanning the parking lot of the Oasis Bar for an empty space. Other tanks, troop carriers, jeeps, chariots, and the occasional civilian vehicle cluttered the lot on the edge of the New Hell harbor. Paradise cast its usual ruddy glow through banks of black thunderheads rolling in from the east. Out beyond the mouth of the harbor the *Titanic* rumbled as it slid under for its nightly sinking, its survivors getting their dunking before they hit the streets in drag. Job squinted in the mustard-yellow glare of the parking lot lights, spied a space at the edge of the lot next to the harbor.

A pink VW convertible—license plate NORMA— had parked across the line next to a dusky gray Jeep Wagoneer, taking up two spaces. The Wagoneer had to belong to some merc, Job figured—it *looked* armored, with the fat tires and the funny sheen to the windows—but the Bug looked safe: civilian. Job drove up to the VW, lowered the blade on the ACE, and rammed the Bug, pushing it over the edge of the lot and into the New Hell harbor. The Bug splashed into the slimy waters, listed to port, then righted itself and drifted out on the tide. Job popped back down into the dozer, shut it off, and yanked the keys out of the control panel. Grabbing his Skorpion submachine gun, he climbed out, dogging the hatch behind him.

The Oasis covered half a block from North Road to the harbor. Just north of the long wharves, and on the main thoroughfare that snaked out of New Hell and into the mountains, the Oasis had become a crossroads for mercenaries moving back to the capital after long campaigns, heading out to sea, or slouching their way to the swamps south of town. Three stories high, the Oasis looked like a squat concrete cube, windowless except for a few small, barred ports on the sea side. A low wall ran around the roof of the building, with gun slits every ten feet, machine gun nests and mortars at the corners, and barbed wire strung halfway up the sides. Job walked around to the street side of the bar, pushed the heavy oak door inward, and walked into the Oasis entry.

The bouncer at the door—a brute Neanderthal with teeth the size of walnuts—stopped Job, grunted over to the hat check girl watching a big locked cage containing a small armory. A sign next to the cage read: ONE WEAPON, ONE MAGAZINE, NO SHIT. Next to that another sign read: ROOMS TO RENT

BY THE MINUTE, HOUR, DAY, WEEK, AND
MONTH. A narrow staircase next to the ammo cage
ran upstairs. Job laid his Samopal 68 and a magazine
of 9mm parabellum rounds on the counter, slipped
off his ammo belt and handed it to the girl, then
stepped through the metal detector at the end of the
counter.

"He's clean," the hat check girl said, signing the
words to the Neanderthal. She handed Job a little
disk of metal with the number "7" stamped in it,
pushed the Skorpion and the magazine back at him.
Job slid the magazine in the SMG, checked the
safety, and slung it over his shoulder.

"Any action tonight, Shanidar?" he signed to the
Neanderthal.

"Quiet, Job," the bouncer signed back. Shanidar
lifted a moth-eaten velvet rope and waved Job in.

Pausing at the top of the stairs to let his eyes
adjust to the dim light, Job pulled the hood of his
robe down, let it fall back on his shoulders so the
Beirut marines standing at the bottom of the stairs
could see the blue hem around the hood, the Star of
David glinting on a gold chain on his neck. A big
black marine grunted at him as Job walked into the
bar, and Job smiled. He'd always been a little jumpy
around the Americans, worried that they might mis-
read his Semitic features and add him to the body
count of their eternal feud.

Sam nodded at Job from behind the bar, and Job
nodded back at the man in the white suit and string
tie. A nasty lot of greasy, grimy, mud-smeared faces
turned to look at Job as he walked around the edge
of the bar, toward a corner table where a man with
dreadlocks sat smoking a joint of ganja about the size
of a panatella. Job glanced up at the newly emplaced
machine gun nests in the upper corners of the big

warehouse-like room, tried to pay no attention to the little red dot on his chest as the laser sights of the guns tracked him—just for practice, he hoped.

Rubbing a gold diablo between his left forefinger and thumb, Job stopped short when a merc in tiger cammo stood up from a table on his right and came at him. The guy reached to grab Job's throat, but Job swung his right hand up, caught the merc's wrist, and brought it down.

" 'Budsman, you owe me," the man growled.

"I do," Job said. He twisted the man's hand around, palm up, then dropped the diablo into it. "We even, Zebediah?"

Zebediah looked down at the gold coin, squeezed it, held it up to the light. "Yeah, sure Job. Sure." He smiled, a gold canine gleaming. "*Yeah.* When'd you get flush, 'Budsman?"

"Oh, you know . . . got the new budget, Zeb. Things are looking up."

"Sheet," Zeb said, shaking his head.

Job pushed him aside, went over to the corner, and sat down to the Rastafarian's left. He slung the Skorpion over the arm of the chair and stared across the heavy walnut table at the man Sam called Rasta Bob but Job knew as Jareem, Son of Zion. The big Jamaican sucked at the joint, breathed in the dope, and blew it back out into Job's face. Job held his breath, felt the dope ooze its way into his eyes. Reem nodded.

"You're looking well, mon." He jerked his head over at Zeb's table.

Job motioned to a barmaid, pointed at Reem's empty beer bottle, raised two fingers. The barmaid, a black-rooted blonde in cammo undershirt and panties, nodded, went to the bar, came back and set two bottles of Tsing Tao down. "Your beers, Mr. Ombudsman," she said.

"Thank you, uh—" Job squinted at the name embroidered in olive drab on her shirt "—Norma Jean."

She smiled, ran a hand through the dark roots of her hair. "Marilyn, actually," she said. "Norma Jean quit last week. This was her outfit. I'm new here."

"Well, Marilyn, then," Job said. He reached into his robes, pulled out a lumpy bag, shook two coins out onto the table, handed her a diablo. "Tell Sam to apply that to my bill." He smiled, picked up one more coin. "And that's for you."

"*Thank you*," Marilyn said. She blushed, took the empty bottles, and walked back to the bar.

Reem snorted. "You *are* flush. Since when does the Ombudsman go around buying drinks—or tipping barmaids?"

Job took the beer, sipped it, grinned. "Since the Devil increased my budget, that's when."

"*Increased* your budget?" Reem shook his head, his dreadlocks swaying in front of his eyes, then back. "Jah be praised, I find that hard to believe."

"Yeah?" Job reached into a fold of his robe, handed the keys to the ACE to Reem. "Thank Odysseus for the loan of the dozer," he said. Job poked a finger into the bag on the table, took out four diablos, pushed them over to Reem. "For his trouble." Job hefted the bag, smiled, tucked it back in his robe.

"I don't believe it."

"*Believe it*," Job said. "Don't ask me how or why, but when I finally made it to my desk today—you should have *seen* that ACE cut through the clutter in the warehouse—there was an open safe with about 10,000 diablos in it. A little note from the Attorney General himself said that it represented 'the commitment of the Department of Injustice to the fine work the Office of the Ombudsman is doing.' "

"No shit?"

"No shit."

"Okay, mon, so how come?"

"I got a case—a real case. Devil wants someone out of here, Reem. I've been empowered to do it."

"Soon come? A soul out of Hell?" The Rasta man shook his head.

"Soon come, Jareem. I'm supposed to meet a messenger here tonight to—*shit*." Job grabbed his Skorpion, swung the Czech gun out, clicking the safety off. He heard the snick of rounds being chambered into guns, chairs falling back, mercs standing and cursing. Job glanced to his right, saw Reem reaching behind his back, then looked to the front of the bar.

A tall, emaciated man pushed his way down the stairs of the Oasis, past the marines, Shanidar sprawled at the top of the stairs clutching his stomach. The thin man's lizard tail whisked behind him, scattering stools as the marines scrambled to get out of his way.

"Son of a bitch," someone said loudly. "A fucking lawyer."

The lawyer's tail ran from just below his neck 15 feet behind him. Boils and pustules oozed from the man's back and dripped down the tail, and he dragged a line of slime behind him. The man walked in sort of a swishing way, turning his body almost all the way to the left, then right. As he turned, Job saw that the base of the tail ran under his buttocks and up through his legs.

Big coke-bottle-bottom glasses had been shoved into the orbits of the man's face; thin, white hair swept back from his forehead. A little demon hovered next to the man's right ear, buzzing loudly. The lawyer kept swatting at the demon, but it would fly away and then dart quickly back. The man wore a tailored pin-stripe suit, blood oozing from the pockets. Across the top of the breast pocket the word ROY burned through the suit from his skin.

"Hold it there, counselor," Sam, the bar owner, shouted behind the bar. He held up a short-barrel bear shotgun, slid the receiver back with a loud snick. Someone shined a spotlight on Roy's pasty face, but even in the bright light Job could see a small red dot centered on his forehead: a laser sight.

Roy stopped just inside the bar, his tail twitching back and forth. He held a neat roll of white parchment in his right hand and raised it up, shielding his eyes. "I'm from the Hall of Injustice," Roy said. "I have something for the Ombudsman."

"Kaka," Job muttered. He looked at Reem, shrugged. "My messenger." He put the Skorpion down, clicked the safety on, stood up and waved at Roy. "Yo, over here."

"Stay," Sam said to Roy. "Job, go to him—I don't want the fucker getting my bar all scummy."

Job went up to Roy, spread his robes back, held out his hand. "You have something for me?" Job felt an itching in his back; the thought occurred to him that he was in the line of fire of about half the weapons in the room, and he didn't doubt that they'd shoot through him if they had to take out Roy.

"Your case," Roy said. He handed him the scroll.

Job took it, tensed as he saw Roy's hands drop to his sides, relaxed a little when he saw that Roy kept his claws in plain sight. He unrolled the scroll and glanced at the writing. Job nodded—the illumination was superb. "Good," Job said. He waved Roy away— the thing exuded a horrible stench that overpowered the rotting smells coming in from the wharves. The lawyer didn't move.

"Sir," Roy said. "Uh, the Attorney General asked me to speak to you about the, uh, importance of this case."

"Yes?" Job scanned the scroll, glanced up, then looked back down.

"It would please the Attorney General if you did your best to process it."

"Sure, sure," Job said.

"It would please the Attorney General—it would please Lord Satan—if you did your best to process it."

Job looked up. "Of course." He felt the bag of diablos tugging at his belt. "I mean—" Job rubbed his eyes. "You mean . . . you mean the Attorney General *really* wants me to do my job?" He'd hoped —hoped—no one had been really serious. Wrong, he thought. *Wrong.*

"Yessir."

"Well." Job smiled. "*Well.* Well, it's not as if I haven't tried. I mean, given my limited resources . . ."

"Exactly," Roy said. "Which is why they are no longer limited." He reached slowly into his suit pocket, pulled out another lumpy bag. "Your latest appropriation." Roy tugged open the bag, poured a small handful of diamonds into his rough calluses. The mercs whispered behind Job's back, and he felt more intensely the eyes of all those guns burning at his back.

"I see," Job said. "Well, would you tell the AG— *and* Lord Satan—that I will do my best?"

"As expected," Roy said. "Lord Satan will be most interested in the results. *Most* interested. Should you fail to deliver satisfaction—should you not give this case your utmost attention—well . . ." Roy grinned.

"Well, what, slimeface?" Job moved toward the lizard man. "What? What can Satan possibly do to me that Y—— already hasn't? *What?* Boils? Kill my children? Burn my crops? Come on, Roy. You're talking to *Job*." He patted his chest with the palm of his hand, looked around the room at the mercs, waved his hands. "These guys know what I've been through—you don't scare me. You know that." The crowd of soldiers muttered, laughed.

"If you fail . . . If you fail, Lord Satan will Reassign you."

"*Pfah*." Job spat.

"The Pearly Gates," Roy said.

"*What?*"

The room fell silent.

"The Gates . . . the Gates to—" Roy pointed up. "Well, someone has to do it. Someone has to sit outside and shove the Damned back down. They do slip through occasionally, you know, just as the Blessed sometimes get placed here. Oh, *He* catches them, but they do slip through." Roy swished his tail back and forth. "I understand it's a coveted assignment, so near to the LORD and all that. So near to your *Redeemer*."

Job stumbled back, reached for a bar stool, sat down. The Gates to Heaven? Nearer my God to thee? Just outside, in Divine shooting distance, close to the Being who had caused him his torment? Job winced at the recalled pain. Never. *Never*. He had chosen Hell, chosen it over Paradise, over Purgatory, chosen it because . . .

. . . because, he thought, whispering the secret thought in his mind, because Satan and YHWH were the same being, two sides of the same entity, an antimony, good and evil together in one. Hell is being without God, Job thought, and God is in Hell,

God is in Satan, and Satan, despite his incredible evil—no, *because* of it—could be trusted to be *not* trusted. *He*—Him, the Other One—could not be trusted *at all.* Job had seen that, had learned that horrible lesson in the most painful way possible. And yet Job loved Him, loved Him with all his heart, and though he loved Him, because he loved Him, Job knew he had to be as far from Him as possible. And so he had come to Hell, the thought occurring to him that perhaps not only did he belong here, he deserved it.

But no, Job thought, The Gates of Heaven? I can never be near the Gates of Heaven. *Never.*

He sighed. "Tell the Attorney General I will not fail. I will do my best to get a soul to Paradise." He held the unfurled scroll up. "I'll do my best to get *this* soul out of here."

Roy nodded. "*Good.* Very good, Ombudsman." He poured the diamonds back into the pouch, held it out to Job.

Job stood, took the pouch, shook his head. He glanced at Sam, glaring at him. "Get the . . . get out of here, lawyer."

The lawyer turned, swished his tail at Job. Job jumped back as the tail swung around, knocking the table over. The lawyer waddled up the steps and out of the Oasis, his demon fluttering along next to his ear, whispering, whispering, whispering.

"Damn it, Job," Sam said. "Can't you do your business someplace else?"

Job reached into the bag, placed a particularly large diamond on the bar, and shrugged.

Roebling. Who in the name of Y——— was Roebling? Job asked himself. He stared down at the bleached parchment, traced his fingers over the illuminated manuscript, felt the faint grooves of the palimpsest in the lambskin. He rubbed his eyes, leaned back in his desk chair.

While he'd been at the Oasis, a squadron of wraiths had descended on the Auxiliary Records Depository, Office of the Ombudsman, Department of Injustice, and cleaned up the place. The great hemlock doors he'd shattered with the ACE had been replaced. The eighteen titanium panels depicting Job's torments—crumpled by the treads of the dozer—had been hammered back into shape, polished, and rehung on the doors. Carpet—carpet!—had been laid on the floors of the warehouse, and the millennia of records had been reformatted, stacked, and filed in row upon row of gleaming brown spheres, like shelves of dog's eyes—the new biologic records Reem had assured Job were all the rage in micro-encoded binary storage. A glassed-in office had been built in one corner of the warehouse, with a heavy oak desk in the middle of the office, a velvet upholstered chair behind, in which Job sat. On one corner of the desk the dead grey eye of a Hitachi CRT stared back at him, its cable twisting down into the floor, a little depression for the bioware in its keyboard. Waiting.

Roebling, Job thought. Why Roebling?

He spread the curled parchment out, read the soul's biography. "Colonel Washington 'Washy' A. Roebling, builder of the Brooklyn Bridge," he read. "Born May 26, 1837, died July 21, 1926. Son of John Roebling, designer of the Bridge, husband of Emily Roebling, whom he loved dearly. Civil War hero, kind to dogs and cats. No known major sins. Resisted corruption. Hard worker."

Why Roebling? Why in Hell?

"Condemned to Hell on order of Y——, LORD of All Creation, for sins committed against Nature and

Man," Job read, "to wit, responsibility for and causa-
tion of the deaths of at least 20 men in the construction of the Brooklyn Bridge, among them: Pat
Daugherty, crushed by a granite block fallen from
derrick, 10/23/70; John Myers, death from caisson
sickness, 4/22/71; Patrick McKay, death from caisson
sickness, 4/30/71; John Elliot, killed in fall from New
York tower of bridge, 5/15/76; Samuel Cope, killed
when leg was caught in cable drum, 6/17/76; 15
others killed in miscellaneous accidents. Also responsible for death of unnamed man, suicided Thanksgiv-
ing Day 1856, after he was refused affections of W.A.
Roebling."

He shook his head, stared at the passage. Damned
to Hell because men had been killed in construction
accidents? Damned because he refused to engage in
a homosexual act with a suicide? Job rubbed his
eyes. *Those* were sins? That was reason to damn a
man to Hell forever? He looked up, stared upon the
rows of brown eyes staring back at him, each eye
containing the sum known facts of a damned soul's
life. If Roebling could be damned, no one was safe.
Job looked at the eyes, the dog's eyes—*God's* eyes,
Reem had called them—and wondered how many
souls like Roebling had been unjustly sent to Hell.
How many had been sent here by mistake? How
many had been processed too quickly? He shuddered again, thinking of his own torment, thinking of
the Injustice of Y——.

I had thought I was the only one. The only one.

Job picked up the brown eye sitting on the desk,
dropped it into the depression on the terminal, flicked
the screen on, *Location,* he tapped in, *roebling,
washington a.* The scanning laser spun over the eye,
transferred its contents into the main banks of the
Net, cross-checked the Reassignment files, and came

back with *slab z, central morgue*. Job smiled, amazed that Roebling would be so easy to find. *Latest reassignment?* he typed in.

None, the screen replied.

First assignment? Job typed.

None, the screen answered.

No Reassignment? Job thought. No Assignment? That couldn't be. Roebling had to have been Assigned, at the very least. Had to have been.

Current status? he typed.

Dead, the screen answered.

Job took the eye out, turned the screen off.

"Kaka," he said, reaching for the phone and dialing the number of the morgue.

The Undertaker pulled back the sheet from Roebling's body. He lay on the marble slab in the inactive area of the morgue, surrounded by racks of dead in dusty sacks and sarcophagi waiting for the Undertaker or one of Old Shit Mouth's crew to revive them. The sheet covering Roebling's body was clean and white, and though his body had that pasty grey look of the newly dead, it seemed to glow in the dim light. His grey beard had been neatly clipped, like that of General Grant, Job thought, and his blue eyes blazed with a life that made the body seem to be only resting and not dead.

The Undertaker checked the toe tag, nodded at Job. " 'Roebling, Washington A.,' " he read. " '5/26/ 1837–7/21/1926.' This your man?"

Job nodded, sighed. He'd expected trouble finding Roebling, thought he might be off in some hinterland, maybe mind-wiped, maybe body-wiped so he'd never find him. And there he was, newly dead, lying on Slab Z, ready for resurrection. "That's him. He just come in?"

Turd Breath turned the tag over, shook his head. "Been here since . . . since he died."

"This is his first trip back to you?" That was pretty amazing, Job knew. Most of the damned seemed to die regularly, at least every few years.

"No. His only trip. He's never died here." The Undertaker shrugged.

"Never? Wait a second—hasn't . . . hasn't he been, um, processed?" Job shuddered, remembering the Awakening, the coming to, that every one of the damned had gone through, even him.

"No. Never." The Undertaker smiled, then shrugged his thin shoulders. "It happens. Not too often, but . . . well, sometimes we get a soul through here who doesn't wake up. They belong here, of course, else they wouldn't be here. But there's not enough sin— enough evil—for them to come alive here. There's not enough good for them to be elsewhere, either. These things are very delicate, you see." He coughed, bit at a long fingernail. "We, uh, we don't like to advertise them."

"He'll just lie there?"

Fart Face held up his hands. "Probably. Maybe. Devil knows." He smiled. "And *He's* not telling, eh?"

"But . . ." Job held up the rolled parchment of Roebling's case. "Roebling's filed appeals. He *has* to have been processed."

The Undertaker pulled the sheet back, looked at his watch. "I'm a very busy man, sir. He has not been processed. I would know." He grinned. "I would know."

"Thank you," Job said. He turned, let the Undertaker lead him out of the maze of the morgue, back aboveground to the lobby of the Admin Building. Roebling not alive? And yet in Hell? It couldn't be, he thought. *It could not be.*

* * *

"He's in Hell, Job." Reem held the rubbery eye of Roebling's file between finger and thumb, squeezed it gently, handed it back to Job. Job had loaned it to Reem to run a hack on it, to see if Reem could get some data out of the Reassignments net that Job just wasn't capable of getting.

They sat at the same corner table in the Oasis, ruddy light streaming through a skylight overhead, the bar almost deserted except for one or two Americans at the door, a drunk merc sleeping in the back. A ganja cigar smoldered in an ashtray on the table.

"I didn't think he could be dead," Job said. "He's *got* to be alive. Who filed his appeals?"

"Not alive." Reem held up a skinny finger. "But he's around. Oohh, yeah. He's around." He held out his hand. Job handed him another biochip, some random file, one Reem could use to bust his way into the Net again. Reem took the eye, held it up to the light.

Job watched him fondle the rubbery eye. Reem smiled, put it in a little wooden case, pocketed it. Reem had a thriving business going in Reassignments. Somehow he'd figured out how to get into the Net and put worms into people's files, get them Reassigned wherever they wanted to be. It didn't last—the Angels usually noticed the switch and called them back—but it lasted long enough for some damned to rendezvous with a lost loved one, long enough for another round of a feud to be played— long enough for Reem to turn a profit.

Job shook his head. "You're starting to sound like the Undertaker. 'He's not alive.' 'He's around.' What is it? Is Roebling dead or not-dead?"

Reem picked up the joint, inhaled, let the smoke curl out of his nose. "Dead *and* not-dead. Both,

mon. You don't understand, do you?" Reem laughed.
"Roebling's a *shade*."

"A shade?"

"Shade, shadow—a wisp, man, a *soul*," Reem
explained.

"We're all souls here."

Reem shook his head, dreadlocks whipping around
like hunks of molasses pasta. "No, no, a soul of a
soul. Part of the soul—the *shadow*. I mean, Roebling
came down here *corporeal*, exactly the way he'd
died. You know what killed your man? Bends, mon,
the caisson disease. Bends and nerves, though he
took a long time to go—lived to be 89, mon. Fucking
ancient for the early 20th century. Guy was wasted,
not even fit to torment. Satan sent him to Reassignment immediately to see if he could be patched up."

Job tapped the table, grabbed his beer, sipped it.
He glanced around the room at the Oasis, looked at
the hard men by the door, the even harder women
along the south wall, the mercs slipping in in ones
and twos as the afternoon wore on and the night's
arrangements started to be made. He looked at the
soldiers, the irregular and regular troops, guerrillas
and terrorists, generals and privates, ranked and
freelance, all with automatic rifles or sub-machine
guns casually slung over their shoulders, probably a
round already chambered—enough mercs and soldiers and armament to fight a couple good old-
fashioned Biblical battles in less than a second. He
shuddered.

"Okay: Satan wanted him patched up. And . . .?"

"The Undertaker couldn't do anything for him—
the body wouldn't *dissolve*. The guy just couldn't be
touched. Roebling—" Reem looked around, then whispered, "—Roebling doesn't belong here. That's what I
hear. He belongs to . . . well, he doesn't belong here."

"How do you know this?"

He sat up, stroked his chin. "First thing I tried when you asked me to look at his file was to get him Reassigned. I ought to charge you double. No could do. Fucking net ate my program—might've eaten me, if I hadn't shut down fast enough. Roebling cannot be Reassigned 'cause he never was Assigned. Got it?"

"Yeah. Undertaker made that clear. But how could he be—I mean, *Be*—if he doesn't have a body?"

Reem sat back, bit his lip, took another toke. "Like I said: he's a shadow."

"A . . . a wraith?" Job remembered the wispy, see-through souls that sometimes made deliveries, the ones who had cleaned up his office after he'd broken into it with the combat bulldozer. You saw them sometimes, little outlines of bodies visible only in dust or the right kind of light, pushing a package along the street. They were like half-souls, bodies that had been used up—great for pushing paper.

"Nope—a *shadow*. We're talking the evil, nasty, cruel, demented, tormented side of Roebling. We're talking a part of him that is so little it can't *move* his body, so it has to cruise on its own. You can't find it because it really doesn't exist. It's a demon, mon."

Job sat back, rubbed his chin. "The shadow . . . the dark side. But it *is* part of him." Reem nodded. "Sophia, Sophia . . . This *thing*—I'm going to have to find this thing, get it back to—" he shook his head, sighed "—that body on Slab Z to get Roebling out?" Job felt the floor shudder a bit.

"Or at least on his way." Reem put the ganja down. "Soon come, feels like a temblor."

Job grabbed his beer, steadied it. "Or—"

"*Incoming!*" someone yelled.

Reem and Job dove for the floor, covered their

heads and crawled under the table. Job stared across the floor, stared as the concrete slab buckled, a crack zigzagging toward him . . .

The floor cracked open before Job, and like a chick poking its head through an eggshell, a horrid thing rose up out of the slab. It had the head of a goat, the snout of a wolf, the body of a woman, and the legs of a jackal, all covered with oozing boils. The thing stood before Job, spread its arms, revealing leathery wings hanging from its fingers. It pulled the wings around it, then opened them up again. The wolf snout diminished, the goat horns shrank, and the head transformed itself into a woman's head. Her hair, like the horns, curled back from her forehead in a hard carapace; her face was covered in fine grey fur. She smiled, and little red drops of blood dripped off her long canines.

"Jooobbb," she moaned, pointing a claw at him. "Ombudsman? We must talk."

"Fuck," Sam muttered from the bar across the room. "Damn it, Job, I told you . . ."

Job got to his feet, dusted himself off. He heard the other patrons of the bar get up, coughing in the acrid smoke, muttering. Extending a hand to Reem, Job helped the Rastafarian to his feet, started to sit back down, thought better of it, and remained standing.

Job smiled at the demon, opened his hands. "Yes?"

"I am Lady . . . *MacBeth*," she said. "Yes, MacBeth will do, Ombudsman. Your . . . *assistant*—" she pointed at Reem "—has been most helpful to you, and to us. We understand you are looking for *Roeb*-ling, yes?"

"Uh, sure," Job said. "Found him, though. No problem."

The demon scratched a breast with a claw, then

ran it up the side of her snout. "Found his *body*, you mean. We know that. No, we do not want his body." She bared her teeth. "We want his *shadow*. You search for his shadow?"

"Yes, yes, his shadow. It seems that is the crucial, uh, element, yes, Lady."

"Gooood. Good. Find his shadow, Job. Find his shadow and bring him to me at—" she rubbed her chin "—at Ilium, and I will give you something valuable, something that will *enhance* your position, and help you end the Injustice you seek to end."

"What do you mean?"

"I will give you the files—not the God's eyes you think so precious, but genuine files, intact souls, as it is—to four beings damned to Hell that may not belong here. Use them. Use them to get this *Roebling* creature out of here. Maybe you will get the four souls out, too. Do you understand?"

"Yes," Job said. "But why . . . why? Who do you work for, Lady?"

She raised a hand, spread her claws, waved it. "It is not . . . important. But we work for the same interests, the same side. Help me, you help yourself. Do you see?"

"Uh, well—"

"To get Roebling out, you must capture his shadow, send the shadow back to Reassignments. We will Assign Roebling to you, to your office, and Roebling and Shadow together, you will come to me. Do you understand?"

"Yeah, but—" He glanced over at Reem; Reem nodded. "Okay. Done."

"Good," Lady MacBeth said. "Good. That man is wise; heed his counsel." She pointed again at Reem. The demon slid her hand into her crotch, pulled out a black silk pouch, handed it to Job. "For your services, and to facilitate your task."

Job took the pouch, hefted it; it had a nice, clunky feel. "Lady." He bowed.

"One more thing," she said. "You will need some assistance. A woman will approach you after I leave. She will offer you her services. Use her, and when you have used her, return her to us."

Job nodded. "Thank you." He bowed again. "Thank you, Lady."

"At Ilium," Lady MacBeth said. She sank into the floor, smoke following her down, the concrete healing behind her.

Sam walked around the bar, held out his hand. Job sighed, opened the pouch, spilled out perhaps a pound of cut emeralds into his palm. He selected one, handed it to Sam.

"You're getting to be a real pain, Job," Sam said. He picked up the two empty beer bottles on the table. "Two more Tsing Taos?"

"Two more," Job said.

Job put the emeralds back in the pouch, shrugged, sat back down. Reem chuckled, shook his head. "You got any bright ideas?" Job asked him. "Would this shadow show up on the net? Could we find him that way?"

Reem shook his dreadlocks. "Jah be praised, no. Enough static as it is."

Marilyn, the barmaid, came up to their table, set two bottles of Tsing Tao beer down. "Your beers, Mr. Ombudsman," she said.

"Thank you, Marilyn." He slid a diablo over to her, turned to the Rastafarian. "Okay, Reem, what's your idea?"

"Mr. Ombudsman," Marilyn said. "Excuse me, can I ask you a favor?"

Job glared at her, sighed. He could smell it coming: now that he had a little power, every soul in Hell would be hoping that he could do for them what Job was trying to do for Roebling. "Yes?"

"I—I need work," she whispered. Marilyn glanced around the bar, looked at Sam. "This . . . this just isn't cutting it. I thought, well, I've heard that you might be having some openings, and I . . . Mr. Ombudsman, I can do a lot of things. A lot. I can type. I can, uh, do fun things. I can perform." Job looked up at her, smiled, glanced at her body—the fine hips, the well-shaped breasts, the face . . . "I can *act*, sir. Do you need an actress?"

Job reached into the sack, handed her a small emerald. "I'll call you if something opens up."

"Thank you, sir." She smiled, knotted the emerald in an end of her shirt. "I'll work hard for you, sir. You'll see. Thank you." She walked away.

Job shook his head. "Women," he mumbled. "Your idea, Reem?"

"Not her," Reem said. "The Devil's, maybe?"

"What? I'm talking about finding shadows."

"Oh," Reem said. He reached for the ganja, took a toke. "No, I thought—Job, that was the Devil's secretary, Marilyn—former secretary, actually. She's on his shit list, I mean, *bad*, Job. Ran off with DaVinci, I hear, then shacked up with Mr. Revolution himself, Che Guevara. Devil yanked her back and Reassigned her to this scum pit. She turns a trick now and then, if that's what you like."

"Not really, Reem. Your plan . . . ?"

"Ah: find the shadow. You don't want to put a trace on it, but there's something just as good. Just as good." He grinned, pulled another eye out from a pocket. "Job, you're an aye-ree mon. Funny that the Lady MacBeth would tell you to seek 'my wise coun-

sel.' I was going to give you this—it's on the house."
He held up his hands as Job reached into the bag of
emeralds. "*No.* On the house, mon. What you want
to look for is shadows of shadows. You read that file
on Roebling again, and you ask yourself, if you were
Roebling's shadow, the evil, nasty part—the *guilty*,
nasty part—what would you do? Shadows of shadows, man." He held out the eye for Job. "This little
bit of bioware, let it be your Virgil, mon. Let it
guide you through Hell, eh?"

"To Beatrice," Job muttered, remembering what
Lady MacBeth had told him: "a woman will approach
you . . . she will help you . . . use her and return
her to me."

"*Beatrice?*" Reem asked.

"Dante's Beatrice," Job said. "Didn't you ever
read that little slime's book? It's in the Welcome
Women's package. Beatrice—the woman who would
help Dante get to Paradise. And Roebling." He jerked
his head over at Marilyn, taking a tray of beers up to
the Marines by the door. "I think I see what you're
getting at, Reem. I think I see." He took the bioware
from Reem.

Job ran a hand over his neatly trimmed beard—
clipped in the U.S. Grant style—and stared down at
the people entering 110 Columbia Heights. He smiled
at the brick street, at the facades of the buildings
lining it, at the little corner of Brooklyn resurrected
on the west coast of Hell, just across the Sea of Sighs
from Pompeii. He leaned over the balcony, adjusted
the drape of the banner hanging from it. "WEL-
COME BROOKLYN BRIDGE BUILDERS," the
banner read. Job waved at a red-haired man entering
the door below. The man stared at him, smiled,
waved back.

Roebling, Job thought. They have to think I'm
Roebling. He took out a pipe, filled it, played with
the tobacco as he'd seen pipe smokers do. Damn
cursed stuff. A breeze blew in from Pompeii, and Job
sniffed at the faint odor of sulphur coming from the
smoldering volcano. In the mountains east of Brooklyn, at the edge of the sham city, he could see lights
moving on the hills. A light at the top of a mountain
blinked twice at him. Job checked his watch, nodded
to himself. Oh-seven hundred, he thought. Right on
time.

He'd been amazed at how easy it had all been.
Remembering, he thought of the sudden power the
Ombudsman's office had acquired when given the
Roebling case. Lady MacBeth's emeralds had allowed
him to commission a replica of early 19th century
Brooklyn. Reem's bioware had given him a list of all
the Brooklyn Bridge veterans in Hell and their addresses. The bag of diamonds had made it possible
for him to organize a reunion. And with the crossing
of a few palms—rough, calloused palms—with diablos, Job had his own freelance mercenary army. So
simple, he thought.

Job turned to go inside, but as he turned, he
noticed a thin man in black watching from across the
street. A match flickered in the man's hand, and for a
moment Job had a better view of the man's face in
the dimming light: neat, clipped gray beard, piercing
blue eyes, a long nose. The match went out, and the
man fell back in the shadows. Job caught the glint of
brass, then heard a faint click as the man moved
down the street, his cane tapping as he walked away.

"Washy," a woman said from behind him. Job
turned, smiled at the brown-haired lady in the long
skirt. Good, Job thought. She didn't call me by name.

"Emily?" he asked, continuing the charade.

"They're waiting for you, Washy."

"Yes, dear." Job stepped to the woman, let her take his arm. He smiled as he felt her smooth hand, glanced covertly at her figure. Marilyn. As Lady MacBeth had said, a woman had walked up to him after the demon had left, and Marilyn had practically thrown herself at Job. It hadn't taken much—a few more emeralds, a diamond or two—to enlist her services. Marilyn, the Devil's former personal secretary— the great actress herself—was his for the night. Marilyn.

Job had thought her a harlot, but her performance as Emily Roebling changed his mind. She was the consummate professional, completely in character, perfect in her disguise. She had become Emily, become Washington Roebling's wife. Job knew he couldn't fool the bridge veterans, knew he couldn't circulate among them, but none would expect him to: Marilyn as Emily would play hostess, would do his duties. But he would make a brief appearance.

Job let Marilyn lead him downstairs, to the head of the staircase leading into the main salon. The bridge veterans stopped, turned, stared up at him and the strong, handsome woman at his side. Marilyn— Emily—held up her hand, and the murmurs of the crowd subsided. The veterans—the Irish, Italian, German, and Scandinavian immigrants who had built the bridge—looked up at the Roeblings. Marilyn smiled, squeezed Job's elbow.

"Gentlemen," she said. "Gentlemen. Welcome, welcome to the First Annual Reunion of the Brooklyn Bridge Veterans. Colonel Roebling and I are pleased that so many of you could make it tonight, though we do, of course, miss those who are unable to attend." She smiled, and the men laughed slightly. "Colonel Roebling is still recovering from the unfortunate effects of his illness, acquired, as you know, from the rigors of building the bridge back in the world. He has asked me to make a brief speech on his behalf." Job nodded, reached into the breast pocket of his coat, and handed her a sheet of crisp white paper.

" 'Welcome, bridge veterans,' " she read. " 'It is with great pleasure that I have the privilege of meeting with you tonight. Aware as we are of the unique events that bring us together here—' " Marilyn spread her arms " '—we must also be aware of our great accomplishments in other worlds and in other times. We gather here tonight to celebrate those accomplishments, and the heroism of those who so nobly gave their lives in the building of the earthly Brooklyn Bridge.' " The men began to clap, but Marilyn held up her hand. " 'But I have asked you to gather here tonight for another purpose. We cannot rest on our laurels—' " Job smiled " '—even in the situation we find ourselves. I have gathered you together tonight to ask your aid in another great undertaking—an undertaking more arduous, more ambitious, and, indeed, more dangerous than that which unites us here tonight. What is this Great Undertaking, gentlemen?

" 'You may have noticed the great chasm separating our Fair City from the great island of the Old Dead on the opposite shore. Gentlemen, you may have heard of the great danger there is in crossing to that shore, even in sturdy warships. You may have heard of the Great Monsters that lurk in the depths of the Sea of Sighs. But you may also have heard of the great riches that await us on that distant shore. Gentlemen, there is one way, and one way only, to get to that shore. I have sent emissaries to the island of Vesuvius and the cities of Pompeii and Herculaneum, and the Old Dead have agreed to join us in this Great Undertaking, if you are willing. Gentle-men, are you willing? Are you ready to join with me and build—rebuild, here in this Hell—the Greatest Bridge of All Time? Gentlemen, will you join with me to build the Brooklyn Bridge?' "

The men stared up at the Roeblings, looked at each other, whispered to each other. One man said, "You've got to be out of your fucking—" but was punched into silence. A tall, beefy man raised his arm, glared around at the crowd, then nodded. "Col-onel Roebling, I'm with you." He stared at the crowd. "John Myers is my name, and you know who that is. I died in the caissons, sir—the first man to do so, but I don't care. I'll die again—hah, I've died ten times already! What the Hell! We'll build your damn bridge!" The veterans roared their approval and others chimed in with Myers.

"Daugherty, sir! I'm with you!"

"McKay, sir! I'll do it again!"

"Cope, sir! Count me in!"

Men began shouting their names, and Job smiled at their willingness to torture themselves again. Did they really think they could build a bridge, he thought. In Hell? He was amazed at the perseverance of the human spirit. Even in Hell they struggled. Even in Hell they would attempt the impossible. He smiled at the idiocy of such souls, at the idiocy of his own soul.

"Let the fireworks begin, then!" Marilyn shouted.

Job started, glanced at her, then nodded. That would be the signal. The men turned, went to the great open windows looking west, to Pompeii. Out on a raft just off the coast a cannon shot shells high over Brooklyn. Streaming fountains of flames roared forth from the waters. The darkness overhead van-ished in the stroboscopic glare of exploding shells.

Rosettes of sparks flowered in the sky. Then Job heard another sound, a faint thumping that grew louder and louder until the windowpanes rattled with the noise.

Choppers.

Job nodded at Marilyn, and she ran down to the main floor, past the men, out to the front doors. Job heard shouting, some sort of commotion, then saw Marilyn being shoved back inside by a man in desert fatigues, a black and white kaffiyeh covering his face.

"PLO!" a man shouted—Mullen, Job saw. Mullen ran toward the fireplace, grabbed a poker, and rushed the man holding Marilyn by the throat. One of the guerrillas turned toward Mullen, raised his AK, and fired a quick burst at him.

"Damn fool," Job muttered. Job moved to the far end of the landing, out of the line of fire, and watched as a squad of IRA regulars burst through the French doors on the sea side of the main room.

Plaster flew as the IRA troops fired bursts across the room. The bridge veterans ran from side to side, first to the exit, then back to the French doors, then from one end of the room to the other. More PLO guerrillas poured into the room, and the two armies slowly squeezed the veterans into a huddled mass in the middle. The armies circled them, automatic rifles pointed down, occasionally jabbing someone trying to escape.

Two PLO fighters dragged Marilyn toward the French doors. She looked up at Job, ducked down on the railing. Her mouth opened. "What?" she seemed to be saying. Job shook his head. That hadn't been in the plan. That hadn't been in the plan at all. Job waved at them, and the taller of the two nodded, then shoved Marilyn outside. In the light of the still exploding fireworks he saw them drag her across the lawn to the sea, and then she was gone.

The bridge veterans sat in a heap in the middle of the salon, hands locked behind their heads. The PLO and IRA mercs stepped back, rifles pointing at them. One guerrilla looked up at Job, motioned with his rifle at the men on the floor. "Now?" he seemed to say. Job stood up, shook his head. The bridge builders looked up at Job. One of the guerrillas raised his rifle at Roebling.

"No!" Myers shouted.

"*Yes,*" a man said from a small balcony opposite Job, looking down at the room. Job smiled, eased his cane forward, slowly raised it up.

The man looked down at the guerrillas. He stepped into the light, tall, erect, his steel-blue eyes seeming to glow, even in the bright light of the chandelier. The man stared across at Job, down at the men, then back at Job. Job looked at him and he looked at Job, and for a moment Job felt like he was looking at himself, then remembered who he was and who the man across was and what he had to do.

"Colonel Roebling?" Myers asked, looking up at the man on the balcony. "Colonel?" he said, looking over at Job.

"No," Job said.

The man on the balcony smiled. "Yes," he said. "I am Roebling." He glared down at the guerrillas. "Put your weapons away. I presume you are paid. Whoever paid you, consider your price doubled if you spare these men."

The guerrillas looked up at Job; Job nodded. Their rifles snicked as safeties were clicked on. They slung the rifles over their shoulders, nodded at each other, relaxing, and moved out of the room and onto the lawn, like football players after a long game.

Roebling looked over at Job, the end of his cane between his feet. Job raised his own cane up and over the top of the railing, let it rest gently on the top of the rail. He pressed a stud in the head of the cane, listened as the cane began to hum faintly, and waited for the hum to cease.

"You wanted me to come here, didn't you?" Roebling asked.

"Yes," Job said.

"Emily," Roebling said. "Was that Emily?" Job nodded. "Where have they taken her?"

Job motioned toward the sea. "Pompeii, probably. I don't know."

"It was really Emily?" Roebling asked.

Job shrugged. "That's who she said she was," he lied.

"Emily . . . Why have you called me here? Why these men?"

The veterans looked up at the two Roeblings, from one to the other. They brushed each other off, some moving toward the bar near the fireplace.

"To build a bridge," Job said.

"Really?" Roebling asked.

"Really," Job lied again. The hum ceased on the cane, and he moved it slowly toward Roebling, until its end pointed at him.

"Who are you?" Roebling asked.

"Job," he said.

Roebling raised his eyebrows. "The Ombudsman?"

Job nodded. "The Ombudsman."

Roebling closed his eyes, let the cane drop to his feet, and gripped the rail. "Why are you really here?"

"To take you," Job whispered. "To kill you, sir."

Job felt for the little stud on the cane and touched it. A light shot out from the end of the cane, and a flash of silver flew across the room, hitting Roebling in the chest. Blue sparks shot across Roebling's chest, flashing into sparkling webs, shimmering around his body, enveloping it in a plasma cloud. Roebling raised his hand, pointed. His mouth opened, shut, and he shook his head. The blue web wrapped around and around Roebling's body, covering him until he was a mummy of blue light. The light spun faster and faster, a waterspout of energy, whirling around and around, shrinking into a sphere the size of a beach ball, then a globe, then a baseball, then a marble, and then a dot that vanished into a faint pop. Roebling's cane wobbled on its tip, and gently fell to the floor.

Job walked across the glass plain of Ilium. His bare feet left faint footprints in the fine ash covering the plain. A rim of rubble ringed the crater, and beyond the ring Job saw wisps of smoke curling into the ruddy sky. Which battle was it? he wondered. What armaments had they used this time? Clouds of ash rose up behind him, soiling his coarse, woven robe. Roebling walked beside him, still stiff from his resurrection. He walked like an automaton, his movements clunky. The Undertaker had told Job he would be like that until his shadow got adjusted to his body. Job stopped, and Roebling came to a clumsy halt next to him. The colonel leaned on his cane, glanced at Job.

"Soon come," Job said, repeating the words Reem used to say to him. Soon come: be patient, you know that your Redeemer lives. Soon come.

The glass before them cracked open, and Lady MacBeth rose up out of the glazed dirt. She stood before Job, spread her arms, flapped her wings, wrapped them around her, and emerged, a woman's face this time, with golden ringlets curling back from her forehead, hardening into gold on her shoulders, flowing over her body in spun cloth. Two hooved feet poked out from under the gown. She let her wings fall back, held out a clawed hand to Job.

"You brought the shadow," Lady MacBeth hissed. Job nodded. "Good. *Good*. And where is . . . the woman?"

"Marilyn?" Job asked.

"Yessss. Satan is quite displeased at her absence." Job shrugged. "The mercs took her. Pompeii, I think."

"*Pompeii*? That was not in the plans." Job shrugged again. Lady MacBeth sighed. "Well, Satan has ways of dealing with the Old Dead."

"Did you bring the . . . material?" Job asked.

"Yesss," she said. She looked at Roebling. "He is intact? Body and soul together? There are no little Roebling shadows running loose?"

"Intact," Job said. He smiled at Roebling, looked down. "The plasma gun Satan acquired for me did its trick, thank you." And, Job thought, Reem's bioware did its trick, helped him get the bridge veterans together, helped him set the trap that would bring the Shadow Roebling to defend his men when they were endangered by the PLO and IRA troops.

"Goood," Lady MacBeth said. "He looks whole enough." She poked Roebling's arm with a tip of her finger, and his flesh hissed at the touch of the claw. "But some things aren't quite working right yet, eh? Ah, well, perhaps it is good not to feel pain, is it, Colonel?"

Roebling grinned, said nothing.

"Well," she continued. "Yes, I have the material."

"Good," said Job. "Very good. How did you get it, anyway?" He thought of Reem—Reem the hacker and his ganja-inspired forays into the Net.

"New programmer," Lady MacBeth said. "Ada Lovelace. Know her?" Job shook his head. "Crackerjack computer jock. She plucked 'em out of one of those new biochip arrays. Damn shame, though—she had to reference them through a data block search, by vocation, as it were. Still, they're files." She waved her hand, and four bioware spheres, the God's eyes, appeared in her palm. Job reached for them.

"Uh-uh-uh . . . not yet," she said. She pulled her hand back. "Do you understand how to use these souls? Do you have any sort of idea for getting them out? I must know before I trust them to you. What are you going to do with them?"

"Going to do?" Job asked.

"How will you use them? How will you get Roebling out of Hell?"

Job sighed. "The souls you have brought me— whoever they are—may not get out; that remains to be seen. Roebling—" he glanced at him "—Roebling will, Y—— willing. Roebling will lead them out, lead them to their Judge, to Roebling's Judge, to the Judge of their times. If they find their Judge, and if they can convince the Judge of the merits of their case . . . ?" Job shrugged.

"You will give us Roebling's shadow?" Lady Mac-Beth asked. Job nodded. "Goood." She pinched Roebling's shoulder. "The Shadow Roebling will be of great use."

"His shadow must stay here in Hell," Job said. He smiled. "It is only a little evil, and so weak, as it is."

"Powerful enough," Lady MacBeth said. "Powerful enough." She smiled, her canines oozing blood, her long tongue licking around her mouth. "Very well, Job, very well." She held out the eyeballs of data. "These are not like your . . . *dog's* eyes, yes? These are true God's eyes, every nuance of the soul. Just add blood, stir—bubble, toil, and trouble, eh? —and you have the soul."

"Uh, could I have them in hard copy?" Job asked.

"*Hard* copy?"

"Please."

Lady MacBeth sighed. "One moment." She popped the eyeballs in her mouth, chewed and swallowed them, rubbed her stomach, then puked up a stream of putrid white stuff. She rolled the stuff around in her claws, patted it, and squeezed her hands together until the white stuff began to smoke. She opened her hands, and handed four small leatherette-bound books to Job.

Job took them, read the names still smoking on the covers: "Crane," "Pound," "Whitman," and "Dickinson." "Who are they?" he asked.

"Poets," the demon said. "That was the category Ada managed to call up. Poets. I don't really know them myself."

"Poets," Job murmured.

"Poets." Lady MacBeth sneered. She reached with a claw toward Roebling, touched his throat, and drew it across his neck. A cut opened up, and a line of blue blood oozed from the wound. Lady MacBeth grabbed Roebling's beard, yanked his head down so the blood dripped to his feet. The pool of blue blood whirled, grew, and shaped itself into a replica of the engineer. She released his beard, and Roebling fell back into Job's arms. The wound at his neck knit itself together.

Lady MacBeth reached for the shadow's hand. The shadow grasped the claw, let himself be led to her. He shimmered, slowly coalescing into real form. The shadow looked back at Roebling, smiled, then turned away. Roebling shuddered, looked to Job.

"Come," Job said. "Come. We will find these poets." he held the four booklets in his hand, then stuck them in a pocket inside his robe. "Poets," he said.

"Poets in Hell." He took Roebling's elbow, and walked away from the demon, across the plain of Ilium.

The demon wrapped her wings around the shade, gathered him up into her, and sank down into the depths of Hell.

BARGAIN

David Drake

There was one named Thorir, called Paunch, who had been a great berserker. He was dead, and the Hell-wind settled crystals of ice in his marrow as he staggered across the snow-rimed lava, tugging the slave behind him in a habit older than death.

"Would you like to live on Earth again, Paunch?" asked the voice.

There was no voice in Thorir's existence. He didn't ignore the words: the part of his mind that should have processed them was as frozen as every other part of the present cosmos.

The ground underfoot was volcanic hraun—old lava worn by wind, frost, and the tiny roots of lichen that adhered to it even here where nothing truly lived. The rock had flowed into pillows and crevices, their lines softened and hidden by the ice that scoured all surfaces and lurked in the lee of the wind that drove it.

Every step meant slipping—on the ice, in a con-

cealed crack, over a block of lava that could have
been a hummock of loose snow until it tripped the
foot that plodded into it. When Paradise burned
through the mist and there was color, the landscape
was gray: gray rings of lichen on gray rock beneath
ice of dirty gray.

But generally the mist covered everything, and
the mist was gray as well.

"Come now, Paunch," wheedled the voice. "This
isn't what you want for yourself for eternity, is it?"

Thorir turned with an inarticulate snarl . . . and of
course his ankle turned as well. He fell with a jet of
hot pain shooting up his leg, supplementing rather
than replacing the blue chill that pervaded every
atom of his being.

There was no one behind him except Kjarten, his
Irish slavegirl. His grip on the rawhide thong dragged
her down also, bawling in the apathetic fear that was
her being as surely as cold was all this cosmos held
for Thorir.

Kjarten hadn't spoken those words. She hadn't
spoken anything since the night Thorir, drunk with
loot and slaughter at the dwelling to which the girl
had led him, had torn out her tongue. He couldn't
recall even the next morning why he'd done that;
Kjarten could scarcely have been more biddable since
he'd come upon her unexpectedly in a field. She'd
been quite willing to sacrifice her whole family to
save her own life.

But whatever the reason he'd mutilated her, Thorir
rather liked the result—until he found himself here,
with no other company than grayness and a girl
without a tongue.

Thorir struggled to his feet. He was a big man,
fond of saying that the paunch wobbling beneath his
powerful chest and shoulders was reservoir of strength

that made him the match of any three other men—or any ten, when the berserk rage was on him and he ravened, champing at his shield edge and swinging an axe already slick with the blood of earlier victims. Certainly no one in life had been able to stand against him. Not until the night he and his followers swaggered into the house of Thorfinn Karson. . . .

"Who are you?" he asked in a rusty, ice-choked voice. He meant the words to be savage, frightening, but they came out as a stutter at whose meaning even he had to wonder.

"I can let you walk the Earth again, Paunch," said the voice, "if you pass my test. Wouldn't you like that?"

There was something in the mist, now: glowing chips that could have been eyes as yellow as pitch flames. They burned in the grayness, as high above the volcanic waste as Thorir's own eyes, and as empty of mercy as the berserker had been empty of hope until this moment.

Thorir swung at the eyes. He missed, or they weren't there after all—phantoms in the chill-saturated air, as surely as the body that wasn't there to support the glowing eyes. He fell again, tearing his left palm on the lava. Ice gave edges to the tangles of his long, red-gold hair as it slashed across his cheeks and eyeballs.

Kjarten watched in terror as she knelt on the bitter rock. She did not reach up to loosen the thong that had chafed an eternal weal around her throat.

"No one can offer that," croaked Thorir as he struggled to his feet again. "No one . . ." But at the repetition, a hint of question had crept into his mind, if not his words.

The eyes were back where they had been, and the voice said, "To walk the Earth, to live a human life

. . . or as close as only God could tell the difference,
Paunch. . . ."

The tone was playful at first, but no one could
have doubted the acrid certainty of the emotion in
the word "*God.*"

Only one being in this place dared speak of God.

"Why . . .?" Thorir said. His voice was beginning
to gain authority with use and with the memories of
his past life to which speech returned him. He scowled
at Kjarten and tried to tug her upright with the
thong. The girl, already trying to rise, slipped again
and mewled.

"Do you get bored, Paunch?" the voice asked mock-
ingly. There was a smokiness in the yellow eyes;
they began to darken with sparks of fitful orange.
"I get bored. I have a very long time for that. . . .
And so I set little tests for my charges, and I reward
them if they succeed."

"Liar!" shouted Thorir. He lunged toward the disembodied voice and Kjarten, forgotten at the end of
the thong in his bleeding left hand, jerked him off
his feet like an anchor. The girl skidded into her
fallen master, her screams retaining the same timbre
when he beat at her and when he stopped.

"Of course," said the voice. "But if you pass my
test, you will live a full adult life on Earth as if you
had never come here. It will be our joke, Paunch—
yours and mine—on the . . . others who placed us
here."

The second time, the word "*here*" had the vicious
force of "*God*" a moment before.

"What is your test?" Thorir demanded as he got to
his feet for the third time since the voice had entered his existence. He spoke without emotion, but
the mind behind his words blazed with a joy as
incandescent as the eyes that glared into his soul.

Never in present eternity had the sky above Thorir cleared fully. Now, slowly, but with the increasing speed of an avalanche pulling itself down a steep slope, the mist began to burn away from the desolation it cloaked.

Paradise was a pitiless dagger point on the horizon. Its light fell on the ice-laden lava fields, spangling them with a myriad of crystalline jewels as bright and fearful as the source they reflected.

"There . . ." said the voice softly.

Thorir's eyes were drawn toward Paradise. Despite the pain, that spot above the line demarcating dark land and pale sky was the first feature Thorir had seen during the ageless eternity he had spent marching across the face of Hell.

And there were features on the landscape as well, now that they were free of the haze that had swaddled them like oil-soaked cotton. In the middle distance across the waste that lava had made its own and nothing else's, was a pillar. It was a cairn built of small stones, flakes chipped from the lava by cold and the roots of lichen—piled here by men or the souls of men as a guide in the wilderness. Everyone who passed would place another bit of rock atop those that earlier hands had raised. Standing up above the snow that swirled across the desolation, the pillar would lead other travellers to safety.

If there were other travellers. If the mist and biting ice crystals permitted anyone else to see the cairn.

If there were any such thing as safety in Hell.

Beyond the cairn and in direct line with the searing radiance of Paradise was a gout of steam knotting sky and land at the horizon. This was not the haze that had hidden the landscape from Thorir until the present moment. The cloud was white and angry, roiling with occasional colors that were not sodden gray. Dimly visible through and above it was spike of land larger than the rubble cairn and perhaps not artificial.

"A woman lives there," said the voice with a touch of harshness. "Because she offended me, you might say. If you can reach her, Paunch—"

Thorir shook himself. He felt as if he were awakening after a long sleep. He was aware of his body as more than a repository of pain for the first time in timeless ages.

"—and receive from her the thing she least wishes to grant you—"

Thorir began to laugh, a booming, barking sound as hideous as the hummocks of icy rock surrounding him.

"—then you will live a human life again—or very like it," the voice concluded. "But you must pass that test."

Thorir began stalking toward the cairn. He could see his footing, but despite that he slipped and hammered his hip on the frozen rock.

Kjarten sprang along beside him on all fours as soon as she was sure that her master was moving. "Bitch!" he roared as he fell, the first words he had deigned to direct at her in . . . well, duration had no meaning in a wasteland without incident.

The glowing eyes slitted, as they might have done in a face convulsed with silent laughter. "Are you in a hurry, Paunch?" the voice asked. "You needn't be. Wait a moment and I'll tell you some things you may find useful."

Thorir paused unwillingly, not because the voice offered to help him . . . but rather, because the voice, for all its playfulness, was master here. Moments ago that wouldn't have mattered—because "here" was ice and haze and lava. But now there was

hope, and with hope came the fear of losing what the
future might bring.

"What is it you want to tell me, then?" Thorir said,
truculence and concern mixed in his words and tone.

"There are two men you'll meet on your way,
Paunch," the voice went on. The eyes glittered momentarily with a blackness that was nonetheless light,
a hellish reflection of Paradise. "They'll have things
you'll need for success—if you have wit enough to
know what they are. Do you like guessing games,
Paunch?"

"Two men," Thorir repeated. He flexed his arms,
clenching and unclenching his hands as he stared at
them. His skin was sallow, chafed and scarred by
falling on rocks whose every crack was a chisel edge.
His limbs were stiff and felt brittle, ready to flake
away like bits of the ice-shattered hraun on which he
stood.

He could not trust his strength, not in this place.
"Two men . . ."

"And the woman," the voice said. "I think I should
warn you—" though the tone was one of slobbering
expectation, not concern "—that she doesn't in the
least like men. That will make your test much harder."

Thought of two men to fight had raised fear in
Thorir. It melted away in a gush of laughter as rau-
cous and masterless as the roar of a glacier-locked
pond bursting its ice barrier and pouring devastation
on the valley below.

"Doesn't like men?" the berserker gasped through
his laughter. "And this should concern me, Voice?
She can't have met the right man, then, can she?
She can't have met Thorir Paunch. Many a wife and
daughter there were who wailed when I took them
away, but none of them disturbed any pleasure I
chose to take!"

"As you will, then, Paunch," said the voice with silky good humor. "Give my regards to Sappho when you've finished with her."

The eyes shrank, the hollow light of them growing brighter and viler in a myriad of shades as their compass lessened. Thorir blinked, uncertain even when they seemed to have disappeared that there were not two dots of scintillance in the air where the eyes had been.

Then he grunted and started for the stone pillar, tugging Kjarten along with a motion that had become an instinct.

In the distance behind Thorir was another cairn in line with the one toward which he trudged. The pillars marked the course of a track across the waste. Perhaps there was a terminus in the other direction as well, a place of warmth and drink and food—

And perhaps the track ended in mist and desolation as complete as that in which Thorir had until now ground out his existence, ever since he thought to repay Thorfinn Karson for the ill service that rich farmer had done him by convincing the king to outlaw berserkers from Norway.

It didn't matter. In this direction lay the chance of real life and a liar's promise of a woman, a fresh woman. . . .

Thorir began to laugh. When Kjarten whined at the end of her tether, he laughed more loudly.

The lava, with its covering of snow and lichen, was as difficult a surface as it had been before, drawing most of his attention. When Thorir lifted his eyes from the underfoot patterns of gray on gray on gray, it was always to focus on the cairn.

Kjarten keened at him. Instead of considering that the girl might be trying to articulate a warning, he jerked her forward with the rawhide.

She fell, and Thorir fell cursing. And Thorfinn
Karson, rising from the crevice which he had roofed
with chunks of lava corbelled into a dome, was on
the berserker before he could get up.

Thorfinn carried a knife with a long, single-edged
blade. It rasped the skin beneath the berserker's
throat, one of the few places on Thorir's body which
the lava had not already gashed innumerable times.

"Who are you?" Thorfinn asked in a voice as rusty
as Thorir's had been earlier when he spoke to the
mocking eyes for the first time. Then, "The fog—
what have you done with the fog?"

He didn't recognize Thorir, and he was just as
confused by change after the changeless eternity as
the berserker had been.

Thorir knew what he was intended to get from this
man. No doubt about that.

"I'm lost," the berserker whispered in a voice that
the knife-edge made ragged. Its chill penetrated
him as even the wind could not, because what the
blade threatened was not Thorir's body but his new
hope. "You mustn't hurt me, I'm—"

Kjarten cried out in fear as fresh as her master's
hope. She had just realized that they were no longer
alone, she and Thorir.

"Eh, child, did I hurt you?" Thorfinn said, shifting
his weight from where it pinned the berserker to the
frozen rocks. "I—I've been here, I lose track of
time. . . ."

The farmer reached out with his free hand to lift
the slave to her feet. Kjarten cowered away from
him, sliding like a broken-backed lizard. Her eyes
stared up at her would-be helper.

"Child," Thorfinn repeated with the sharpness of a
man with good intentions—and the anger of seeing
them misconstrued.

Thorir didn't act hurriedly—the voice had warned him he would need to use his wits. Only when he was quite certain that the other man was occupied with Kjarten did the berserker rise to a half-crouch and grip one of Thorfinn's ankles.

Thorfinn shouted as he fell, twisting with the knife raised. His right elbow took the shock of the ground, spinning the weapon away. His fall doubled the force of Thorir's right fist swinging toward him with a rock.

"Have me killed, will you?" Thorir shouted as he twisted on top of his victim. He slammed down at Thorfinn's broken face with a chunk from the farmer's makeshift shelter, lava hammer on lava anvil, and flesh the work-piece between them. "Kill me? *Kill me!*"

When at last he stopped shouting, his throat was hoarse from unfamiliar use and his limbs were weak . . . but he felt warm for the first time in eternity— loose and warm with the rage and joy of killing that had left Thorfinn unrecognizable and made the rime smoke from the rocks with his blood.

"Kill me . . ." Thorir whispered as he leaned on the corpse of the victim who had already been dead, as everything here was dead forever.

Kjarten snuffled where she lay. She could have run when Thorir dropped the thong during the fight. There was no place to flee—Thorir's eyes searched their surroundings at the thought. The fierce light that limned the ice and stone, throwing shadows from every tooth of rock, did not make the place less an empty wasteland than it had been when the mist concealed it.

But she could have run away from Thorir. He couldn't imagine how she could been more afraid of freedom than she was of staying with him . . . but she was a woman, and therefore there was only one thing that a man needed to know about her.

The dagger had fallen hilt-upright into a crevice in the lava. It was a fine weapon, the blade carved and the design filled with silver wire. It was the sort of thing a rich king's-man like Thorfinn Karson might have been given by the monarch himself after they discussed outlawing Thorir Paunch.

Thorir laughed as he tucked the knife beneath his belt. "I thank you, gracious host," he said, his toe nudging the outflung hand of the corpse. "You have provided what I will surely need for my business."

Kjarten was standing. She handed Thorir the end of the rawhide cord about her neck. He took it and, with playfulness rather than malice, pushed her down again as he started toward the plume of steam.

It should have been easier to walk with the landscape lighted and his muscles quivering with blood and triumph, but Thorir found he was slipping just as frequently as he had before. The impacts with the rock hurt as badly also.

Paradise was a point in the sky that sparkled all the way to the back of Thorir's skull, even when he closed his eyes. It seemed to be warming the landscape enough to cover the ice with a film of water invisible until droplets glittered in the air, slung from the berserker's feet as they flew out from under him.

The shape beyond the steam was a rock outcrop, as natural as anything was in this place. As he neared it, Thorir thought he caught a glimpse of a woman there, but the vision of diaphanous garments could have been a trick of the steam that clung with sluggish power, ragged on the lee edge, but constantly replenished from beneath to deny the authority of the wind.

Thorir tugged the dagger out of his belt. It made walking even more difficult, but he would not be

surprised again as he had been by Thorfinn. All that
had saved him from Thorfinn was the farmer's softness: the fact that he had not been willing to kill a
stranger in a landscape where no one was a friend,
the fact that he had turned his back on a man because a girl was whimpering in fear.

But Thorir wouldn't need luck anymore, now that
he had a blade in his hand.

A man appeared from the edge of the steam cloud
so abruptly that reflex almost put the knife through
his belly and up the line of soft cartilage tying his
ribs to his breastbone. He screamed and threw up
his hands in startlement. By falling down on his
back, he saved his life—or what passed for it in this
place, this existence.

Thorir was laughing with triumph and the absurdity of the pudgy figure who flopped before
him, but that did not keep him from wrapping the
fingers of his left hand in the man's black garment
and putting the knife to his throat, just as Thorfinn
had held the berserker moments before.

"Please, please," the little man was bubbling in a
voice whose low volume was a subconscious attempt
to placate the fury he saw in the eyes of Thorir
Paunch. "I'm sure we can, I'm sure we can . . ."

"Who are you?" the berserker demanded. He shook
his new captive hard enough to make the fellow bawl
in abject terror when his head brushed the rock on
which he lay. The air was full of roaring, like that of a
waterfall but of a deeper timbre. The vapor that
swirled around them was hot, not spume dashed
from cold stones.

"I'm Father John Ryan," the smaller man said. His
eyes were shut, as if by not looking at Thorir he
could make the berserker disappear. "I'm, I'm,
I'm . . . I work in an office, or I did, but I—came

here. I'm really a priest, and I shouldn't be, I mean . . . ?"

He opened his eyes, then swallowed in resignation.

"A mass priest," Thorir said.

He lifted Ryan without taking the knife away from the other man's neck. The threat wasn't necessary, that was clear, but it amused Thorir to see how Ryan tried to lift his double chin away from the steel without giving possible offense to the man who held it.

"Do you think your prayers will help you, priest?" Thorir added as he pulled Ryan with him deeper into the billowing steam. "Many have prayed, and it's never saved them from me before."

"I . . ." said the priest. "I'm very glad to see you, sir. I say that in all sincerity, because since I've been here alone in this—"

Thorir shook him again as he dragged him, a warning for silence that would have been followed by a blow if Ryan hadn't understood.

Dividing the current of a small stream was the basalt outcrop that Thorir needed to gain to complete the voice's test. It was no more than twenty feet from where Thorir stood to the outcrop—almost close enough for him to chance leaping the gap.

Almost. The stream was not water but molten rock. The black crust that covered most of it radiated heat as intense as the chill of the wind that still raked Thorir's back. The cracks that webbed the surface glared with the light of the eyes that had accompanied the voice.

"Ah . . ." murmured Thorir, because even his soul was stunned by the lowering presence of the stream he had to cross.

If the fluid had been water, it would have been dashing its way through shallow rapids. After the magma burst from the side of a basalt cliff, it spread around the wedge base of the outcrop and plunged back into the solid ground again, having dropped about six feet of elevation in the hundred feet or so it ran on the surface. The gases it gave off were bitter and throat-searing, even in this place. Their precipitates colored the stone of the channel blue and pink and especially the sullen yellow of sulphur.

As slowly as the stream moved, it crumbled chunks from the walls of its channel, and the roar of its progress was so loud that not even Thorir could hear the demand he shouted to Father Ryan.

He slapped the black-suited man anyway, then pulled him far enough back from the lava flow that the sound was no longer deafening. They bumped Kjarten, who had followed not to look but to be close. The berserker started to kick her, but he knew he would fall down if he did so. His mind was working better now. He was beginning to understand his environment—now that he had the chance to escape it.

"How do I get across the stream?" Thorir demanded in the high wheeze which was all the voice the hot fumes had left him. The wind across the hraun whistled through the passages of his nose and throat from which sulfides had scraped the mucous protection, but the cold air was no anodyne.

"I've been trying to solve that dilemma myself, my friend," said Ryan, nodding his head portentously. He was trying not to look at the dagger that Thorir had lowered to his side, but instinct drew his eyes sidelong to the gleaming steel. "There's a person on the rock, you see . . . a, ah, woman. I thought that if I could reach her, we could—that is, since I'm here, then it follows logically from the divine wisdom of the Almighty that there's a reason. Therefore—"

Ryan was not as self-involved as he seemed. He leaped backward, avoiding the blow Thorir aimed to silence him.

"Girl," Thorir said, motioning Kjarten even closer so that he didn't have to bend to pick up the end of her short tether.

"Sir, for both our sakes—our souls," said Ryan with a touch of desperation. "I can help you if you'll listen to me. I, ah, I'll try to adapt my idiom to the circumstances, rather than use the terms of theological debate in—"

Thorir looked at Ryan when he heard the word "help." The berserker's eyes slitted and the dagger drew back for a disemboweling stroke when the priest continued to yammer.

Ryan closed his eyes and fell to his knees in an attitude of prayer. Either he knew that Thorir could run him down if he wanted to, or emotions had leached the strength from his legs. "For the sake of argument," he cried in a pinched voice, his face lifted up and his pudgy hands clasped before his breast, "let's say that I, during life, exhibited insufficient concern for others. Let's say, ah, a *lack* of concern for others, despite my conscious intention to follow the tenets of the Church and our Savior."

Thorir looked at the priest. His throat was as open for the knife as that of a goat with its muzzle lifted. Ryan wasn't worth the step toward him and the chance of falling. Thorir stalked back into the bitter steam, pulling Kjarten with him.

She would no doubt have followed as she had before, but this time the berserker didn't want to take the chance. He had a use for the girl.

The roaring came from the cleft in the rock from which the magma rolled. The sound was the result of steam jetting around and through the boiling rock.

Ground water—seepage melted from the ice and snow that covered the wasteland beneath which the pipe of lava flowed—was heated to enormous pressures until it reached the opening here and a chance to escape.

The steam was as dense as cloth to those who stepped into its pall. The gases that hissed with it from the magma gave the vapor the slightly yellow tinge of a linen burial shroud.

This time as he stood on the edge of the lava stream, Thorir could see the woman twenty feet away on the other side.

She was short, barefoot, and dressed in a garment that could have been an afterthought of the steam which parted momentarily to expose her. She had black hair and eyes set wide in a face swarthier than Thorir was used to seeing when he walked the Earth.

Not that it mattered. There was only one thing that mattered about any woman, and Thorir did not need the voice on the empty hraun to remind him of that.

Father Ryan must have followed the berserker back into the mist, because Thorir could hear him keening over the steam's roar, "I'm sure it must be the land of the Almighty, because His mercy is divine, that souls be able to seek salvation even here. . . ."

Thorir pulled the slavegirl next to him and transferred his left-hand grip from the cord to her thin shoulder.

The lava stream itself was fully visible. Heat radiating from its surface kept the air above it clear, though vapor boiled up like a wall to either side of the channel. The crust that formed almost as soon as magma touched the atmosphere was a black so deep that its webbing of orange-red cracks gave it a purple cast.

The surface was a viscid mass moving but without apparent direction. Blocks of stone floated in it, broken from the channel by the stream's weight and the enormous thermal energy locked up within its fluid mass. The solidified lava was lighter than the magma by the volume of the gas bubbles it had cooled around, so the blocks followed the contours of the surrounding land, sloping downhill toward the lower opening at the speed of an old man walking.

If you hopped from one block to the next, perhaps you could reach the outcrop and the woman upon it.

"If I can help *you* find salvation, my friend," the priest was maundering in a voice that could have filled a cathedral to be heard over the roar, "then perhaps I, too—though this is not the most important factor—can, ah, rejoin the, ah . . ."

"Go across, girl," Thorir said to the girl. She couldn't hear him. He swung her out over the blasting heat when a block of lava floated close enough for her to leap onto.

She screamed instead of jumping, a tongueless fluting that pierced Thorir like the wind across the wastes. He jerked back in amazement. Kjarten managed to keep her balance there on the edge by twisting, her arms wide.

Thorir reached in and pushed her with the flat of his hand. She catapulted out over the magma, her thin shift lifting in the draft flung upward by the glowing rock.

Across the stream, the other woman watched Thorir with a face like hardened lava.

Kjarten could still have touched the drifting block if she'd thought to try, but the girl's eyes were wild and blind as she pirouetted through the air. Her feet starred the crust. Purple-black splashed to furnace-bright orange. Kjarten leaped away like a frog on a hot grill, her toes black and trailing tendrils of smoke that the convection currents whipped around her.

Almost, Thorir thought that his trial had been a failure, that Kjarten would not test the stability of the floating blocks as she fled across the stream of magma. Behind her were dimples in the crust, pools of yellow-orange that darkened as they cooled—sometimes centered about a charred bit that had clung to the lava as the mad girl leaped forward on disintegrating feet.

At the last, scarcely her own height from the farther shore, she touched a block, fell across one, and sprawled full-length on the crust. The slab tilted, dropping beneath her so that the other end rose, sticky with magma and its own melting substance.

Thorir could not trust the blocks to support him, even if he were willing to chance an alignment of two or three slabs floating like stepping stones in the stream.

The woman on the other side bent over the magma and gripped Kjarten beneath both shoulders, though the heat made her own diaphanous garment crinkle with the incipience of bursting into flame itself. She tugged at the slavegirl to break her loose from the clinging rock, then jerked her to the shore with strength that belied her slight form.

The stream was very shallow. Kjarten's right hand had sunk only to the wrist when instinct threw it out to break her fall.

Thorir turned. Father Ryan was no longer behind him. For a heart-stopping moment, the berserker believed that he had lost his chance by not seizing it in time.

Steam swirled and he caught sight of the priest's hunched back, walking away from the blazing stream. Thorir followed at a lumbering run, managing—for a wonder—not to fall before he had grabbed Ryan by the shoulder.

Then they crashed down, and the frozen lava was as painful as it had been throughout Thorir's present eternity.

"I must recognize the will of the Almighty and accept it," the priest was mumbling. "I must find the faith to carry me where logic will not . . ."

"I have a use for you, priestling," Thorir said in a voice that shivered with the wind and anticipation. He rolled Ryan over on his back. The priest was unresisting, but an awkward task for his softness and the way he flopped as a dead weight. "The eyes warned me I'd have to keep my wits about me to figure out what good you were."

"I must remember that everything that happens, even here, is the will of the Almighty," said Ryan with his eyes closed. "I must—"

His eyes shot open when the blade forced its way through the black silk of his shirt and on through skin, fat, and the cartilage joining his ribs to his breastbone. Ryan saw Thorir's shaggy savagery framed against an empty sky. The berserker had the fleeting impression that it was the first real thing that had impressed itself on Ryan in all his life or his existence afterward.

For some reason, the words ". . . is the will of the Almighty . . ." echoed in Thorir's mind, though the priest's mouth was already filled with blood. The long knife had severed the veins and arteries connecting Ryan's heart with his lungs as Thorir ripped the body cavity open from collarbone to diaphragm.

The priest's eyes emptied of meaning and the semblance of life . . . but life or its counterfeit would come again on the Undertaker's slab, and meaning—that would not be lost either.

What Ryan did with what he had learned was of no interest to Thorir Paunch. The berserker's business was with the fat corpse for the brief time before it melted into a slime of Hell's own making, for recycling into more damned uses.

Thorir worked quickly. Even though there was a purpose behind his activity, it gave him a warm glow of remembrance for all the times he had cut the blood-eagle on the bodies of his victims—chopping through their ribs and tearing out their lungs to flop over their emptied torsos. Good days—

Days that would be his again to live, if he passed the test the voice had set him. Now, thanks to the priest, he was quite sure of success.

Thorir's boots were worn to useless scraps that did nothing to protect his feet from the frozen edges of the landscape. He hadn't discarded them because of the same mindless apathy that kept him staggering across the hraun with neither hope nor destination. . . .

Until now.

And now there was purpose as well for the remains of the boots—the long leather thongs that bound the uppers to calves which the leather chafed but did not shield from cold. Working with fingers numb from wind and disuse, Thorir untied the thongs and laid them aside.

Then he pulled Ryan's lungs the rest of the way out of the body, cutting through the bit of bronchial tube that tugged against the berserker's first attempt. He slit both of the flaccid, spongy masses and fitted them onto his feet.

They slurped as Thorir tied them in place with the boot thongs. The blood that filled the soft tissues would not protect him long from the molten rock, but he was willing to bet against the pain of failure

that they would last for the three long strides between him and success.

Because the prize was worth even the chance that
his own feet would burn and slough away as Kjarten's
did when she tested the route for him.

Haste made Thorir careless, but he did not fall,
even when the sulfurous steam wrapped him again
and hid the treacherous footing. Certainty of success
filled him as it always had when he prepared for
battle—the assurance that later his enemies' goods
would be his to loot, their women his to rape and
degrade in the ways that more than anything else
proved that he was a man and the world's master.

The woman across the magma watched him. She
cradled Kjarten in her arms. She had thrown aside
the slave's shift, but the stumps of Kjarten's limbs
still smoldered.

Thorir took a deep breath, coughed at the bitter
vapor he inhaled, and stepped into the stream.

He hadn't allowed for the *weight* of the magma
being so much greater than that of water. Shallow as
it was, the molten rock threw his foot sideways and
threatened a disaster for which Kjarten's ruined body
was a template.

Thorir twisted, remembering how the slavegirl had
pirouetted in an attempt to save herself—but Thorir
succeeded, because there was no hand thrusting him
back out of the safety his sense of balance had gained.
He strode onward, surprised again by the viscosity of
the stream that made it grip him as surely as it had
almost thrown him down. His stride was half the
length he had expected from it, and he lunged forward against his memories of Kjarten writhing,
burning. . . .

The woman, Sappho, struggled with the girl she
had saved from extinction and rebirth in still greater

agony on the Undertaker's slab. She was trying to lift Kjarten, to carry her away from the edge of the lava torrent and the berserker crossing it . . . though she must have known that there was no escape—that the outcrop, a fortress until its moat was breached, was a narrow trap thereafter.

Sappho and her mewling burden disappeared behind the curtain of steam, but Thorir was so filled with his expectations of triumph that he forgot his danger until he took a third stride and a block of floating lava struck his trailing foot.

The stone that seared his calf above the wrapping of lung tissue was not fluid, but its temperature was within a few degrees of the magma that carried it. Thorir screamed. His eyes and mind saw nothing but red terror, and it was reflex that lifted his foot in a convulsive leap.

The bundle of lung pulled off with a sucking sound that the bones of Thorir's feet transmitted, though his ears were filled with the roaring of the lava vent.

His bare foot touched the outcrop's firm edge. His toes gripped as though the rocks were not blazingly hot as well, and the toes hadn't been mutilated by tramping innumerable miles of the chill hraun.

Thorir's leg flexed and flung him full-length to safety. Sappho, hunching under the weight of the maimed Kjarten, stared at him with empty eyes. She glanced toward the molten stream behind her, escape if not safety—

But Kjarten moaned something through a mouth whose lips had burned off when she sprawled.

Sappho laid the girl down gently and stepped away from her. The woman crossed her rosy arms over her breasts as if she were hugging her thin garment closer against the cold. She did not speak as Thorir got up and walked deliberately to her, his left foot still squishing with the remnants of Father Ryan.

"You know what I'm here for, girl," he said to the woman. He smiled.

Sappho's face scrunched up in preparation to spit. Thorir's arm was already swinging. The flat of his left hand knocked her sideways. She fell; Thorir knelt between her legs. The ground was hard and cold even here, but anticipation cushioned Thorir's stance.

"Don't be a fool!" he shouted as Sappho tried to struggle away when she came out of her daze. He pushed the edge of the knife toward her face. She lunged forward, trying to cut her throat with it. The hem of the light shift pinned beneath Thorir's knees tore.

He hit her again with his balled fist. When she flopped back, he put the knife down to have both hands free. It was not the first time Thorir had dealt with a difficult wench: he was careful to set the weapon at the end of his own reach, where the woman's shorter arms could not touch it, even if they thrashed about somewhat in the next minutes.

Thorir lifted Sappho by the throat and slapped her—palm, backhand, and palm—with enough force that her teeth cut her cheeks on both sides.

"Don't be difficult, girlie," he said, through jaws clenched with anger because she was trying to balk him. "It won't make any difference—and anyway, you've never had such a man as me."

When he reached down to tear her shift out of the way, Sappho spit in his face. Her saliva was mixed with blood.

He hit her again, stunning her and breaking a tooth.

Were the eyes watching him now? Thorir wondered as he got down to the only business a man had with a woman. But the thought made him pause, for the glowing eyes had been as cruel as his own and the voice was a trickster's voice, a liar's.

The thing she wishes least to grant you, the voice had said. Of course, they thought to fool him. . . .

Thorir rolled his victim over so that she lay belly-down on the rock. Then he proceeded.

The pain of her flesh tearing awakened Sappho. That pleased Thorir, for it was the only pleasure he was taking. Things weren't right. Everything *worked,* but it was an empty exercise, like the ages of tramping across the wastes . . . and as cold, almost as cold.

So there was pleasure in the woman's waking pain. But when she twisted her head to look at him, there was no fear in her eyes—only contempt, as utter and complete as the emptiness in Thorir's existence on the lava.

"Don't!" he shouted at the woman as his fingers sought her throat. *"Don't!"* with his voice rising in something like terror. . . .

Perhaps Sappho's look did change as the berserker battered her head against the stone, but the eyes and scorn were bright in his mind, freezing him as the wind across the hraun had frozen his marrow. Her body spasmed as she died, but not even that brought Thorir to release—

Except that it released him from the need to continue with a pointless exercise.

Thorir stood up. He was shaking as if with the chills that follow fever, and his knees hurt from the scraping they had taken as they bore his weight. He felt—

He felt empty.

Kjarten made a whimpering sound. It had nothing to do with Thorir, but it recalled him to his surroundings. All trace of Father Ryan had disappeared. Sappho's body lay faceless and unrecognizable. It would soon be gone as well—a puzzle for the Undertaker and a lingering agony for the soul whose form would reknit to bear the further tortures of existence in this place.

But Thorir Paunch would be leaving. He had *won*!

The mist was beginning to gather, dimming Paradise and covering the wasteland with a batting no more featureless than the rippled lava itself.

"Voice!" Thorir bellowed. "Voice!"

"Well, Paunch," said the voice, from behind him. "Have you succeeded in gaining the lady's respect? With our Sappho's prejudices, that was a very hard test . . . was it not?"

Thorir whirled around and stumbled. He was beginning to lose the agility that had returned to him when the landscape cleared. "I won your test," he muttered, trying to focus on the eyes. They were a deeper amber than he remembered. Other colors swirled in their depths like currents in the magma. "I'm *here*. I won!"

"Thorfinn was a hard man," mused the voice. The eyes bubbled, and the landscape darkened all around. "No lack of reasons for him to be here, surely. But he had a way of being kind to the helpless that I thought might stand you in good stead."

"I took his knife," Thorir said. He shook his head, trying to clear it of the confusion that invaded him like cobwebs of mist. He looked around, but he couldn't see the blade anymore. Even Sappho's body was almost hidden.

Kjarten mewed.

"Yes, he had a knife," said the voice softly. "And there was Father Ryan, who knew all the things he had never thought to practice. Too late now, of course. This isn't a place that *mercy* penetrates. . . ."

Thorir blinked, lashed from his growing chill by the venom in the word "mercy."

"But perhaps you could have learned enough to

succeed in my little game with you, Paunch," the voice continued. Its tone was the bloody sharpness of a cat's claws, toying with a helpless victim.

Thorir knew the sound very well.

"She could have watched you learning to help your little slave—not that there was much you could do for her in this place."

Much anyone can do for anyone in this place— echoed words that no one had spoken.

"But trying," the voice continued. "Who knows? It was a hard test, to be sure, for our Sappho is a difficult woman . . . but in time, as she watched, who knows? And you had no shortage of time, Paunch, not here."

"I crossed the fire," Thorir said, through lips choking with a variety of emotions. "I *came* here!"

"Very impressive," the voice said in what was not agreement. "Needless, of course, but very impressive nonetheless."

"You have to give me life!" the berserker shouted as he lunged toward the eyes, swinging his fist.

His hand shattered against nothing. The emptiness it hit was as hard as the frozen hraun, as all-devouring as the magma in which Kjarten's limbs had dissolved.

"Must I, then?" mocked the voice as Thorir screamed. "But perhaps I will, Paunch. After all, you've amused me. I'll give you an adult body and as much time as you can find with it to walk the Earth."

Thorir was doubled over, as if that could armor him from the pain blossoming from where his right hand had been. That was only a hint of the life-blasting agony that enveloped him in the next instant. He was whirling, spiraling, and his direction was uncertain until he struck, and felt every atom of his being *smear* into another plane of existence.

"I'll be seeing you, Paunch," the voice whispered in his mind.

There was a fire roaring nearby. Its heat hammered him. The air was thick with the smoke of wood and turf and human flesh. Men were shouting. They had thrown down their shields when the brief resistance ceased, but they still carried axes or bloody swords.

Thorir recognized the men. Less familiar was the rage-inflamed face of the man who held him now by the jaw, and shouted in a voice reeking of looted beer, "Who told you to cry, girlie? Who did, tell me?"

It looked different by a night lighted in the fire of a blazing Irish farm, but Thorir had seen his own face before in clear pools and the polished metal he had torn from monastery altars.

The berserker's thick fingers squeezed both sides of Thorir's girlish jaw-hinge while his other hand reached into Thorir's mouth. The fingernails were black and as hard as claws.

The pain was terrible. Worse than that was the memory of the maimed thing still whimpering on a rock in Hell.

Thorir had a pretty good idea of how he was going to spend the rest of eternity.

PAWN IN PLAY

C. J. Cherryh

Augustus was becoming accustomed to the idea of replaceable rosebushes in the garden outside his study window—replaceable rosebushes, replaceable windowpanes, and (he winced) twice having to go to Praxiteles with the hope that he could repair the finish on the priceless bronze of Iris. ("What are you *doing* with it?" the aggrieved sculptor had protested—with admirable restraint, Augustus thought. Augustus had shrugged in embarrassment: "Viet Cong. A few overshots. I promise—*this* time we won't set it near any windows.")

There was sawing and hammering downstairs. There was the smell of new varnish and paint in the air. All of that was work of the sycophants, the lost souls who mended and polished with manic zeal as if to make up for their desertion under fire—sycophants *never* stayed around when the going got truly rough, and it had lately, with the small matter of a grenade in Tiberius' atrium and more than a few grenades in Assurbanipal's palace, gotten very rough indeed.

But normalcy, as far as Hell had normalcy, settled like a sigh over the estates on the edge of the Lake. Tiberius seemed to have forgotten who had thrown the grenade, his statue was repaired, and his new preoccupation was Caligula, who, Tiberius insisted, had shown up again in the guise of a baboon. And while Assurbanipal quite well remembered who had thrown the grenade at his doors, he had enough trouble with Administration asking questions, nor was he likely to reclaim the baboon.

So Augustus settled into paperwork, into the endless governmental forms and requisitions and accountings which were too sensitive to trust to the staff—which in fact were a monumental construction fabricated of interrelated half-truths and bureaucratic persiflage, on which their lives and well-being depended.

Julius fought for the Roman West in the field. Augustus' field of combat was somewhat smaller, in fact, the six by five expanse of a mahogany desk buried in paper, ledgers, and miscellaneous notes. There were the militia accounts: those, Julius' staff handled. But the civil ones took a special skill, the ability to recognize alarm signals and traps designed to turn up discrepancies. Accounting was only a part of it. Hell's forms-in-triplicate were an art form, and the Hall of Injustice was full of papers constantly cross-compared by endless supplies of clerks and functionaries. Hell *had* no statute of limitations, and a report filed a thousand years ago could suddenly surface, in the hands of a clerk who had just Gotten Around To It in the mounds of papers which lay in the never-purified vaults of Infernal Revenue and the Department of Injustice, not mentioning entities as apparently innocuous as the Park Department, which was in charge of Decentral Park and the Viet

Cong who ran riot through its rhododendrons and ancient oak groves. One never knew: that was the main thing to remember. One never knew when some bit of paper would come back to haunt its creator.

And Infernal Revenue constantly changed the forms.

While the Insecurity Service had its own ongoing inquiries and wanted depositions from a number of witnesses to Assyrian misbehavior.

Naturally, there was no dearth of volunteers among the legions. But these had to be primed, most carefully, and warned what they could answer, what they could say, what they might be trapped into saying, and what line they must follow in any related questioning. They were not fools, who had served the Eagles for more than two thousand years. Bluff, square-faced Baculus, the First Lance Centurion of the 10th, might look like a country bumpkin, and talk like one—no surprise, since his folk were shepherds—and he was a veritable map of scars, the sort of man whose honorable wounds made him suspect in Polite Society; but *pro di immortales*, there was a canny good sense behind those deep-set eyes, and the mind that reacted so quickly to shifting conditions on the battlefield could quite well handle an interviewer's tricks. Baculus was, in fact, Augustus's favorite sacrificial lamb: "Oh, yessir, our orders was to go knock hell out of the Dissidents, and then these damn—beggin' yer pardon, sir, well, you know—Tiberius, he ain't so well wrapped sometimes. We was already having trouble there, an' then them damn—(damn, *sorry!* sir)—them Assyrians went and grabbed them boys and there we was—I mean, wasn't much we could do, them holding Caesar's kids an' threatening Tiberius—oh, yes, they did, sir! I was out there on that line. I heard that with my own ears, yes, sir. And we didn't have nothing, I mean, one damn jeep and a truck we was hauling supplies in—oh, munitions, the 14th requisitioned it. The Dissidents, you remember. Well, and this rocket launcher, against the Dissidents, yes, sir. . . . I mean, we had nothin', and them Assyrians was sitting there with all this stuff and them mines and the machine guns— They wasn't talking. They was going to cut those boys' throats. What was we going to do?"

Investigators always took Baculus for slow-witted. And that broad, dumb grin of his could charm the right words right onto paper in the Administration interviewers' own writing.

In that department Baculus was better than Niccolo Machiavelli: *everyone* suspected Niccolo. And Hatshepsut, thank the gods, had Pentagram connections, not that Rameses loved her, far from it: but Rameses did not want her or Kleopatra interviewed, for reasons which had to do with the fact that Rameses' aide Mithridates was under investigation and Rameses' own position as Supreme Commander of Hell was shaky. Rameses had no wish for *anyone* who had been in his office recently to be interviewed by the Insecurity Service; and he used the fact (which he had tried hitherto to ignore) that they were Egyptian and both pharaohs to fling a protective blanket over them and *their* activities in the Assyrian affair.

That left Sargon, whose bull-like strength sometimes tempted the clerks to suspect he had slow wits: wrong. The Lion of Akkad had ruled by cleverness as well as force, and could charm or intimidate—alternately.

Then there were himself and Julius—enough said. Intrigue was meat and drink to Julius, and no inquiry made points off Octavianus Augustus, who had installed the Roman bureaucracy that kept the Empire

running for centuries after, even with dead hands or
dead wits at the helm.

In fact, Augustus settled to his work quite cheer-
fully, finding himself far more in his element than he
had been since he had innocently walked down a hall
and precipitated Caesarion's flight, —which had precipitated everything else.

Caesarion, thank gods, was reputedly back at Tiberius' villa, gone home to his foster-father Antonius, who had his hands full over there, what with
Tiberius' latest fancy and the necessity to garrison
the line between Tiberius' palace and the Assyrians.

Antonius . . . had been handed command over the
Praetorian Guard. It was, for Marcus Antonius, a
pleasant circumstance, even given the Assyrians: it
kept him a great deal out at the barracks, and it
might even keep him sober, if Caesarion did not
drive him to drink.

At least the boy *was* home, and not gallivanting off
and about with the Dissidents. That meant Julius
was far easier to live with.

There remained only the small matter of Rameses,
who was anxious enough to be dangerous. Rameses
wanted very much to know just *why* Julius had taken
the convalescing former Supreme Commander, Aelius
Hadrianus, the *emperor* Hadrian, out of the remote
house where he had been—*on ice*, Julius called it;
and moved him back to the New Hell.

But there had arrived among the morning's mail a
letter from Rameses to himself and to Julius (no
outsider could exactly figure out protocols with the
villa, forgetting that Rome from the time of the wolf-
suckled twins had always had a double leadership
. . . two thrones in the days of its kings, though one
was always empty; two consuls thereafter, in a system of precedences sometimes by simple alternation,

sometimes by experience, sometimes by differing expertise: Romans found no difficulty understanding it at all, but it confused hell out of the god-king).

So did Rameses confuse hell out of Augustus.

"This came," he said, having asked Hatshepsut to see him.

Pharaoh was mostly lavender today—lavender metallic jumpsuit shading to absolutely transparent here and there by unpredictable turns: a body could become quite—ahem—mesmerized. Her uraeus-crown was silvery but not silver, and flickered with internal lights, a thread running decoratively beneath pharaoh's thick black bob and into pharaoh's ear, where it whispered gods knew what.

But pharaoh had saved no few lives lately, among the legions, and Augustus, who suspected everything, suspected pharaoh less for that.

He watched anxiously as pharaoh read the paper, which to his eye was a mishmash of scrawl: he read a few hieroglyphs, enough to give him addresses; but this was demotic, below the formal salutation to the Julian house. Rameses was being informal, and his handwriting was execrable.

Hatshepsut read it with a slight pursing of her lips, and looked up with a flash of kohl-painted eyes and a wicked, small smile that betokened pharaoh amused on the surface and *not*, decidedly not amused beneath. "This is an invitation. The Osiris Rameses has written to you, in his own hand: an honor. In most obscure language, which requires my translation: he will know this. He desires to meet with you and with Julius in his offices, and wishes to discuss what he calls matters of import. He suggests that you have listened to untrustworthy influences which he neglects to name and he wishes to 'make open the way' for you. *I* am the influence he means; and 'opening the way' is polite, but ominous as well, since it also refers to another sort of passage than the one to his offices. He knows that I will tell you this."

Augustus leaned his elbows on his desk. "A meeting in his offices. Both of us."

"I would distrust it."

"I do distrust it. I see no polite way out of it."

"That is his intent, *Auguste*. He is a snake. And *very* disturbed that his predecessor is in your hands, and outside his surveillance. At worst case—assassination is not beyond him. Reject the invitation."

"We cannot afford it."

"You cannot afford to accept. It would expose you to hazard. It would serve no one but him."

"He calls you an untrustworthy influence."

Hatshepsut lifted her brows. "Would you know what he calls you?" She smiled, a cruel curve of the lips. "Be quite plain with him. Tell him you do not trust the influences that surround him, which he will translate as Mithridates, which is precisely the influence you would have removed; and hint that you will remain estranged from him while Mithridates' agents have the freedom of the Pentagram. Therefore if he wishes to see you on a friendly basis, the old crocodile will have to take measures to rid himself of what may be his strongest support—cast himself on your protection or continue to rely on aides who may be compromised with you and, more, potentially vulnerable to Administration charges, should Mithridates come under further scrutiny. Rameses lacks imagination, but he does understand innuendo. He is quite good at it, in fact."

Augustus leaned his elbows on the desk and smiled. Hatshepsut smiled. "Turn up the heat on Mithridates," Augustus translated it.

"Exactly so."

He had never had an outstanding fondness for Hatshepsut. Hatshepsut was Klea's guest in the house, and Klea's ally—He and Klea . . . got along, that was all that could be said for it: none of Julius' close adherents ever quite trusted him, and that was a fact he knew. None of his own family trusted him, nor did he trust them. And as for the few he did fully rely on, like Agrippa, *Julius'* people refused to accept and Julius, do him credit, had *tried* to get along with them, but *they* were uncomfortable with Julius. It bewildered him. His personal isolation in this teeming house of which he was co-ruler was, when he thought about it, precisely his misery in life, and Hell had, if anything, increased it.

So he always suspected help when he had it, and suspected it doubly when it came from a source to which he had no personal ties at all. But there was an exhilarating little warmth, a dangerously untrustworthy warmth that he tried at once to quash, that leapt into his heart at that look of Hatshepsut's, whose mind, he had long recognized it, was *very* political, and who was in many ways his match: a woman without illusions, a woman likewise isolate and lonely, and beautiful—

—a woman who carried a personal armament capable of wholesale slaughter, and whose eyes positively lighted when it came to blowing things up. One could not imagine a woman more his opposite—

But he had always admired intellect in a woman, and a political mind. And, gods, she was a mind as well as a—

Ahem. As the wandering transparent patch began to travel from pharaoh's shoulder downward. *Prodi,* how did a man think when this woman was in front of him?

"You can—draft an answer."

Hatshepsut smiled and leaned back, which changed the course of the traveling spot. "Trust me," she said, and crossed shapely legs which had a wandering spot of their own. "Tell me, *Auguste*, do you ever—"

O gods, not in far too long!

"—no," Hatshepsut said, veiling the fires in her eyes with a lowering of lavender lids, a cooling of the temperature in the room which had Augustus sweating. "Of course not—I'll write your letter, in the best priestly hand. I am, you know."

"What?" Augustus asked thickly. "What are you?"

"A priest." The marvelous eyes half-veiled again, and the smile grew lively and wicked. "But so are you, aren't you? A priest. Isn't that unlikely of us." She rose and sighed, and rubbed the back of her neck as she turned, which view hypnotized no less than the wandering spot—then smiled at him from the corner of an eye. "I want to think what to say to the old crocodile."

"Be careful, for godssakes!"

"Of course I'll be careful." She retreated to the door, went out of it, and put her head back through.

And gave a most conspiratorial grin.

"O gods," Augustus moaned when the door had shut. But it had nothing to do with Rameses.

Things had gone back so quickly to boring. Two days ago Marcus Brutus would have sworn he wanted nothing more than his own bed, his own room, the sound of "Don't bother me," from Sargon and "I'm busy, kit," from Hatshepsut, who passed him on the stairs with a clatter of boot-heels and a retreating view which—

O gods—

Brutus, in a Police tee-shirt and faded, frayed

jeans, sat down on the bottom step right where he was, holding his tennie-clad ankles, arms between his knees, and stared after the pharaoh with a thumping of his heart and a feeling elsewhere which scared hell out of him and made him a little crazy. He was only seventeen. He was always seventeen and he was always going to be seventeen, he had come to that realization. He had a half-brother, his father with Klea having produced Caesarion, who had Julius' dark good looks and Julius' dark eyes and the soul of a rebel—Caesarion, who had come into his life and out again with the swiftness and the force of a thunderstroke, leaving a weakness in all his bones.

Caesarion had slept with women.

Caesarion had fought in battles.

Caesarion knew all the places they went to and knew all the people there, even the Assyrians—was never at a loss (even if he had nearly gotten them killed) and never took anything off anyone.

Caesarion was seventeen, too, but Caesarion had done so much more and been so many more places, and all Brutus got out of Hatshepsut was a chuck under the chin when she had the time.

Which she didn't, today.

His father Julius was at the armory with Mouse and Scaevola and everyone except the soldiers who were on guard, and who wouldn't move for anything. Dante was keeping to his room, complaining of headaches.

The phones kept ringing, which might be good or bad news coming in: Brutus had no idea.

Phones.

Telephones.

He snapped his fingers. His own personal syco-phant popped into existence, a glowing green dot an inch from his nose. He swatted at it, recoiling, till it assumed the proper distance. It was *cold* when it got that close.

"Sorry," it whispered miserably.

"Just watch it, will you?" It was a very new sycophant, and he was very new to having one all his own, which was better than having, say, Hatshepsut's, which were terrified of her and snobbish to all the others. He leaned forward a bit, elbows locked beneath his knees. "Do you know how phones work?"

"Yes-yes-yes," it said, brightening after its gaffe. "Oh, yes."

"Can you show me?"

"Yes, yes." Brighter still. It positively bubbled. "Follow."

"Augustus is having it translated," Mouse reported, flipping through the reports the courier had just brought down from the house, and Julius took the sheet Mouse handed him. "We don't have it yet, but it's at least movement."

"Rameses is getting nervous," Julius said, elbow-deep in reports and long list of quartermasters' reports. Numbers still orbited and circled in his head, and surfacing from that web of data made his eyes ache. "He has to know where Hadrian *is* now. He has to be damned careful getting at him. And even if he suspects the French connection, he'd be a fool to challenge them. Napoleon's a quiet sort. But he's not to be pushed."

"Napoleon is surely," Mouse said, in his stiffly proper way, "growing somewhat discontented with matters: his house is somewhat strained at the seams just now: more to the point, he knows he's being set up as a decoy, he knows that Rameses knows by now where Hadrian is—mad Louis has turned in innumerable disturbing the peace complaints—and Napoleon somewhat suspects the game, surely."

Julius sighed. "I'd say he does. I'd say he's going to have a thing or two to say about it when we *do* have that long-postponed poker game." Letting Napoleon stand proxy for Rome was not precisely a betrayal, though he was not sure how Napoleon would see it: it was a delicate position, to be sure, to be set in the Pentagram's view as Hadrian's jailer or Hadrian's refuge, ambiguous which—and certainly a reminder to the reckless souls in the Pentagram that Hadrian was either in or out of play very much as Rome wanted to have him, in neutral hands at the moment, in hands that might not remain neutral and which were fully capable of playing their own game if Rameses wanted to push.

While it stalled off Hadrian's own demands to be reinstated. ("We're keeping you safe, *m'sieur*, we certainly are *not* your enemies: we assuredly will not betray you—")

And *that* kept Rameses in suspense, uncertain whether Napoleon was still neutral, ready to be pushed by some hostile act into becoming the power he could be—or whether Napoleon was still in retirement, doing a favor for Rome.

It was Rameses' weakness that he simply did not understand the West. Certainly the god-king of Egypt, believer in his own divinity, came nearer understanding Tiberius than he did understanding Julius— or Napoleon.

And Klea, via Hatshepsut, had made sure Napoleon had more defense than Napoleon wanted to have.

Napoleon, in fact, would have apoplexy if he learned what armament was in his house, or where the Uzis they had shipped him with the wounded de Vauban were from.

Ah, well. But sometimes one had to do things, even when friendship was at issue.

He had the other reports Mouse had supplied him and bit at a hangnail. "Damn. No sign of Alexander, no sign of Welch. With what's going on downtown, I can understand anyone who'd rather stay under the table."

"The word is," Mouse said, "that Stalin's position is eroding."

"Good. That's one we won't miss."

"There's a new man: Molotov. We're researching him."

"Good." Julius took out a cigarette lighter and flicked it. The flash paper notes went up in a puff of fire and left a stench behind them. "We just keep our heads down. We don't *do* anything, we don't make a move. Let everyone else scurry around."

"What about Hadrian?"

Julius pocketed the lighter. "*That*, that is a problem or an advantage, and Rameses may tell us which."

"Information?" Brutus asked of the operator, and: *What city do you want?* came back at him. He was dumbfounded. "Rome," he said, on an instant's inspiration. He had not known he would have a choice. *Mother*, he thought desperately, as he had not thought—almost since coming here.

But: *That city is not on the network. Sor-ry.*

"Wait!—*wait!*" As his sycophant hovered near and burbled anxiously.

What city?

"What's Tiberius' villa?"

In what city, ple-azzzz?

"In New Hell!"

That's ni-ane ni-ane oh oh oh oh.

The voice clicked and vanished as if the line had been cut.

"You have to hang up first," the sycophant said, and the cradle went down under an invisible touch. The thing the sycophant called the *dial tone* was back. "Now dial."

Brutus dialed the numbers. "Now what do I do?" he asked furiously, hearing the sputter and bleep. "What's that?"

"It's dialing!"

"I just dialed!"

"*Hello!*" a male voice said, in Latin.

"Hello," Brutus said, delighted and anxious at once. "Is this Tiberius Caesar's villa?"

"Who *are* you?"

"This is Marcus Junius Brutus. I want to talk to Caesarion."

There was a long silence on the other end.

"Hello?" Brutus said.

"Wait," the voice said.

Brutus waited, planted his shoulders against the wall, and listened anxiously as someone passed in the hall. He wasn't exactly supposed *not* to use the phones. No one had ever told him not to use the phones.

But Uncle Tiberius and his father were not exactly on the best of terms. He was sure that that had not been Tiberius who answered. Tiberius was supposed to be crazy, and that man had not sounded that way. One of the staff, he thought. One of the Praetorians.

The phone clicked.

"Hello?" he said.

No one answered. It was only one of the noises the phone made, he thought.

Someone else walked down the hall. And did not come into the drawing room, thank the gods.

"Brute?" the phone said into his ear, so loud he jumped.

"Caesarion, is that you?"

"What in *hell* do you want?"

He was taken aback. He had not expected open-armed welcome from Caesarion, but he had not quite expected to be snarled at.

But that was, in all his pricklish ways, Caesarion.

"I—th-th-thought—" Oh, damn, the stutter was back, whenever it was important to get the words out.

"It's you, all right," Caesarion's voice said, easier-sounding. And more gently: "Brother, *what* do you want?"

"I j-j-j—"

"Has the Old Man been beating on you?"

"N-n-*no!*" There was no love lost between Julius and Caesarion. And Caesarion always expected the worst. "I'm just b-b-b-bored, that's all. I w-w-wanted to t-t-t— *Prodi*, I wanted to s-s-see you."

There was a long silence on the other end. "You're nuts."

"I'm s-sorry," he said through a lump in his throat. "G-g-goodb-b—"

"Wait!" Caesarion shouted into his ear. He waited, hopeful. And a moment later: "Are you there?"

"Y-yes."

"What in hell's the matter?"

"I j-j-just th-th—"

"Oh, hell. Get it out."

"It's n-n—" It was not like people. It was a thing he was talking to. And the stammer grew worse and worse.

"*Brute. Brute*, there's a stand of old pines out over the hill, toward the villa, this direction. You know where they are?"

"I don't know, I never walked out there."

"Well, just take a hike. You'll find 'em just fine. I'll meet you there. All right? Is it all right?"

"I'll b-b-be there," Brutus said, and heard the phone click and then click again. "Is that all?" he asked of the sycophant.

"Hang it up, hang it up." The sycophant danced and darted. "Dangerous."

He thought that it was. He thought too that Caesarion was going to run some risk in getting there, and that the worst thing he could do now was not show up, because if he did not, Caesarion would come here, and somehow there would be a fight—there was always a fight, where Caesarion was concerned.

"Just stay here," he told the sycophant. "Go put on my record player. Like I was in my room. Don't tell anyone."

"Dangerous," it said, "dangerous."

". . . demned Roman snob," Wellington said, his face well toward matching his British army coat. He paused for breath. "That— That— That *outrageous*, overbearing, dictatorial, *arrogant*—"

"Easy, *mon ami*," Napoleon said, and shut the door of Wellington's front hall behind him with both hands, gently, as if all such openings and closings went straight to the ears of the Pentagram—as, considering Goebbels, well it might. He knew better than to ask precisely what was the matter: he *knew* what was the matter. "Patience, I beg you—"

Wellington seized him by the arm and dragged him through the entry hall, through the living room, where a litter of newspapers, cigarette butts, popcorn, and beer cans surrounded a makeshift bed of cushions on which two DGSE men snored with their rifles, where a glaze-eyed trio of Huns occupied the cushionless couch, tilting sort of toward each other, their glazed eyes reflecting the television glare.

One would have wondered if there was a pulse, but his own living room looked much the same, and the radio still blared Heavy Metal rock, while de Vauban and Marie played poker at the dining room table—Marie with a de Vauban hyped to the gills on pain pills, in a game which had been three-handed and now became two without disturbance: Marie was into her third day with no sleep and de Vauban was too stoned to know an ace from a king. They might not even miss him.

But Wellington had marched in with the force of a hurricane and marched him out again and next door; and now dragged him further, through the reek of kumiss, stale beer, horse-sweat, popcorn, and garlic.

Mon dieu, it was a disaster area.

And much more, the dining room, where Hadrian, a shaven, toga-clad Hadrian, sat in regal splendor, amid a clutter of silver dishes and TV dinners.

"My sheets," Wellington declared.

"Satin?" Napoleon said, and regarded Wellington in amazement.

"My silver. My food. *The last demned bottle of Lafitte-Rothschild!*"

"Ah, Bonaparte." The Emperor waved a fork. "Wellington. My hosts. A token of civilization in this sty. Sit, sit. I'm only finishing." He raked another TV dinner from its silver platter onto his plate. "Well, well, I *have* found the right combination for this tolerable wine—"

"*Tolerable!*" Wellington breathed.

"It needs garlic, however." The Emperor raked sardines onto the edge of the plate. "Enchiladas. I don't think I've ever had enchiladas. —Well, well, will you have a chair?" He took a healthy swig of the Lafitte-Rothschild, and dabbed at his lips with a linen napkin. And belched. "Sit, sit, we're not that prig Rameses. We're all honest soldiers."

There was a hard glitter to the Emperor's eyes. A challenge.

"Of course," said Hadrian, "we want to know what the hell we're doing here. And why there are no telephones."

Wellington leaned on the edge of the table, knuckles white. "Because, *sir*, Rameses is looking to find you, and he needs no help from—"

"Wellington," Napoleon said gently, then took Wellington by the arm and pulled him aside to the doorway. "*Wellington, pensez—*"

"I *am* thinking! I'm thinking."

"Let me talk to him."

"Be my guest."

Napoleon drew a large breath and strode to the middle of the room. "*Monsieur*. We are playing a most difficult game with an Administration in which you have few allies. You must understand—"

"I *understand*, Bonaparte, that I am being held prisoner, and that Julius is playing his usual game—feint to the center and strike from the flank. I have no confidence that I am the beneficiary of this maneuvering, and as for prisons, my last was preferable."

"Ah. Now I hear the man who was leading the armies when *I* held my commission. And *monsieur le commandant* always had the great good sense to delegate and trust his generals. Patience. Patience. And believe me that we are being watched, that there is no phone that we would dare trust, and that there are those working to purge Administration of contrary influences. There are newspapers. Read them and see."

"Believe the *Daily Hell?* Not likely."

"Then you must believe *us*, and trust someone, *monsieur*, which I assure you is safer than running the streets in a dressing gown."

It was dangerous, should this man ever regain office. Hadrian's face went a luminous red. "Thanks to your drugs."

"I would say," Wellington said, strolling over from the door, hands in pockets, "that his lordship the Commander *does* trust us more than he trusts some agencies downtown. After all, he could try hanging himself. He could take his chances with Reassignments."

Perhaps there was a wistful little hope in that quirk of Wellington's brow. But it was ever so subdued.

"Damn you," Hadrian said. "Get me a safe phone."

"There *isn't* one," Napoleon said. "Believe me. If you have a message, give it to us. We'll see if we can arrange a courier. But bear in mind that *any* attention to any of us right now could send us on worse than the Trip. A tribunal is in session in Administration."

Hadrian's face went a shade pale. And very, very sober. "An Administrative Tribunal?"

"Exactly so," Napoleon said. "We *don't* think it's the moment to make ourselves conspicuous. We are taking an enormous risk, you understand, for your sake, *monsieur*."

"Well, well," Hadrian said, and took a swig of the Lafitte-Rothschild. "One can understand. But—" He waved a hand toward the disaster of the living room. "This is so—squalid."

Napoleon caught Wellington's arm and dragged him back to the doorway. Wellington's face had gone an alarming color. His mouth was clamped and his nostrils flared in an intake of breath that threatened subsequent explosion.

"Patience," Napoleon said, and shook at him. "Courage, *mon ami*."

Wellington exhaled. "I—" he said. "That—"

"A little longer. Only a little longer. We can last."

"*You* can last. *I* have him."

"You can move in with us."

Wellington rolled his eyes. "And leave this juggernaut unencumbered in my house? Damme, no."

"You have that keg of French brandy," Napoleon said.

"Secreted. Safe!"

"*Give* it to him."

"Give—" Wellington began. Then the idea glimmered wickedly in his eyes. He grinned, clapped Napoleon on the shoulder, and advanced on the Emperor Hadrian. "Commander," he said, "join me in an after-dinner drink. Or two. Or three."

Hell's sky was always cloudy, always a murky red, but there was an uncommon edge to the wind that made Brutus wish he had worn his jacket.

But *that* might have raised suspicions when he strolled out the back door and skipped down the steps.

And ambled through the parking lot, around by the remaining pines, and so down a little roll of the land that gave him cover behind the trucks that were parked there.

Then he lit out at a steady jog, looking back now and again to be sure no one had spotted him, and headed in the general direction of the boundary between the Julian villa and Tiberius's estate.

There was sort of a road: the trucks and the legions had flattened the grass in their passage out and back again to Assurbanipal's palace, which had just happened to take them through Tiberius's land. He had seen this edge of the estate once, with the legions, but all the landscape then had passed like a dream, an endless succession of hills, and he was not sure what was theirs and what was Tiberius', or where he had seen trees and where not.

The old pines, Caesarion had said. A stand of pines.

He saw something like that as he came over a roll of the land. *You'll know it*, Caesarion had said.

So he went toward it.

"Here you are," Hatshepsut said, triumphant, and laid the meticulously composed letter on Augustus's desk. Her eyes danced. So did the traveling transparent spot; and so did Augustus' pulse rate.

"Marvelous," Augustus said without more than looking at it. He gazed up at pharaoh. "Have you a transcription?"

"Of course," Hatshepsut said, and sat down on the corner of his desk, leaned on an arm and leaned across to show the paper beneath. A long lavender nail indicated the Latin version. "I was very diplomatic, very brief. I didn't even insult the fool. I held out every hope of your cooperation—if Mithridates were not in the way. Our language is such a fine tool for diplomats—you can imply everything, saying nothing specific. Latin is so mercilessly blunt, don't you think?"

"We have our subtleties."

"Oh?"

Augustus cleared his throat, his head, the center of his desk, and opened a drawer for his sealing wax. "Baculus can run courier on this. He's safe. They've already interviewed him. Gods save us if Rameses gets caught up in the probe."

"Water runs off that one," Hatshepsut said. "Have

no worries. Rameses is a fool in military matters—
but not in politics. Never in politics. Mark me, *we*
are the only ones who could hang him: no one else
has both motive and opportunity. He surely has no
desire to see us go down: we would assuredly impli-
cate him. He surely has no desire to move against
Bonaparte directly: Bonaparte lets Louis XIV *have*
his fetes and his amusements and the French are
tranquil—but if Bonaparte wakes, so will Wellington;
and Hell will see changes in its geography, indeed."
A tap of the lavender nail on the desk. "The armaments we give him—registered to Rameses' own
guard—Rameses would *not* want to find, would he?
Just like that little present Klea slipped Marie
Walewska."

Dante, his phone lines restored in the hours since
the Assyrian affair, had ventured one highly dangerous
and very essential dive into the Pentagram computer
system. And they were all a great deal more comfortable knowing that the records were very, very clean.

"We might gain far, far more," Hatshepsut said,
"by cultivating Rameses now, than by doing anything
for the ungrateful Hadrian."

Augustus looked up at the kohl-rimmed dark eyes,
his heart beating harder for more than simple lust.

"Meaning rapprochement with Egypt?"

Hatshepsut smiled, and the long nails touched
Augustus' hand, tracing a small pattern. "I know all
the pitfalls. And the advantages are enormous. I can
lay them out for you. You can present them to Julius.
Oh, don't doubt the letter I've written for you. I'm
absolutely discreet. You know I'd never betray you.
But think of it. Napoleon installed in a seat of power,
at your right hand, a friend who would never turn on
you; the might of imperial Egypt at your left—"

"Who would rule it?"

"Oh, Rameses is an adequate figurehead." Her hand curled into his. "Of course you don't want to rush into things. But times are so uncertain. It's worth considering—amid all the changes in the wind. And right now Rameses is crying out for allies. Don't forget, too, there's Wellington. There's a chance of drawing the British Empire in as well. And with them—the Americans. NATO. The—"

"*Pro di immortales*, woman, your ambition is boundless."

"We, on the other hand—we Egyptians—have our contacts too. You established the *Pax Romana*. You closed the doors of Janus, put the world at peace for the first time in human history. What could we do with an alliance like that? A *Pax Inferna*. An alliance that could turn Hell's energies to—other than internal war."

"Like what?"

"You're the ideal focus of a union like that. A born diplomat. A man of—" The nails traced the palm of his hand. "—such abilities. *Talk* to Julius. You always know the best approach with him. You *are* the one who built Rome—what was it you said: you found it a city of brick and made it a city of marble? You might have said, you found it a city in civil war and made it the center of a world at peace. That, far, far more than the marble."

He blushed. And drew his hand back. "What you propose is reckless."

"So was taking command of the legions when Julius died. You might have lost your life. So many did. But you have a talent for peacemaking, even in your ruthless acts. Even Klea respects that, you know. Why else would she live under your roof? She admires you, in her way, the man who accomplished what she so much wanted. Even if it had to come with her death. Klea is so volatile on the surface. But very deep. You should know her better. You should know me better—after all these centuries."

"You know Julius has his doubts about you."

"Julius has his doubts about all of us," Hatshepsut said, flashing perfect teeth. "But he's a generous man. And prefers the active role. So do I. I absolutely *hated* the throne. I'd make Julius's choice—to command the armies."

"If you'll forgive me—Egypt would find that very hard to accept, even yet."

"*Trust* me. I ruled. I ruled and died of old age. I have my adherents among the officers—the same who put me on the throne once. I *even* own a few priests. It's very easy—to take that power back again. But I would be very reluctant to leave this house. The throne is a trap I don't want and I have friends here, friends I am more than fond of—" She leaned forward and touched his face lightly with fingers like ice and fire at once. "I'm your friend. Whatever the fortunes of this place—always your friend. We have so much in common." She drew back the hand, enough to rest on his. "I leave it to you to approach Julius. You'll see. I *know* Egypt in a way Klea can't. She's Alexandrine. I'm an Egyptian of the Egyptians. I know them the way my grandfather knew them, down to the farmers and the boatmen. They're Egypt. And I'm a god of Egypt. Time and mortality were the only enemies I couldn't defeat."

"So with us all."

"You see. We have the same perspective. We both ruled long. We both died old. And we have our youth again. With all it means."

He cleared his throat. "You're trying to seduce me."

She grinned at him. "Have I succeeded?"

"Oh, yes. But I warn you it has no effect on my judgment."

"I should expect as much. In that we're very much alike. Tonight? Are you busy?"

"No," he said, finding breath tight. "No, I'm not busy."

Thunder rattled in the sky, and a gust of chill wind blew the grass as Brutus ran the last gasping step to the pines. *"Iuppiter!"* he swore, shivering, and leaned against a shaggy trunk, casting about the pines and the shrubs that clung to this rocky spot. "Caesarion?"

No answer. He gasped for breath and slid down the side of the tree, reckoning that he might have run faster than Caesarion or maybe it had not been so easy for Caesarion to get away or the way might be longer. He did not know. His side hurt, and the wind bit through the tee-shirt and the jeans, so he tucked his bare arms between his knees and tried to keep the tree between him and the wind.

Bang!

The thunder cracked and lightning chained across the ruddy sky, one stroke and another one, like artillery out of Paradise.

(Could it be? Would Paradise, that made the daily journey across the sky to light Hell's clouds, make war on Hell? His mother was in Paradise, he thought; and perhaps his father Junius was; his father had been a good man, *was* a good man, who had not rejected a bastard son, but brought him up a Junian and lived a lifelong jaw-clenched lie in front of all the relatives and the neighbors and the loud, loud whispers when Julius had yearly gained more and more notoriety— Such parents belonged in Paradise. He hoped that for them, at least, not knowing what a seventeen year old boy could have done that would have exiled him here—except he was Julius' son, and Julius was here, a power in this place, and Fate had perhaps known what it was doing when it cast him here, with his true father. Elysium could not be Elysium for his mother and father while he existed: that was the bitter truth, which thought bit like the cold of the wind and made his heart ache, but he had no wish to find them. Julius was enough. To have found a brother was an unexpected bonus. To have a brother who knew all about him and still liked him—)

He sneezed, shivered, and tucked up the tighter, blinking, for the clouds must have gotten thicker and ruddier, casting the whole landscape in a lurid twilight.

It was colder, too. He clambered to his feet and walked a little, hugging his arms and shivering. He imagined Caesarion having arrived, tucked up against some bush the other side of the ridge, both of them freezing like fools. He climbed the hill and shouted his brother's name, and looked outward from that high point to the view lakeward, where black night raged, speared through with red lightnings, where Tiberius' villa—it could only be that—hove up as a shadow against the flares on the shores of a red-glowing lake.

"Caesarion," he murmured between chattering teeth. "O gods. Caesarion—"

He was afraid then, afraid for where he was standing, thinking of his brother out there underneath that.

"*Caesarion!*" he yelled into the oncoming storm.

Surely his brother would have had sense enough to turn back.

But he was dealing with Caesarion, to whom pride was more vital than common sense: and worse, Caesarion was dealing with *him*, who in Caesarion's eyes was an unworldly fool.

Caesarion being Caesarion would come after him, that was what.

No matter what.

He ducked his head into the wind and ran, half-blind in the gusts that carried dust and dead grass, toward that looming villa by the lake about which clouds swirled and lightnings flashed; and when he was out of breath he stopped again and looked all about him.

"Caesarion!"

He saw him then, running for all he was worth, a white speck dyed red in the glare of the clouds. He waved his arm, gasped for breath, and ran to meet him, while lightning struck to left and right and thunder deafened him.

Caesarion was wearing a Roman *tunica*, no more than that—not so much as a cloak between him and the cold. They reached each other and Caesarion grabbed him by the arms: his hands were like ice and his black hair was wild in the gusting wind.

"Fool!" Caesarion yelled at him.

It was true. He was too out of breath to talk, and the thunder drowned whatever else Caesarion said. The wind chilled the sweat on him and his teeth began to chatter again.

"I kn-kn-kn—" Between the damnable stammer and the shaking of his jaw he was as good as mute. He only grabbed Caesarion by the arm and tried to get him to come with him, back where the storm had not come yet, back to the villa where they could find warmth.

"Dammit, no," Caesarion said. "Not to *him*."

Meaning their mutual father, whom Caesarion did not forgive, even yet.

"I w-w-w—" He clenched his hand on Caesarion's arm and pointed again where he would have him go, because he could not talk, he could not hope to talk; and his side hurt and they were going to freeze out here, that was all.

Caesarion shook his arm free. "Damn!" he said, and yielded then and struck out in the direction Brutus was trying to take him, dragging *him* along at a jog.

The world blew up, like a grenade had gone off in their faces, and suddenly Brutus was on his back, blind, with more light in his eyes than eyes were meant to stand.

"C-C-C-Caesarion?" he gasped, flailing out and trying to rise.

Somehow they found each other, arm crossed arm, and they embraced each other while the thunder racketed about them, and more such strikes slammed the ground.

"I c-c-c-can't *see!*" Brutus cried.

"Down!" Caesarion yelled, and pushed him flat and landed on top of him.

The world was all sound and light then, a flat and open space under the hammer of the lightnings while two motes of human substance flinched and winced as if their nerves were linked.

Then the wind swept over them with a spatter of dust and debris, and roared with a voice like angry gods.

Brutus wiped tearing eyes, a vision across which a jagged trail was branded in shadow, and gulped as he saw fingers of cloud wreaking havoc across the landscape, toward the woods.

"G-g-g-gods."

"*Brute*—" Caesarion gasped, jerking him by the shoulder, turning him half about to see the very skin of the landscape break and rise and take the form of walking corpses.

Brutus scrambled for his feet: they climbed each

other getting up, and they both lit out running, with the wind blasting into their faces and no sense of direction any longer, nothing, but the terror of what was behind them.

"Wh-wh-wh—?" he asked.

"Liches," Caesarion managed to answer.

No stopping, no looking back—but Brutus felt the tremor in his knees, the weakening of his ankles as the shock of the lightning had left him, and he found himself falling behind, found it harder and harder to keep the pace.

But it was Caesarion who fell, who went skidding on his belly and half-rolling as he tried to get to his feet. Brutus stopped for him, grabbed him by the arm, and got a look at what was following them, at the very skin of Hell risen up in rotting flesh, yellowed bone, reaching hands. He hauled, hard, got Caesarion up, and they staggered into a run for which neither of them had breath left.

He led for the moment, catching at Caesarion's arm to keep them together. His heart was pounding in his ears, his mouth tasted of blood, and at every step his legs threatened to go out from under him.

He fell and brought Caesarion down, and this time, getting up took more out of them. The liches had gained on them, a solid mass of them, legions of them. There were riders among them, on horses with red-blazing eyes.

"Run!" Caesarion yelled into his ear, pulling at him.

And suddenly a roaring came from behind them both, and a horn blared.

It was a jeep. O gods, it was a jeep from the villa, coming toward them all out, a race between it and the liches with them in the middle; and Brutus ran, pace for pace with Caesarion, what limping steps they could manage, with a tearing pain in his side.

The jeep pulled up between them and the lich-riders. The legionary driver braked hard, and gave them time to clamber in and fall into the back seat before he jerked the wheel over and gunned it the hell out of the reach of the liches that raced to overtake them.

A rider raced along with them a space. Brutus looked up over the back of the jeep into a close-up view of a red-eyed horse with yellow teeth and bone showing about its jaws.

But the horse could not keep up. It fell farther and farther back, and Brutus sagged into the seat, bowed over Caesarion's heaving back.

It was all right. It was all right. It was young Valerius driving, and they were going home, they were going back.

They roared over the rise by the pines, and passed a line of legionaries formed up out by the parking lot. Brutus put his head up again, saw the liches coming, saw the legionaries take aim and deliver a barrage of rifle fire.

"That's got them," Brutus breathed, pounding Caesarion on the shoulder. "They'll st-st-stop them."

Caesarion said nothing, only stared at the sight of liches mowed into pieces and still coming, but fewer and fewer of them.

"It's all r-r-right," Brutus said, shaking at his shoulder.

"The hell," Caesarion said, and caught himself as the jeep bucked over a rut and onto the asphalt parking lot.

Valerius braked. And there were more legionaries with rifles, going out, Brutus thought, to the defense of the villa.

But it was the jeep they came to meet. It was
Paulus in command, a *legatus*, lieutenant general;
and a man who took no nonsense.

"Don't do anything," Brutus said, holding Caesarion
by the shoulder, pressing hard. "Don't. It's all right.
I swear to you."

"Sure," Caesarion said.

Brutus managed to climb out of the jeep, landing
on legs that threatened to buckle. Caesarion landed
behind him.

"Come with me," Paulus said, in the singular. And
to Caesarion: "*You* go with them."

"Sure," Caesarion said, and gave Brutus a sidelong
look, his jaw gone tight. "Welcome home, brother.
Tell papa hello for me."

"Let him go," Brutus said when the legionaries
took Caesarion by the arms. "Dammit, let go of him.
That's my brother."

There was a strange look on Caesarion's face,
through the rage, through the exhaustion. "Hell," he
said, while rifle-fire kept up a steady din behind the
parked cars, and he did not fight at all when they
hauled him away.

Brutus did. He ran the few steps after them and
jerked at the legionaries that held Caesarion, but
other soldiers caught him and pulled him back.

"Don't do that," Caesarion said. "They'll beat hell
out of you." He gave a jerk at the soldiers who were
taking him away, but it gained him nothing. And
the soldiers took Brutus the other direction, shoved
him toward the garage where the guard-station was.

"Let him g-g-go!" Brutus shouted. "It was m-m-me
c-c-called him!"

They said nothing. They hauled him toward the
guard-station and inside, fighting all the way, for

what his seventeen-year-old strength was worth against two burly legion regulars.

He had expected Furius, or maybe even Scaevola.

It was not a Roman who met him. It was Niccolo Machiavelli, black and lank and ominous, who looked at him with cold eyes and said: "I will take him, *signori*."

And the legionaries, who should not have obeyed him, drew his hands behind him.

"No," said Niccolo, taking Brutus by the shoulder in a grip stronger than those scholar's hands ought to have. "He will not need the handcuffs. Will you?"

"That d-d-de-p—" Brutus shut his eyes and took a deep breath, the way Welch the American, had told him once. "-pends. Wh-wh-wh—where did they t-t-take C-C—"

"Use the cuffs," Niccolo said.

"No!" Brutus cried. But they did, faster than he could do anything about it, then spun him around and took him down the steps into the garage, where the Ferrari was parked.

Niccolo followed, and had the keys.

"Your father wants you," Niccolo said, opening the passenger-side door. "And *perdio*, you will not make more trouble. Do you hear me?"

Brutus got in, turned sideways for his comfort and to turn his face from Niccolo, who slammed the door shut.

He turned his face again when Niccolo got in on the driver's side.

The shooting had mostly died away. The thunder still rumbled, off over New Hell itself, as they backed out of the garage, turned about, and headed out.

He had never seen the armory. He had always wanted to. But not like this, not hauled out of a car in handcuffs, in Niccolo's keeping, in view of the soldiers. "Please," he said, "I'll walk. Take them off."

Niccolo considered, and for a dreadful moment he was afraid Niccolo did not even have the key. But: "Turn around," Niccolo said, and Brutus leaned against the fender while Niccolo unlocked the cuffs.

Even so, he did not look at the legionaries who stared at them, and who muttered softly among themselves as Niccolo brought him through the halls.

Worse and worse: it was Mouse who waited for them, it was Mouse who took him in hand next, without a word, and who shepherded him deep into the heart of the armory, down an echoing, empty hall and into another room, dark, and lit only by braziers.

Eagles were ranged all about the walls, the enshrined Eagles of the legions, gathered there, more of them than he had ever seen at once.

And in that dark place, before the fire and the glittering gold, the shadow of a man in legion khaki, who stood with hands locked behind him.

Brutus knew that stance, knew it before his father turned and looked at him with a coldness Julius had never shown him.

Julius only looked beyond him, a lifting of his chin, and Mouse left like a ghost, a soft closing of the door.

Brutus wanted then to sink through the floor. To fall on it, and beg Julius not to have that expression on his face. But that would shame them both, him for weakness and his father for siring him. He could only stand there, with his knees shaking under him and his teeth all but chattering again. He was going to stutter if he had to talk. He could *not* talk. He would not be able to explain, and Julius would not listen, and nothing would be right again.

"What were you doing?" Julius asked.

His throat froze on him. His jaw trembled and locked, and he could hardly breathe. He only bowed his head in token of respect and looked up again, his lips clamped.

"Did I sire a fool?"

He nodded, mute, and clenched his jaw the harder. Tears blurred his vision, making the fire glitter.

"Or a traitor?" Julius asked.

He lifted his chin in the Roman *no*. He wanted to shout out: *I never meant any harm, I was only stupid, I never thought it would make trouble*.

But it had, of course. The soldiers had had to shoot, the liches were stirred up, gods knew whether they would come at the villa again, Caesarion was in the basement again, and most of all they had made a commotion when the villa could least stand it. It was all supposed to be secret. And he had been selfish and stupid and betrayed everyone, that was what he had done.

Julius turned his back and walked away from him, and stood a long time in front of the Eagles, a shadow without detail.

"F-F-Father," Brutus managed finally, burning with shame. "I'm s-s-s-*sorry*—"

"Do you know what you've done?"

"N-n-n-*now*. I d-d-do." The tears ran on his face. He took a hand from behind him to wipe them, quickly, and put it behind him again. "Th-they c-c-caught C-C-C—my b-b-brother. D-D-Don't b-blame him. M-M-My f-f-fault. M-M-Mine" He quit while he was ahead. Before he got some damned word he could not get out, and made himself altogether detestable. Julius was an orator. His son could hardly get out a sentence.

Julius turned finally, still faceless to him, all in

shadow. "So you just called Tiberius' villa and thought you'd pay a visit, did you?"

"I w-wanted to s-s-s—"

"See Caesarion. *Did* you?"

He nodded. Brought his hands before him to help his speech. He made them an appeal. "N-n-not his f-f-fault. I—"

He could not get it out. The words loomed up like an unscalable mountain, too many and too hard. He made a helpless gesture. "M-my f-f-fault."

For a long while his father said nothing. Then: "What do you think I ought to do with you?"

He tried to think. He could only see Caesarion, in the hands of the soldiers. In the basement. "R-r-rods," he said finally. It was a soldier's punishment. A man's punishment. He had never seen it. He had never wanted to. He looked at his father's dark outline and felt steadier then, as if maybe he could endure it, if that was going to be the way out for them, to save their honor, his and Julius's.

Julius walked a pace, turned a profile against the light, head bowed. "Did you even think?"

"N-no."

"Do you understand we could lose everything, all of us—that you've put all of us at risk?"

"I d-do n-n-now."

"Whose are you?"

Brutus lost his breath for the moment. "Y-Yours," he managed to say; but that was not what Julius meant, he understood that. He understood the suspicion behind the question—that it was Mithridates who had sent him, Mithridates who was their enemy and Mithridates who stood to benefit if what he had done brought them down. "M-M-Mithri-d-dates is m-m-m— *Damn!*—enemy, t-too."

"Does this act like it? Is this the way you treat your own?"

"N-no."

"Then why?"

"I'm a f-fool." His chin trembled. He fought the tears back. "I'm s-sorry."

"That's a real easy way out, isn't it?" Julius turned his back again, and reached to the wall, where trophies stood, glittering in the firelight. Steel rang and gleamed in his hand as he turned.

He threw it. Brutus turned his shoulder in shock, and the sword flew past him and clanged to the floor somewhere against the wall behind him.

"Pick it up," Julius said.

Brutus stood there, cold through and through.

"*Pick it up,*" Julius shouted at him.

He wanted to say no. But it was an order. It was his father telling him. He walked over and found the sword against the wall.

A second blade rang out of its sheath behind him.

He looked at Julius in horror. And dropped the sword he held.

"Pick it up!"

He kicked it away with his foot, and edged away from it, far as he could get. He was shaking. It was Julius' right, as head of house. It was always Julius' right over any of them, even his sons.

Especially his sons.

But it was never a son's right to fight back. He stood there. Death was not forever in Hell. It was not like it was forever. Julius might even get him back again. The soldiers he had twice endangered might forgive him.

If Julius would take him back.

"You asked me a question once," Julius said. "I told you to wait. Do you remember it?"

"I as-asked you how I d-d-died." Damn, the stammer gave him no grace at all. And he did not want the answer. It was one cruelty more than he could bear, he foreknew that.

"Suicide," Julius said. "It was suicide. You were twice seventeen. You lost a battle. Do you have another question?"

"Did I l-lose the w-war?"

It seemed to startle Julius. The brows went up. The laugh lacked humor. But it had something of respect. "You might say. Ask on."

"W-Who was I f-fighting?" Questions became easier. It became a litany, a riddle-game to play out to the end.

"Augustus. And Antonius."

It answered so many things, the little looks, the silences. It fell into place with a sickening feeling.

"Why?" he asked, the next question.

"They were my heirs," Julius said. "I never acknowledged you."

"You mean you had d-died." He made a rapid construct in his mind, jealousy, civil war, bastard son against adopted son and lieutenant. He could understand that. No wonder Augustus had been cold to him at first.

"You killed me," Julius said.

Brutus heard it. It just did not make sense for a moment. He looked at Julius in shock. "I—"

"You killed me. Assassinated me. I was dictator of Rome. You formed a conspiracy with a handful of senators and killed me, in Pompeius' theater. We were still using that for the Senate house. The Senate house had burned in the riots. Remember?"

"Gods," he said, and cold went all through him. "O gods."

"Do you remember?"

He tipped his head back slightly. No. He looked at
Julius and looked at him, and the tears ran down his
face, he was aware of that, and the fire, and the rest
of the world just stopped, that was all, himself and
his father held there motionless forever.

"You got in with a malcontent named Cassius,"
Julius said. "Gods know why. Because I turned you
away that summer, maybe. The assassins wanted me
out—to save the Republic, they said. But it was
personal revenge Cassius wanted. And Casca. Some
said you were the honest one. The idealist. I don't
know. Patricide just isn't a real idealist's choice, —is
it, son?"

"I—" He was lost, that was all, just lost in forever.
He wished the sword would come whistling around
and end it. But there was no ending. There was no
ending, ever, in this place. There was nothing but
the truth, and it was the truth. Julius would never lie
to him like this.

"Mithridates held you out of time," Julius said,
"and sent you to live under my roof, a patricide, with
Augustus, who brought you down. It was his revenge. It was thorough, don't you think?"

He could say nothing. He could think of nothing.
Except none of that memory was there. There was
just the Baiae road, the lazy horse, the sunlight—
forever the sunlight, the last thing in his life. He was
seventeen.

Julius walked up next to him and put his hand on
his shoulder, shook at him. "Why did you do it?
That's what I've wondered. Why did you join them?"

"I don't know," he said. No stammer. Nothing.
Just a hoarse, hollow whisper. That was all that would
come out, and the fire shimmering in front of his
eyes. "I can't remember. I don't remember any of
those things."

"Damn." The fingers bit into his shoulder, turned him roughly against Julius's shoulder.

He stayed there. He did not know whether he was going to live or die. He began to cry finally, and held to Julius and wept.

"Damn," Julius said again, and the sword clanged onto the floor. Julius held him, shook him and made him look at him.

He could not tell with his own eyes blurring, but the fire glistened on his father's face; and Julius held his face between his hands and looked at him a long, long time.

"Anything," Julius asked him, "anything beyond that road, that day?"

"No," Brutus said, in that nowhere where he drifted.

"So much rides on my shoulders. I can't take chances. Do you understand? On me, Rome rests. Everything. If you were to strike at me—you would damn everyone. You know that."

The assassin? Augustus had asked once, the first time he heard the name Marcus Brutus. He had thought Augustus meant his ancestor, who had overthrown the kings. That bewildered moment flashed into memory, a coldness in his bones.

He freed himself, bent down and gathered up the sword; and gave it to his father, hilt-first.

Julius took it. "Go get the other one," Julius said, and turned and put it away.

Brutus did as he was told—brought it back crosswise in both his hands, and put it in its sheath in the trophy rack, beside the other, carefully.

"My b-b-brother," he said then. "Paulus locked him up. It was my f-fault. I c-called him. It was all my d-doing."

"He'll be free to go," Julius said. "I gave him my word on that. I don't break it—oftener than I have to." He laid his hand on Brutus's shoulder, standing beside him in front of the Eagles. "What's yours worth?"

"I don't know."

Julius jerked him about, hard. "You're not a boy any longer. Too much is on your shoulders, too. Hear me?"

"Yes," he said.

"What's your word worth?"

"I'm not a m-murderer!"

"Hell's long, boy. It's very long. What's your word worth, that's the question."

"Everything," he said. "It's worth everything."

"You've got it," Julius said. And turned him toward the door, and walked with him.

Nothing was the same. Nothing could be.

SEA CHANGE

Janet Morris

There was a purge going on in the Pentagram, one result of a skirmish between the Julian Romans and the Assyrians, which had destroyed the statue of Drusus, a great deal of nefariously appropriated warfighting equipment, and a few careers. At least this was the story being floated by Mithridates, Rameses, and others At The Top who were, despite every attempt at secrecy, embroiled in the ensuing scandal.

Whatever the cause of the purge, the very sky was glowering down on New Hell, suffused with red and glaring through the one split-pupiled eye of Paradise. A hot wind blew seaward from the mountains, lashing the coastline as if the city itself were to blame. The fetid gale scoured the streets of Hell's greatest metropolis and whipped the towers of Administration with a fervor that popped glass panes, which fell crashing to the street, stories below.

One of the deadly panes of glass fell on the Undertaker's favorite Mortician and sent the man on the

251

Trip—back to the Mortuary in three severed pieces, where he waited in a body bag among other lesser luminaries for somebody to get around to resurrecting and reassigning him.

Another pane fell squarely at the (clawed) feet of Asmodeus of the Insecurity Service, and the Fallen Angel took umbrage all the way up through channels.

When Asmodeus, in a rustle of wings and a blur of shifting Presence, reached the Devil's office in the Hall of Injustice, His Satanic Majesty wasn't receiving visitors, so Asmodeus had to wait. Wait among the petitioning damned, wait until Hell's fury had abated, until the Devil returned from wherever he'd gone—wait, if need be, until Hell froze over.

Thus the Insecurity Agent wasn't at his desk when an urgent report printed itself out there. If he had been, he might have asked for a retransmission, because his tractor feeder had fouled up, causing the entire fourteen-page report to print itself on a single line, while all the other thirteen pages rolled up and folded up and curled up, blank and pristine, behind the single sheet upon which was one very black, illegible mass of print.

This report also printed itself out on the Devil's personal computer's printer, but that copy was equally unreadable: Michael, the Devil's catlike familiar, had been sleeping below the printer in the paper box when the transmission began; the fanfold tore; the system sensed a Paper Error and stopped, cursor blinking patiently, holding the transmission in RAM until an untimely brownout wiped the data. The buffer of the printer, which was holding the first page of the report, was wiped soon after, when lightning struck the phallic tower of the Hall of Injustice and sent a spike up the Devil's line.

Not that the Devil knew any of this—He was

Elsewhere when Hell's Fury vented itself upon New Hell and its surrounds. He was always incommunicado when the worst storms raged in Hell, causing some of his confidants to believe that the storms were a result of his Infernal temper.

In the Insecurity Service's offices, and in the Infernal Bureau of Investigation, and in the Pentagram's clean rooms, and in Reassignments, and in the Agency's most secret headquarters on Corpse Street, no one believed anything at all. Couriers, all winners of the New York Marathon, ran messages between the Deputy Directors of the services, and the messages all contained repudiations of other agencies' assertions, lists of discrepancies found in after-action reports relating to the Roman/Assyrian affair, denials of responsibility for missing Armory equipment, and blanket disclaimers of complicity in advance of any possible accusations of wrongdoing.

Every agency in New Hell was to all intents and purposes paralyzed by this process of disassociation from error, put into motion by counterclaims issued by Julius Caesar and Mithridates and validated by the sudden storm, which had lasted thirty-six hours, Zulu time. And the Devil wasn't around to kick the required butts into motion once Cover My Ass syndrome started, so inertia took over. New Hell's Administration complex was winding down like a neglected clock.

Meanwhile, Asmodeus sat in the Devil's anteroom helplessly, waiting with his little green ticket, number fifty-two, which he had been given by an ugly woman who insisted he "Take a number, buddy. Siddown. You'll get yer turn."

Asmodeus had *had* his turn—he'd almost been decapitated by a pane of glass hurtling from forty stories above. When he'd come storming up here, he'd meant to file a complaint, tender a personal warning, and let himself be mollified. Now, after so long in the anteroom, his fury had ebbed, his pique cooled, and he wanted nothing more than to be away. But he'd taken his infernal number, and he was helpless to do anything but wait for his audience.

Asmodeus waited like a fly on flypaper, like a cockroach in a roach motel, and behind him the room filled up with others of high degree, who'd also come to see the Devil about the deteriorating situation in New Hell.

He waited until he noticed that everyone in the anteroom was crucial to any restoration of order. His wings rustled in distress, then stiffened in horror, as he looked around more carefully and saw that nearly all the bureau chiefs were with him in that chamber, which seemed to grow larger as he stared about him.

When he'd come in, it had been small, cozy. It was still cozy, in a cavernous way, but only because of the number of bureaucrats who'd joined the line. There were more heads than Asmodeus could count, more worried faces than he'd ever seen in one place. The anteroom now stretched endlessly into shadows. And it was filled with the smoke of myriad cigarettes.

Asmodeus decided to leave. But as he stood up, someone in the desert-cammo uniform of Al Fatah came up to him, rifle at the ready, and pointed a finger: Sit back down.

The pointing finger was replaced by a pointing gun barrel that jabbed his way repeatedly as Asmodeus began to explain who and what he was. The PLO fighter didn't understand English or Greek, and it wouldn't have mattered if he had: no one was leaving this chamber until he passed through the Devil's portal and gave back his audience ticket—unless he wanted to leave by the mechanism of an Express Trip to the Undertaker.

Asmodeus sat back down when the PLO fighter had made his point clear. Sat and fumed. Asmodeus was a Fallen Angel of high rank. The Angels weren't human; they'd never lived and they didn't die as the damned souls did.

But that didn't mean they couldn't be punished, weren't responsible for their actions or responsive to the laws of Hell. If Asmodeus got himself shot, he could be lost in the crowd of stiffs in the Mortuary for longer than it would take to have his number called, his ticket returned, and his audience with Satan.

Or so he thought. So everyone in the increasingly large anteroom thought, until the demons came in with their knives and forks and picnic tables and their portable bonfires, to take their places on one side of the room, which was shifting itself into a perfect example of a twentieth-century courtroom.

And when all the demons (who were the jury of "peers") had settled themselves and tied plastic bibs around their necks and put their salt and pepper shakers before them, and set out their bottles of A-1 and teriyaki sauce, their mustard and their ketchup, and their jointed tools for cracking bones to get at the marrow—*then* Asmodeus understood what was going on here.

When the bureaucracy screwed up this badly, hearings and trials and punishments followed. In this bloated chamber was an executive of every bureau in New Hell who'd been industriously shirking blame and pointing fingers ever since the Roman/Assyrian affair turned into a hush-hush scandal leaking like a bald tire and the weather turned into a commentary on the state of the Devil's temper.

So now here they were, all Hell's supergrades, facing a materializing judge in his stuffed chair covered with human hide, at his bench of human bones.

Here they were, behind a fence—in a cage of chicken wire that hadn't been in front of Asmodeus even a minute ago: the accused in their dock, hundreds of them.

Just like a roach motel, Asmodeus told himself, feeling foolish, and then frightened, and then angry. And then even the great angel bowed his head as, surrounded by Fallen Angels who'd not incriminated themselves by hustling to make excuses, in came Satan himself.

And he was terrible. As terrible as the punishments to be meted out by the jury of hungry demons, who were clashing their cutlery and gnashing their teeth as a voice from somewhere bellowed, "All rise."

For that was what they were going to do, every damned soul of them, Asmodeus knew: rise. It might be the first time a demon had gotten a taste of Fallen Angel. Asmodeus could only hope that his kind wouldn't become a delicacy, and that his resurrection at the hands of the Undertaker would be quick and efficient.

But that was too much to hope in Hell, realized the Insecurity Agent as the Devil in his black robes crooked a claw at the Fallen Angel and said, "First witness, first defendant."

Asmodeus was both. When one of his brothers came to lead him to the witness stand, the Insecurity Agent went meekly. You couldn't do anything else. The Devil hated excuses.

And the only shred of evidence that might have served Asmodeus's cause was a single line of computer printout, fetched from the Fallen Angel's office, that no one could read, overstruck until it was as black as the Devil's heart.

"If there is no new evidence better than this," the

Devil said, sulphur leaking from between his massive jaws, "then I have no choice but to adjudge you, Asmodeus, guilty as charged: guilty of suppressing evidence in the Roman/Assyrian affair." The Devil crumpled the single sheet of computer printout in his clawed fist, opened the fist, and the paper began to smoke. It caught fire. It blazed.

Asmodeus shut his own eyes against the infernally bright blaze of the hell-fired paper, and as he did so he heard: "Complicity to commit treason; incompetence; conspiracy to cover up—and, worst of all, a wretched attempt to make excuses. Failure, Fallen Angel, is our lot. Responsibility is our duty. Asmodeus, I sentence you to a slow and agonizing death, followed by punitive reassignment."

Such a thing had never befallen the Insecurity Agent before. Nor any other Fallen Angel. Asmodeus bowed his head. Falling from God's grace in Lucifer's service had been bad enough. Falling from Lucifer's grace was unbearable. He would probably be reborn as a toad, throat-deep in the Lethe.

His eyes still closed, Asmodeus heard the Devil ask, "Have you anything to say for yourself?" Cattily. Cannily.

To that query, Asmodeus could only shake his head. There was nothing he could say that wouldn't sound as if he were trying to make excuses.

The woman undergoing interrogation had only one nipple.

She was Duplicity Herself. Mata Hari. One of the Devil's Children.

Even the team of interrogators was given pause when they realized whom they had here, no matter that she was helpless, undergoing a procedure called "wall-standing," naked but for a burlap bag over her head so that she'd never know who tortured her. And when they'd opened the file folders and looked over the list of questions to be asked, and asked, and asked again, they shook their heads at one another and huddled together, as far as possible from the silent woman whose bare feet were turning blue on the grid of wet steel beneath them.

"She's got connections all the way up in the Pentagram—and beyond. To the Fallen Angels, to Agency . . . everywhere we don't need trouble," said a blond American with chin whiskers named Custer.

The other man was also an American, a bumbler named Nathan Hale whose ideals had overridden his ability and gotten him killed undertaking a mission for which his Yale diploma hardly qualified him. But Hale was not entirely stupid—only stupid where affairs of honor were concerned. He looked over his shoulder at the woman and said, "We're only here because Mithridates doesn't think any of the Old Dead can handle her." He jerked his head toward the prisoner. "And because one of the Fallen Angels has himself disappeared. Our people need to know what this woman knows. Of course she's dangerous. Anyone who isn't, doesn't know anything worth knowing." He smiled at his compatriot, a rasher man who longed to be a true general, a thing he'd never been. "Colonel Custer," said Hale, "I suggest we begin with this question here, the one about her friends in the Agency. And begin, shall we say, delicately. One catches more flies with honey . . ."

Custer's sullen mouth twitched. Both men knew what the PLO guards and their Iranian compatriots could do with hot pokers applied to private parts. Wall-standing was as rough as the Americans were willing to get—first-hand. If crueler methods were called for, they would absent themselves and come back when it was over.

Before that, there was always the time-honored routine.

Custer said, "All right, Hale, but this time I want to be the good guy. You be the mean bastard who wants to cut off her other nipple."

"Suits me. Fondling Mata Hari is far from my idea of a privilege. Be sure you have a fungicide handy . . ."

All of this was audible to the woman whose head was in the burlap bag, whose feet and legs ached and whose thighs twitched with exhaustion and relief. She'd expected electroshock interrogation. She'd been envisioning herself writhing helplessly, screaming confessions to anything and everything as electricity pulsed remorselessly through the metal grid under her feet. She'd expected the Iranian hot-poker-up-the-rectum trick. She'd expected . . . serious interrogation by professionals.

Not that she was out of the woods with these fools—not by a long shot. There remained the PLO and Iranian guards who'd abducted her from the Admin parking lot; there remained the mechanical aids. But there was a ray of hope now.

And when the questions began, about Asmodeus and a certain missing Agency officer called Welch, Mata Hari realized why she had been captured: Mithridates, et al, were cornered. They were losing, or had lost, the advantage to the Roman Julians.

So now it was not as difficult as it would have been to maintain silence all the way back to the Undertaker's table. Now she knew what lies to tell and what weaknesses to feign to convince the arrogant fools that they had fooled her.

Mata Hari's pride was hurt, though, and her pride was dear to her. Dear enough that she resolved, upon her release into a wet and empty street, naked and barefoot in a devilish gale, to go directly to the opposition and offer them her services.

With his previous Agency contacts gone, Julius Caesar was going to need someone. Even the Julians were wise enough, by now, to know that nothing was over, among power players, until it was over.

And after you'd been here awhile, you learned that nothing was really ever over in Hell—not where revenge was concerned.

As soon as he'd finished the morning's work on his new translation of the Iliad, Lawrence flogged himself hurriedly and had one of his boys dress him.

He had an appointment, and one didn't go to the Oasis Bar in Arab robes. In his British uniform, he surveyed his cottage with its custom-made iron reading stand and iron sitting-rail around the fireplace, kissed his sloe-eyed boys each in turn, and told them, "Don't wait up," with a slap of his riding crop against his polished boots.

Then he spent a half-hour trying to get his shiny BMW motorcycle to start.

By the time he'd reached the Oasis Bar, he was soaked from the rain and covered with mud from two spills he'd taken, cornering too fast on the Beemer in the rain. And he was limping. But the bar had a cure for all of that.

Full of his kind of men, it was dark and moist, and the American Marines at the door waved their victory sign at him as he came in.

Vicious lot, those. They got what they were waiting for, every now and again, when this or that displaced Arab or Persian wandered in by mistake, having heard that there was mercenary recruitment going on in the back room here.

There was, but you had to get by the U.S. Marines first. And this batch, who'd died protecting some Lebanese airstrip, the victims of a suicide bombing, was understandably racist. The oldest among them was still a child, to Lawrence's way of thinking. If he stayed around here long enough, one of these days he was going to sit down with them, in his RAF persona, and try to explain the Eastern mind . . .

But not today. Today he had a special summons to a special table in a back room. When he found it, the rogues' gallery waiting there nearly made him hesitate.

But Lawrence had walked into worse—he'd had to deal with the Home Office, with the War Office, and with the occasional British Matron. At least there were no women here today . . .

There were, however, a pair of Jews in that back room, to which the fat Chinaman, Confucius, introduced him: "Zaki—T. E. Lawrence; Lawrence, Judah Maccabee."

One Jew was short, sharp-faced, with sheep's eyes and curly hair on his head and at his throat. Sephardim. The other was—must be—Ashkenazai, a big man, wide shoulders, clear eyes set so deep that no lid showed under a warrior's brow. Never had Lawrence seen such a Jew in his life.

The Chinaman waddled toward the door through which Lawrence had come, saying, "The others will join you presently. Perseverance furthers."

"It had better further fast," said Lawrence, looking at his tank watch. "I've got other things to do today." *Than sit around talking with a couple of yids.*

"The past contracts; the future expands," said Confucius softly as he squeezed through the narrow doorway.

The big Jew said, "Please, take a seat. We have wine and lamb . . ."

Kabobs, broiled over an open fire; raw lamb, ground sheets of it to be eaten with fresh onion, olive oil, and Syrian bread. Hummus. It was a feast to Lawrence's liking, though he'd pay the price of gluttons in Hell if he indulged.

Which he did. His morning flogging was enough to assure him some leeway. Lawrence kept his own journal of Torments; he was a good accountant of sin.

The little Jew leaned forward before Lawrence had more than wet his lips with the too-sweet wine. "We need to contact the Romans—more specifically, Julius Caesar."

"Machiavelli," the big Jew put in, a single word that sounded like a curse or a cough.

"Which is it then, my men? And what will you give me?" His eyes on the big man, Lawrence began to wonder whether this really was a Jew. "And what did you say your name was? MacAbee? Scottish, is it?"

"Judah Maccabee—Mac's good enough," said the big man in a low, friendly voice that seemed as Americanized as his little friend's.

Were they friends in the way Lawrence made such friends? Then the big man's words sank in: "Judah Maccabee? Surely not the biblical—"

"Then you've heard of me," said the large fellow. "Good. Then you know I will not lie to you. We need a courier to take a message to Machiavelli, for Caesar."

An Israelite, not a Jew, Lawrence realized. "You said that," he reminded Maccabee. "I've got boys who do that sort of thing . . ." Lawrence smiled a smile meant to convey the additional message that payment usually accompanied these sorts of favors. Payment of one sort or another.

"Boys, we can get," interrupted the little hawk-faced man named Zaki.

This Zaki had a rat's nose and was beginning to annoy Lawrence, who was now willing to forego thinking of Maccabee as a Jew. Maccabee was no Jew, in the common sense, but an Israelite. An Israelite, certainly, was a different matter. Fascinated, Lawrence noticed the scars on Maccabee's hands; the sinews of them; the long fingers that had curled in fury against Imperial Rome itself.

"Boys, *phfaa*," Zaki said again. "You, we need. To take our communiqué personally to Caesar."

"To Machiavelli," said Maccabee again.

"You two seem not to be in agreement, or to know I'm not a spy, but a leader of—"

"We know what you lead, and how and why," said the little Jew, who was more and more annoying. "You have men to whom you are *the* man; but to you, Caesar is *the* man. And Caesar needs to know this—" Suddenly Zaki stopped and his liquid eyes seemed to freeze like the rain through which Lawrence had been riding so recently. "You tell him, Mac; I don't think our friend is listening to me."

Caught gazing at the other man, Lawrence flushed. Looking for something to do, his hand started slapping his riding crop against his boot again.

For a time that *thwack* was all that could be heard, and in that time, in Lawrence's universe, all that existed was the strong, sloping neck and shoulders of the Israelite as the big man shifted them, putting both elbows on the table.

"We have information Julius should know," said Judah Maccabee. "If you take it to Machiavelli, then I am done with the matter. If you take it to Caesar, then I need to know what Caesar says. Either way, the Roman power base, on which some think New Hell's stability depends, is at stake. Will you, Lawrence, or will you not, take the message?"

"I—anything, my good man, to ease your mind."
Lawrence drew himself up. "Now, you'd prefer it to
go to Machiavelli, I assume."

The two dark-haired Meds looked at one another.
Zaki's shoulder rippled in an eloquent gesture: Do it
your way.

And Maccabee said, "Tell Machiavelli that Gertie—
Mata Hari—was rousted by the Enemy, who wanted
to know of Asmodeus's fate. And Welch's. And that
she could not tell them where Agency has sent the
latter, because she did not know. But she would
meet with Julius herself, if he is interested . . ."
Maccabee stopped. "You are getting this? Say it back,
please."

Lawrence slapped his boot with an especially resounding thwack. "Of course I'm *getting* it, my
good man. But I'm not taking any such message from
that slut of a spy, Mata Hari, to that greasy rat,
Machiavelli."

"*Now* you say this?" Zaki moved like the blink of a
god, and there was a weapon in his hand, pointing at
Lawrence across the table—a clean shot above the
minced lamb and between the glasses and bottles of
wine.

In the way of moments before one's death, Lawrence had an eternity to study the weapon, to realize
it was a .44 magnum, gas-powered Desert Eagle,
perhaps the most sought-after handgun in Hell. The
accursed thing, made by Infernal Military Industries,
had no more recoil than a forty-five acp, but it would
stop an elephant, a dope addict, or, with a well-
placed shot, a tank. And it was loud—loud as hell.

Lawrence really didn't want the last sound he
heard to be its ear-splitting roar. Sometimes the
Morticians, and especially the Undertaker himself,
forgot details during one's resurrection—something

as small as punctured eardrums might get past him. Lawrence didn't want to be deaf, if and when he was returned to New Hell. And he might go elsewhere; he knew the Nether Hells were there, too. His Arab boys worried about it all the time, crying in their sleep where the demons promised them terrible futures for the evil Lawrence made them do. . . .

"I didn't mean—that is," Lawrence temporized, desperately seeking to back verbally (and gracefully, oh so gracefully, in front of this man called Mac) away from the gun centered on his chest. And started again: "I simply think that, with matters so complex, I should take you, Mac, to Caesar and you can tell him what you will, yourself, face to face."

"Impossible. I am in hiding."

"Oh."

Zaki snorted and muttered under his breath, "I should waste him now, Mac. He knows too much."

"His kind always does," said Maccabee. "He knew too much before he came here. But your own investigation, Zaki, showed him to be trustworthy."

"It could be a trap, and we need you . . ."

"I know, I know." The big man reached out slowly, gently, and put his hand on the slide of the Desert Eagle, inexorably pushing the barrel down, away from Lawrence's shallowly moving chest, until its muzzle rested against the table top. "We are all testy, these days. So much has gone on that no one understands. Whatever was between Mithridates and Julius, only you, Lawrence, can assess. You think I can get in to see the Roman and out safely? Without the Supreme Commander finding out I've been there? Without being followed? Without harm coming to those I represent?"

"I . . . I'm not sure, actually," Lawrence said with quiet wonder in his voice. He'd told this man the truth, just now. And was about to do so again: "I don't understand the message, but I'll learn it verbatim, and I'll take it to . . . Machiavelli, and then go with him to see that Caesar also learns it. They're good men, but sorely overtaxed."

Again, the horrid Zaki snorted. "You're the right fool for the job. The short of it is, Welch could have stopped the trouble, so he was sent to some Nether Hell as punishment for a crime the Pentagram trumped up—Mithridates, Rameses, that lot. We think there'll be more trouble. Asmodeus, the Insecurity Agent who decided things in Caesar's favor—or at least got him off the hook, culpability-wise—has been sent back to Reassignments. Gertie was brought in for questioning by Mithridates' boys. Caesar ought to know."

"For heaven's sakes, why?" said Lawrence, mystified. "I fought in the skirmish—it's over. We won."

"Only to your way of thinking," Zaki sneered.

Maccabee, more kindly, elucidated: "Caesar should see a need to respond. We do. We're going to clear Welch, and free him. We'd also like to get at Asmodeus when he comes out of Reassignments— only Caesar has the resources to get someone out of the Mortuary—"

"This is too complex for me to explain," Lawrence said again, tired of listening, but not of watching Maccabee's lips as he spoke. "You'll have to come yourself. And yes, I can get one man, of your stature, in and out of a meeting with Caesar—and/or Machiavelli—safely. As long as you'll wear the disguise I choose for you." And Lawrence, for the first time during that meeting, smiled his sweet smile, full of boyish mischief and companionable guile.

"One man and a woman," Maccabee said implacably. "Mata Hari comes, too—to meet with Machiavelli."

Lawrence's smile disappeared as if Zaki had shot it away with the Desert Eagle.

The meeting was set for the dead of night, out behind a house Machiavelli frequented—or perhaps owned, for nothing could be known for certain of the greatest dissembler in all of Hell.

But Zaki had been to the house, to the very rose garden where the meet was to take place, and he'd briefed Maccabee extensively. Maccabee had listened, and nodded his head, and occasionally made sure that the woman neither of them trusted also understood.

Maccabee, who feared little, feared the woman called Mata Hari. She was a consort of the Fallen Angel, Asmodeus. The angel had come, long ago, from God. Maccabee knew that God was testing him, that there was a way out of Hell. He had been in one of the nether hells when a companion, Aziru of Amurru, had found that way out.

Maccabee must not blow his chances to befriend the Fallen Angels. Thus he had brought the woman with him to meet Machiavelli. And it had been a great sacrifice to bring the woman. He had wrestled with himself while Lawrence preened and sulked during the meeting, and in the end, his best self had won out over all the others.

He had brought Mata Hari, not because she would have insisted, or because he feared her or her connections, but because he feared himself, what he might do, alone with Machiavelli.

Machiavelli had murdered him, during the Trojan Campaigns, in a deeper Hell where souls were at desperate risk. Maccabee had suffered mightily after that, at the hands of the Undertaker, during disembodied interrogation, and upon returning to the battlefield, where everyone shunned him and the stink of death upon his shroud.

Even now there were holes in his soul, and in his memory, from what Machiavelli had done to him. There were holes in his heart where a friend named Alexander once had been. All of this anguish had been Machiavelli's doing.

Only Zaki knew the truth of it—only Zaki, and Machiavelli himself. The murder had been done through an intermediary, and Machiavelli must have assumed that Maccabee had never learned the truth of it, or the Prince of Lies would never have agreed to meet Maccabee here, among the roses and the darkness.

But here they were—Lawrence, Mata Hari, and himself—smeared with chimney black and crouched in the bushes—Lawrence's idea. Maccabee's disguise was a djeballa, and Mata Hari's another, indigo like shadows in the night. Lawrence's white, modern teeth flashed and he had a penlight he lit too often.

There was no talk among them. The woman's presence had changed everything. And that was a relief for Maccabee: owing Lawrence a favor was unpleasant; the Englishman's assumptions were more so. But Mata Hari served a higher purpose here—Maccabee would not kill in cold blood, or in hot blood, with such a witness.

It was said she slept with Asmodeus the Insecurity Agent, was his mistress. She was the only mortal soul who could call out Angels, borrow the might of Satan himself, for her enterprises. Even Zaki was impressed with her—and kept away from her, for that reason.

Beside Maccabee, in the darkness, she was small and frail. Her breathing was measured. She crouched on her heels, unmoving, uncomplaining, as stolid as a Myrmidon, waiting for the hedge to part, a pebble to be cast, a birdcall to whistle through the night.

When these things finally happened, Lawrence was the first to stand. British audacity, the sort that had gotten him killed in life.

The small, fey man who came silently along the rose-garden path to meet them was a velvet wraith with a serpent's whisper: "Ah, the evening is old, and my friends new," said Machiavelli.

It was the recognition phrase, one of several, but the only one that meant *Let us proceed.*

Machiavelli would not kneel in the dirt. He held out a pale hand as if Maccabee should kiss his ring. The Israelite rose to his full height, one hand on the elbow of the quiet woman beside him. Her hood fell back.

Machiavelli hissed disapproval: "*Pro di.* Let us not be too emboldened. The household has many eyes. Proof, dear lady, of your identity? And quickly. That you keep bad company proves little."

Out came Lawrence's penlight, and out came Mata Hari's nippleless breast. When the light had shone upon the teat, Machiavelli whispered urgently that both be put away.

Then he dismissed Lawrence as one would an employee, saying, "Go to the front of the house, enter and have tea there. We will join you presently."

When Lawrence had gone, Machiavelli kept peering into the bushes, as if expecting someone to be lurking there.

"What is it?" Mata Hari said in a European-accented voice.

"Zaki?" whispered Machiavelli insistently. "Is your trained Jew with you, Maccabee?"

"No," Maccabee growled. "And watch your tongue. We do you two favors tonight, more than you deserve."

"Two?" said Machiavelli with a tentative smile that rested on the small woman.

"Two: Mata Hari's proposal is one. Letting you live is the other." Maccabee couldn't help it. His hands were balled at his sides and aching with rage. He wanted to take Machiavellli by his long nose and make an end to him, as vengeance decreed.

But he could not, now, with the woman here.

And she said, "In case matters have not been clearly stated, let me say this: I offer myself, and my connections, to your Caesar. Only to him. Under certain guarantees. For services to be rendered by him in advance."

"Guarantees?" Machiavelli said. "Services?"

"Asmodeus must be gotten safely out of Reassignments. If this is done, information and aid in the matter of the Devil's Child, Welch, and others from Agency will be forthcoming."

"My man, Caesar, is . . . careful. Cautious. What guarantees. . . .?"

"Your life, Machiavelli, mine by rights, will be guaranteed not to flow from your body like shit into a sewer," Maccabee said conversationally, in as low and measured a tone as the others were using. "Gertie has had a falling out with your . . . Pentagram rivals. We need your resources. Yes or no?"

"To embrace such a flower," Machiavelli spoke to the woman, "will be our privilege. To nurture and comfort you. And yours."

" 'Our privilege?' Do I sense a 'we?' " said the tiny woman in a voice like steel. "Is that the royal we? Can you speak for him?"

"No, I cannot speak for him. I offer my home, now—an interim measure. I must go to Julius. You will stay here. It is dangerous for me as well, you must understand."

"I must understand many things, but your personal difficulties are not yet among them," said the small woman with a bared threat in her voice. "Come back with Caesar's answer, and then 'we' will concern *our*selves with your well-being."

The Italian muttered something, but swallowed what he said and held out a crooked elbow to the woman stiffly. He looked, to Maccabee's ancient eyes, ridiculous, all locked up with his fear.

Fearful or not, Machiavelli led them around to the house, and into it, and put them in the care of his staff to wait with Lawrence, suggesting only that they "Cleanse your faces of that idiotic blacking," before he disappeared into one of Hell's darkest nights.

Once Caesar had acceded, there was only the doing of the thing: the retrieval—the rescue, perhaps—of Asmodeus from Reassignments.

Machiavelli and Lawrence used their access to get into the Reassignments computer. How this was done, they kept hidden from the woman they called Mata Hari, whose real name was Gertrud Margarete Zelle. They didn't trust her, these factionalizers, these cretins responsible for Asmodeus's shame, his pain, his punishment.

She had seen Caesar, seen him only briefly. He looked younger than his busts, but that youth was deceptive. There were centuries in his eyes. Gert knew that Caesar's assassin/son, Brutus, was in his household. It must be a terrible weight for both of them, to live together, remembering what had gone before.

Hell was full of terrible weights, and Caesar wanted to see for himself that she was one soon to be lifted from his neck. She said, "I have it in mind to teach Mithridates and all his cohorts a lesson. Do this for me—return Asmodeus to the Fallen Angels—and the shadows that still hang over you because of your recent adventurism will be lifted, in Authority's eyes."

This was the proposition she could make only to the man himself. He couldn't know whether she could do what she promised, but she was who she was: the offer spoke volumes.

Caesar had said, picking at a bit of lint on his robe, in a room designed to remind petitioners just how old and established the Roman was in Hell, "Madam, we will do everything in our power to aid you. And you, in turn, will discuss with us the matter of the missing Welch, formerly of Agen—"

"I *know* who he is. I know much you would like to know, Caesar. When I know you better, perhaps I'll tell you some of it."

And she had smiled, and he had smiled, and there had been enough in those glances. This was a household, a stronghold, full of agendas. Caesar would make room for one more.

Now, waiting outside Admin's back door, with a dozen men spread about on rooftops and in unremarkable cars, in case there was an attempt by Mithridates' henchmen to stop the pickup of Asmodeus or recapture Mata Hari herself, she felt the first tremor of uncertainty.

Nothing ever went right in Hell. The report, exonerating Asmodeus, that she'd gathered so painstakingly and sent both to Asmodeus's office and to the Devil on his private modem had never reached either source, or things would be different now.

It had all been in vain. The transmissions had never gotten through; the originals were destroyed; the storm had wiped the rest from data banks all the hell over.

Now she was dependent upon Caesar, embroiled.

And upon Maccabee, who was bold enough to walk up to the door of Admin and show a falsified requisition for one Asmodeus, Fallen Angel; to stand spread-legged with crossed arms and wait.

She was not so brave. Her training was different. She skulked with her transceiver and her three Agency boys, ready to give covering fire, concise orders, whatever was needed.

And her heart ached, as it often had in life and more often did in Hell, to know what was going on inside, what her machinations had accomplished. To know how her agents were faring.

Would Asmodeus come out that door? And if he did, what shape would he be in? Had she helped or hurt him? Had the whole plan backfired; was he lost, sent to some nether hell?

Or would they all lose, in a street battle with Mithridates faction? Or with Agency, whose authority she'd used for this but whose sanction she did not have?

A spy's hell was close and fetid, full of doubts and questions never answered. She bit her lip with her teeth and dug her arms with her nails and listened to the pulse in her ears pound away the seconds.

And still the door did not open. Still Maccabee stood waiting, exposed and vulnerable. Still her men held their fire. Still Asmodeus did not appear.

If Asmodeus had truly been, as he was remembered by the living, an evil spirit and king of the demons, then maybe the demons wouldn't have given him such a hellish time before turning him over to the Undertaker.

Legends became garbled, over millennia, and his was not the last or least of those. He was a Fallen Angel—no more, no less—and how far an angel could fall was something he'd never known until the demons began feasting upon his once-supernal flesh.

He had sat once with a damned soul named Welch, getting drunk over a report detailing an abysmal failure of Agency operatives, and Welch had maundered on about his "sea change." And Asmodeus had listened, as a superior will to a troubled inferior, with patience but without real understanding, as the tortured soul had spoken of torments welling from a change of heart.

Asmodeus had not then, or since, understood the anguish of which the damned mortal spoke. But now he did. He had looked upon all the abounds of Hell in one way, for eternity.

Now he looked at infernity and it was different. It was petty. It was horrible. It was useless and unreasonable and venal and old. It was a remnant of the animal mind of man and the animus of God. It was, in short, damnable. And Asmodeus had helped to make it so.

Every bite the demons took of his body, every thrill of pain that went on far too long because Asmodeus's body was not so feeble as mortal flesh, taught him what Hell meant to the weak, to the helpless—to the damned.

And he repented those days, upon the Earth when man was young, when he had gone abroad among the Israelites and the Canaanites, striking the fear of God into primitive hearts; when he had taken the phallus of Pazuzu and the slither of Set and the fire of the dragon Illuyankus for his own. In those days, he had been Lucifer's hammer, Poseidon's trident, Him whose name made children obey their parents and parents quake like children in the dead of night.

In those days, he had been the Scourge upon the land, when the battle was joined on Earth for the

souls of men, when Michael wrestled Satan for Mo-
ses' soul, when every contest between heaven and
hell was fought in person, hand to hand.

Thus he had acquired the apocryphal title 'king of
the demons,' long before God sent his son on a
ministry to man. And now, lying stitched together,
breathing hard, on a cold slab in the Reassignments
elevator, he thought back upon the tortures he'd
decreed, the battle lines he'd drawn, and he . . .
regretted.

The pain that man suffered had come to visit
Asmodeus, and gone, and in its wake had left the
Fallen Angel with a worse malady: guilt. Would Satan
think himself so lofty, so omnipotent; would Hell be
so completely awful; would man suffer all this misery
without complaint, if not for Asmodeus's labors? For
Asmodeus had put in man the fear of Evil, of Shai-
tan, of Sin—the fear of God that could only flourish if
God's opposite were alive and well.

For millennia, Asmodeus had served the Devil in
a changing Hell, because that Hell was as dear to
God as Paradise, as necessary as the pearly gates, as
pure as the Archangel Michael's smile.

Or so he'd told himself; so he'd thought. But pain
was pure and in its wake, its absence was a palpable
pleasure. Suffering, when alleviated, was not an absence but a presence: comfort was defined by discom-
fort; Heaven was given embodiment and substance,
reality and value, differentiation and meaning, by
the vast expanse of Hell.

These sophistries had sustained the Fallen Angel
through the years, through the horrors, through the
indignities of consciousness in Hell. Now they were
no longer enough. Asmodeus, Fallen Angel of high
estate, one-time child of god, Joint Chief of Staff of
the Demonic Host, had finally fallen low enough to
know what a mortal meant by "sea change."

Asmodeus had learned to weep.

The skill had come to him, unbidden, under the knives and forks of demons he'd once commanded. It had been honed sharp before they'd sliced his essence from his bones. And it had been reborn with him, under the Undertaker's clumsy ministrations, when he opened his eyes again and met the rheumy, frightened ones of a team of Morticians who'd never brought such flesh as his to life before, in all the eons they'd sweated over corpses in the bowels of hell.

Some disembodied voice had questioned him unremittingly, the whole helpless time of his resurrection, and all that time Asmodeus had openly wept. To questions aimed at finding out what he knew of treacheries and schemes in the Pentagram, he gave back stories of damned souls he'd sent to final rest.

For there was a final rest. There was Nothingness. There was Non-being. A man could lose his soul, his self, become less than dust, in Nether Hells. And it was this story of punishment beyond comprehension, of neverending incomprehension itself, that Asmodeus told his interrogators who hid behind the cloak of Reassignments.

Lying on a slab, immobilized, devoid of sensory input beyond the single one of pain, was an occasion for weeping, and Asmodeus wept. He wept because the pain would end. He wept because the interrogators were hopeless fools. He wept because what was happening to him now was partly his fault: Asmodeus had helped make Hell what it was today.

The voice without a mouth said into his ear: "But tell us of your last assignment, so we may put you back where you belong."

He knew the interrogators wanted information, wanted to know what he knew about them and theirs. The Reassignments computer didn't care about them and theirs. The Reassignments computer didn't care what these little men who used it might learn from him; the Reassignments computer would put Asmodeus where the Devil wanted him. And these interrogators wanted something else: assurances that Asmodeus would not find them, come after them, make them pay.

So he wept louder, finding his throat and his voice, finding his eyes and cheeks wet with salty tears, and he called upon the Powers to forgive him, for he had sinned.

And that stopped the voice in his ear: there was an inaudible but nonetheless discernible scuttling, away from him, as if the interlopers tiptoed as quickly as they could, back to their desks, out of sight, if not out of mind.

Let them send him to some Nether Hell, the Insecurity Agent thought defiantly. Did he not deserve it? Had he not helped create every nook and cranny of this Hell that man would have his wish, if not there, then here?

For they flooded here in their teeming multitude, as if to the Promised Land. They hastened to the Underworld and the end of their expectations, complex and full of pain, because their guilt demanded pain and their greedy souls would not loose a grip on existence that was far too tight. And now, some of them, foul creatures playing power games in Reassignments, dared to try to fool a Fallen Angel.

He wept for them, for their punishment to come. He wept for himself, who must mete it out. And he wept for the Devil, who had allowed the demons one Power Breakfast too many, when he'd directed them to chomp on Asmodeus's hallowed bones.

The orderlies who wheeled the weeping ex-stiff

into the Reassignments elevator were glad to be rid of it, to hand the gurney over to the big ancient at the back door who had the requisite paperwork.

Inside the body bag, when Maccabee opened it with trembling fingers, was Asmodeus.

The Insecurity Agent opened his eyes, and for an instant they glowed hellfire red from lid to lid. And in that same instant, before the huge Fallen Angel came up out of that bag in a rustle of half-manifested pinions and infernal strength—for just an instant, Maccabee thought he saw the glitter of teary streams upon Asmodeus's dark face.

Then the Angel was out of the bag and off the gurney, and the gurney itself was spinning crazily under Asmodeus's pointing finger.

"Come on," Maccabee pleaded softly. "The paperwork's not kosher. We've got to get you out of here—"

But the Fallen Angel's attention was still fixed upon the gurney, which started to spin faster, without a hand touching it, in front of the back door to Admin under a streetlight.

It spun yet faster; then faster still. It shook on its casters and it careened like a wobbling top. And as it spun it began to glow, and as it glowed it seemed to melt and spark. And then, with a sound like a clap of thunder, it burst into green flame and disappeared.

Maccabee had his hand out to jerk the Insecurity Agent away from the gurney, but he couldn't make his fingers close over that arm.

Asmodeus was nude but he was not naked. A darkness like fine veiling covered a form too perfect for a man's. An angel from God, Maccabee reminded himself. A warrior in Satan's cause, cast out from heaven to minister to the damned.

But an angel, nonetheless.

"Come, please, Asmodeus. Mithridates and that

lot may find we've tricked them any minute—" Frozen there, arm extended, Maccabee willed his hand to close upon that arm, to tug upon it.

But he could not, and he ramped miserably there, trapped as if tethered in the light by some invisible thong to the Angel who wouldn't leave.

Then Gert's voice called out, soft urgency and an incomprehensible word.

And the huge Fallen Angel turned his head. Dark eyes in a shadow-face glowed slightly; chin raised; shoulders squared. "I'm coming, Gert," the deep voice said, and Maccabee could have sworn it was quavering.

They ran together, the Israelite and the Fallen Angel, across the cobbled sidewalk, the macadam street, into the bushes beside the covered parking lot, where Mata Hari and her men from Agency waited.

Even hurrying, with his back twitching because Maccabee's every muscle sensed the snipers on the rooftops, and Mata Hari's snipers were not necessarily his—even hurrying, Maccabee was distressed by the tears he'd thought he'd seen, and by the nudity of the angel.

Before he knew it, Maccabee had unclasped his cloak from his throat and thrown it across the Fallen Angel's shoulders.

For a moment it seemed suspended on wings like a tent on its poles, and then it fell about Asmodeus, who turned and glanced at him.

Again, the red-in-black eyes, the face that couldn't quite be seen. And, too, a glitter of tears.

Could Fallen Angels cry? Could demon lords feel sadness? Or was it just the pain of resurrection? And if it were not, was it any business of Judah Maccabee's?

Just as Maccabee was deciding that the answer to

the last question he'd asked himself was a resounding no, he and the angel reached the shadows. The sniper on the garage's roof called an alert through his transceiver, and Mata Hari threw her arms joyously about the Fallen Angel's neck.

The two were off in a corner, murmuring and kissing one another. Mata Hari had to feel every inch of Asmodeus, to make sure he was unharmed. Asmodeus had to do whatever such a one did with a damned female soul.

Maccabee turned his face away and yelled for the van. The sniper who'd called the alert thought he'd seen vehicles approaching.

It was possible they'd have to fight their way out of here, if the fake requisition for the Fallen Angel had been discovered. Somehow, it wasn't worrying Maccabee. Mata Hari's lover, their new ally, Asmodeus the Insecurity Agent, ought to go a long way toward evening their odds.

C'MON DOWN!!

Is the real world getting to be too much? Feel like you're on somebody's cosmic hit list? Well, how about a vacation in the hottest spot you'll ever visit . . . HELL!

We call our "Heroes in Hell" shared-universe series the Damned Saga. In it the greatest names in history— Julius Caesar, Napoleon, Machiavelli, Gilgamesh and many more—meet the greatest names in science fiction: Gregory Benford, Martin Caidin, C.J. Cherryh, David Drake, Janet Morris, Robert Silverberg. They all turn up the heat—in the most original milieu since a Connecticut Yankee was tossed into King Arthur's Court. We've saved you a seat by the fire . . .

HEROES IN HELL, 65555-8, $3.50 _____

REBELS IN HELL, 65577-9, $3.50 _____

THE GATES OF HELL, 65592-2, $3.50 _____

KINGS IN HELL, 65614-7, $3.50 _____

CRUSADERS IN HELL, 65639-2, $3.50 _____

Please send me the books checked above. I enclose a check for the cover price plus 75 cents for first-class postage and handling, made out to: Baen Books, 260 Fifth Avenue, New York, N.Y. 10001.